FACE OFF

A Novel

Jennifer Willcock

CW01000658

FACE OFF
Copyright © 2021 by Jennifer Willcock

All rights reserved. Neither this publication nor any part of this publication may be reproduced or transmitted in any form or by any means, electronic or mechanical, including photocopying, recording or any information storage and retrieval system, without permission in writing from the author.

This is a work of fiction. Names, characters, places and incidents either are the product of the author's imagination or are used fictitiously, and any resemblance to actual persons, living or dead, businesses, companies, events, or locales is entirely coincidental.

Print ISBN: 978-1-4866-2119-4
eBook ISBN: 978-1-4866-2120-0

Word Alive Press
119 De Baets Street, Winnipeg, MB R2J 3R9
www.wordalivepress.ca

WORD ALIVE
—P R E S S—

Cataloguing in Publication may be obtained through Library and Archives Canada

To Mom & Dad
Thanks for always letting me curl up with a book.

ACKNOWLEDGEMENTS

I'm so grateful for the following people and their willingness to jump alongside me for the ride.

Emily Wood and Grant Gagnon are physical therapists and they shared their expertise and knowledge about bone breaks and therapy with me. And answered ALL my questions. Any mistakes are entirely my own.

Although I'm a Canadian, I don't follow hockey closely—I only check to see if we win the big games. When I decided Tristan was a goalie, I needed information. Wes Werner, a goalie with McKendree University ACHA Division One team, was more than willing to share his knowledge about hockey and the life of a goalie with me. Wes was a wealth of knowledge and patiently answered all my questions. Wes provided interesting stories that I found fascinating and I would have loved to have included. Tristan is more authentic because of all the background information Wes shared. Any mistakes about hockey or play are my own.

My first readers, Trina Jones, Robin Livingston, Brenda Tindall and Nicole David, are so fabulous. I can't thank them enough. They questioned certain aspects and gave ideas and made this book so much better. Thank you!

Sara Davison, my editor, thank you for sharing your gift with me and for your patience as I make a mess of so many grammar rules.

The team at Word Alive Press who always make it a pleasure to work with them. Special thanks to Tia for working alongside me again. And to Jen who is doing double duty.

Ross's Elite Athletic Camp was inspired by real life camps my sons have attended. PGC is a basketball program and camp that teaches both the game and leadership. They addressed the campers as "Athletes" which left an impression on me. Getting our son involved in their program has been one of the best investments we've made.

Camp Widjiitiwin is located in the Muskokas in Ontario. Both my sons attended summer camp there. They had an indoor climbing wall that I thought was so cool that it inspired the one in this book.

Thank you to my two guys, Ian and Ben who inspire me every day. As you enter adulthood, know that you are more than enough, so be brave and bold and make a difference in the world around you. I love you so much.

Thank you, Mark, for always encouraging me to chase my dreams. I'd still be wasting time if it wasn't for you.

And to you, the readers, thank you, thank you, thank you. Thanks for reading *Exit Stage Right* and asking about Shelby. I loved writing her and Tristan's story. I hope you enjoy it. And I pray you know that you are more than worth it. You are enough just as you are.

CHAPTER ONE

My mother is ruining my life.

Shelby Wright slumped against the beige leather passenger seat of her mother's forest green Lexus, oblivious to the lush fields and trees flashing by her window. Instead she watched her mind's internal video—barre class with her best friend Madison, stealthy trips to the ice cream store with friends, and, of course, dancing at the Summer Festival at the end of season—all of which she'd miss this summer. Shelby snapped her gum. Once. Twice. She smirked as her mother's knuckles whitened on the leather-lined steering wheel. "Shelby."

She lifted her eyebrow. "What?" Pop.

Her mother huffed. "Stop snapping that gum. Or better yet, throw it out." She fumbled around for a tissue in the middle console of the car until her fingers found one that she shoved at Shelby.

Shelby rolled her eyes as she snatched it and spit the wad of pink gum into the white tissue. Slowly wrapping it up, she stuffed it in the cup holder.

"Put it in the garbage bag." Her mother glanced sideways at her. "Really, Shelby, where are your manners?"

Picking up the tissue, Shelby dropped it into the small garbage bag attached to the side of her seat, then crossed her arms and stared out the window. "We're in the car, Mom; no one can see us," she muttered. Although there was no point arguing. The great Shane Tivoli, principal ballet dancer for the National Dance Company, fan favourite, and her mother, cared about public perception even when they were the only two around. *I'll never be perfect enough for her.*

Her mother nudged her. "It'll be fun."

Shelby's pink-glossed lips formed a thin line.

A sigh drifted over from the driver's side. "Keep an open mind, Shelby. You might enjoy yourself."

She shook her head. "An elite athlete's camp consisting of hockey players, soccer players, and runners isn't going to be fun." *Far from it.*

"Why not?"

"I've already told you—half of them won't even know what ballet is, and they'll ask me why I'm at an athletic camp."

"You're an athlete—in fact, you're in perfect condition, probably superior to most of them. Go and show them that."

Shelby smoothed her long blonde ponytail and ignored the sick feeling in her stomach. She cleared her throat. "They'll make fun of me, Mom. They always do."

Her mother signalled a lane change then tapped her finger on the wheel. "Not if you show them who's boss. Not if you out-perform them."

Shelby rested her elbow on the window ledge, resting her chin in the palm of her hand. Once again, she'd have to prove herself. And she would—no way a bunch of jocks were out-performing her—but she tired of always having to work to belong. "It won't matter. I'll stick out like I have at every other non-ballet function I've attended. The kids either stare at me like I'm a three-headed alien or they tease me. I'm sick of it. I want to go home."

"We've already been through this. I'm in Australia all summer at the Aussie Ballet school. You can't stay home alone."

"You've dragged me all over the world all my life for *your* dancing and the one time I want to go, you put me in camp. Why can't I hang out with Dad and play tourist?"

Her mother barked out a laugh that was more a scoff. "Your father will be travelling most of the time with his own business. That doesn't work. I'm not leaving a sixteen year old alone in a strange country in a hotel room all day."

"That's what I'm saying, Mother. I am sixteen and I can take care of myself. I could've stayed home in Reinholt, either at our house or with Maddie." She already missed her best friend.

Her mother's sigh rang out in the tight space. "This is a moot point, Shelby. We're on the way to Ross's Elite Athletic Camp; I'm not turning around."

Shelby clenched her teeth. "This is so unfair," she hissed.

Her mother kept silent. Shelby sneaked a glance at her, waiting for her retort. When none came, she turned her attention to her fingernails, which she'd bitten down to the nubs. Afraid her mom would notice, she shoved her hands under her thighs. *I don't need a lecture about biting my nails too.*

The exit from the highway grabbed her mother's attention. They took the winding ramp onto a two-lane highway, and Shelby's stomach clenched. *Hicksville, wonderful.*

Her mother's smooth and perfectly manicured fingers loosened on the steering wheel. "I'm so glad we're off that highway. I can't believe how busy it is for the early afternoon."

"How much farther?"

"Not too long now. Maybe half an hour."

A half hour until I die. Shelby barely resisted the urge to press the back of her hand to her forehead. *Melodrama much?* Maddie would be laughing at her right now. Her lips quirked up at the thought.

"I'm glad to see your mood is picking up." Her mother glanced at her, but Shelby only lifted her shoulders, staring out the window at the endless pine trees and large rocks that lined the two-lane highway. Hicksville indeed—they were in the middle of nowhere.

Silence filled the car as they drove. A sparkling blue lake peeked through the trees every once in a while. The knot in her stomach eased at the sight of the sunlight shimmering on the water. A rustic wooden sign attached to an outcropping of rock announced that Ross's Elite Athletic Camp was another ten miles up the road. Shelby rubbed her moist palms on her jean shorts, inhaling short, choppy, breaths. Her eyes scanned the area for the entrance of the camp. The sight of the large blue and white sign announcing that they had arrived at their destination made her heart lurch. As the car wound its way down the gravel drive, Shelby glanced back at the two-lane highway, which looked positively civilized compared to where she was headed for the next month.

* * *

The camp's longhouse—made of real logs and not cheap siding—where meals and gatherings were held, had a homey feel to it. The inside walls were golden, the wood worn down to a sheen. Large woven mats adorned the walls, along with pictures of several famous athletes who had attended the camp at some point in their careers. A large antler chandelier hung from the ceiling in the middle of the room. Tacky yet somehow it worked with the whole atmosphere.

Brown leather couches and chairs had been arranged in a far corner, creating a place to chat and hang out. In the distance a rock climbing wall disappeared into another level of the longhouse. *Is that how you get upstairs?* Shelby glanced around for a staircase, spotted one to the side of the climbing wall, and breathed a sigh of relief. Madame Clare, her dance teacher, would faint if she knew Shelby had to climb a wall every day.

The teachers at the performing arts school she attended were always warning the students not to take chances and injure themselves. Skiing was outright forbidden for students at Spencer School of the Performing Arts. Shelby didn't know if rock-climbing fit that restriction, but her spirits lifted at the thought of doing something her teachers would frown at. Something an ordinary teen would do. Especially since she had her mother's permission since she'd signed her up. *Maybe this won't be so bad.*

Shelby glanced at her mom, standing in the registration line, her posture perfect and her blonde hair, which matched her own, swooped up in a messy bun on top of her head. Her mom was either crazy to believe this would work or crazy desperate to have a place for Shelby to stay for the summer.

Several people waited in line in front of them. Shelby used the time to study the kids who would be her camp-mates this summer. A couple of guys bounced basketballs. Thwap. Thwap. Thwap. Shelby rolled her eyes. *I hope there are no basketball players in my cabin or someone will die.*

Her gaze travelled over other kids lingering around the room. A group of girls wearing the same navy long-sleeved T-shirts and gym shorts giggled, their hands covering their mouths as they checked out the Greek gods standing two feet away from them and holding soccer balls. The boys were tall and almost all sported the man buns that seemed to have taken over the sport.

The door to the longhouse slammed against the wall, drawing all eyes to a tall guy with short auburn hair who barrelled through the doorway, a heavy-looking duffle bag—that he made look as light as candy floss—slung over his shoulder. His lazy grin made Shelby take a second peek as he dropped his bag on the floor and turned to a woman who had come in behind him holding a hockey stick. He took the stick from her and shoved the bag over to the wall with his foot.

Another male with dark curls any girl would envy came over to the auburn-haired hockey dude and they performed a complicated handshake. Shelby frowned but couldn't turn away. Auburn hockey guy, as she'd taken to calling him in her head, turned to take in the room, his glance landing on her. Eyes the color of summer grass locked onto hers and her neck felt suddenly hot and sticky. She shifted her gaze back to the registration desk. *Stop staring.*

Her mom grabbed her arm, urging her forward to the desk. Shelby glanced one more time at the hockey player, now in animated conversation with the dark-haired boy and a couple of girls. As she followed her mother, Shelby shoved away the urge to glance over again. *Who are those girls?* Shelby shook her head. *What is the matter with you? You saw him for the first time ever two seconds ago.*

A tug on her arm drew Shelby back to the registration desk.

"Shelby dear, pay attention."

"Uh, sorry." She smiled weakly at the woman with dark-framed glasses sitting at the registration desk.

Her mother sighed. "Daydreaming."

The woman's eyes flicked from her to her mother and back again. The gap between her front teeth showed when she smiled. "Not a problem. This is probably one of the best places for daydreaming." She winked as she handed a slip of paper with her cabin information to

5

Shelby. "Welcome to Ross's Camp. We haven't had too many dancers here, but I'm sure you'll fit right in."

Shelby swallowed and tried to force her lips upward but the gesture came off as more of a grimace. *Yeah, right.*

"She'll love it," her mom gushed as Shelby picked up her black duffle bag with pink pointe shoes embroidered on it. The girls with the soccer balls glanced her way, clearly catching sight of the bag. A few lifted their eyebrows. Shelby raised her chin and stared straight ahead. *Ignore them. They don't know anything.* She followed her mom toward the door of the longhouse, heat making her ears burn as she passed near the auburn hockey guy. Fumbling with her bag handle in an attempt to avoid looking his way, Shelby tripped, sprawling forward. Strong hands gripped her upper arms, keeping her from face-planting on the hardwood floor.

"Whoa, watch your step now." Auburn hockey guy righted her and pointed to her sneaker. "Better tie those up or it'll be a long summer in a cast here." His voice was chocolate smooth.

I'm dying. Right. Now. Actually, I'd prefer that to this humiliation. She nodded like an idiot and dropped to her knees to tie the laces as her mother spoke to the guy.

"You wouldn't know some days that she can do pirouettes and advanced footwork all on pointe!" She laughed, shaking her head.

Heat crawled up her neck and settled in her cheeks as Shelby finished tying her shoe, then shoved her mother out the door. "Mom!" What if he'd questioned her comment?

"What?"

"You didn't have to tell him I'm a dancer."

Her mother shrugged. "They'll know before the day's end. What's the big deal?"

Shelby glared at her mother. "The big deal is that you embarrassed me in front of everyone. Now they'll all think I'm a klutzy dancer."

"Shelby, calm down. You'll show them all you can compete with anyone here." The great Shane Tivoli waved her hands in the air like a magician, dismissing any other arguments.

Shelby bit her lip, letting that pain distract from her burning eyes. Her mother obviously didn't understand Shelby's feelings—how she'd stick out at this athlete's camp, or how badly she wanted to spend the summer with her mom. But Shane Tivoli always put her career first. And Shelby? She only fit into her mother's life when convenient. *I should know better.*

Furtively, Shelby glanced over her shoulder. The auburn hockey guy stood in the doorway of the longhouse watching them. Whirling away, Shelby marched to her cabin, lamenting her certain doom this summer.

CHAPTER TWO

"HEY, HOW'S IT GOING?"

Tristan finished rolling his blue sleeping bag out on the thin foam mattress that covered the bunks in the cabins at Ross's. Having been a camper the previous summer, he knew to bring a blow-up mattress to cushion his body against the unforgiving wood. After smoothing down the material, Tristan straightened and nodded at the tall, muscular boy standing beside him. "Hey, man. I'm Tristan."

"Kyle." The boy glanced up at the top bunk, frowning. "Are we supposed to fit up there?"

Tristan grinned, taking in the guy's broad shoulders and large feet. "Yup. It's roomier than it appears."

Kyle studied the small cabin then pointed to an unclaimed bottom bunk on the other side. "I think I'll take that one. At least if I fall, it won't be a long drop."

Tristan laughed. "I hear ya. Let the little guys have the top bunks."

A large hand came down on his shoulder. "Who ya calling little?"

Tristan turned around. "Hey, Matty. We were just talking about you."

"Funny." His friend turned to Kyle, "I'm Matt."

"Kyle."

Tristan reclined on his bunk. "We were discussing the five-star quality of Ross's and how they designed everything for short guys... like you."

Matt playfully shoved Tristan's shoulder.

"I'm not short. I'm the perfect height for a point guard. I mean, have you seen Lowry?"

Kyle dropped his stuff on the empty bottom bunk. "Maybe so, but you'll sleep better than the rest of us. I think my legs are going to hang off at the knees." He untied the strings to his sleeping bag, rolled it out onto the wooden bunk, then stretched his tall frame out on it. His feet stuck over the end, and he groaned loudly.

Matt laughed as he climbed onto the bunk over Tristan's. "Definitely five star. The quality of the foam mattresses is out of this world."

Kyle sat up, leaning on his side to avoid hitting his head on the bunk over him. "I thought there'd at least be a better mattress."

"Here." Tristan tossed a small, balled-up blow-up mattress onto his bed.

"Oof. What's this?" Kyle held the ball in front of his face, inspecting it.

"Magic. It might not appear like much, but believe me, it'll improve your sleep a hundred percent."

Matt nodded. "The wonder of the blow-up camp mattress—your best friend over the next month."

Kyle stood and unfurled the rumpled fabric. He frowned.

Tristan pointed to a small tab on the side. "Pull it and it inflates itself."

"Don't you need it?"

"Brought an extra for newbies like yourself."

Kyle watched the mattress inflate. "Thanks. I owe you."

"Nah, that's what bunk-mates are for."

Matt jumped down from the top bunk, landing gracefully on his butt. As he sat there stunned, the other two guys burst out laughing.

Tristan reached out a hand to his friend. "So graceful, Matty."

Kyle remade his bed using the air mattress before plopping onto it. "So you guys know each other?"

Matt clapped his hand on Tristan's shoulder. "Tristan here has the very good fortune of attending school with me and living two doors down from my house."

Guffawing, Tristan shoved Matt away. "Yeah, right. It's more like I'm unfortunately stuck with you." Tristan grabbed his baseball cap and slipped it on his head. "Let's head over to the longhouse. It's almost time for Ross's welcome and pep talk."

Walking out of the cabin, Tristan was blinded by the bright summer sun and all three guys slipped on their shades. A cool breeze blew up from the sparkling lake behind the cabins. The dirt path to the long-house was crowded with kids coming and going from the main building. Tristan recognized a number of people passing by, and he greeted them with either a nod or fist-bump.

Kyle gestured to the grounds. "How long have you guys been coming to Ross's?"

Matt shrugged. "A couple of years. Is this your first time?"

Kyle nodded. "My football coach thought it would help me."

"It will. You'll leave here fine tuned." Tristan searched the groups of kids heading back to the longhouse, glad he had his shades on so Matt wouldn't notice his wandering gaze. Finally, he caught a glimpse of the blonde pony-tail attached to the pretty girl who'd taken a nose dive into his arms at registration. Her blonde hair was almost translucent, he'd noticed when he caught her. And her eyes—sky blue with long lashes. It'd taken a gigantic effort to look away. She was tall but not basketball-player tall. Maybe she played soccer? Her lean body made him think so. The woman with her had said something about point that he hadn't understood. Maybe she did play basketball and played point guard like Matt.

A sharp jab to his side brought his attention back to his friend. "Ow, what was that for?"

Hand waving in front of Tristan's face, Matt said, "You're off in La-La land. What's going on?"

Heat travelled up his neck. "Nothing. I'm... looking to see who I recognize."

Matt gestured between the three of them. "All you need is right here, buddy." He poked Tristan with a finger. "Don't get distracted."

Kyle raised an eyebrow. "What's that supposed to mean?"

"Girls. Don't mess with them and you won't get messed up yourself."

Kyle raised his dark eyebrow. "Really?"

"Really. This guy here," Matt pointed to Tristan, "is going to play for the NHL. I'm not blowing smoke either—he's got scouts stalking him. Girls will only distract him from his game."

Tristan scratched his neck. He hated it when Matt boasted about him. "Don't listen to him. He doesn't know what he's talking about."

Kyle cocked his head, his shades reflecting the sunlight. "He has a point. But I think it's possible to stay on track with your program and still have a girl. I do. And not to boast, but I have scouts following me too."

Matt scanned the area. "You have a girlfriend? Is she here?"

"Nah. Kenesha's a cheerleader, so she's at cheer camp for a few weeks and then she'll be working for her dad the rest of the summer. But she understands that football is my priority."

Tristan let out a low whistle. "Wow. She must be like one in a million." The girls he'd dated were interested in him because of his prospective future, but they still didn't get why they weren't his top priority.

Kyle's face lit up with a huge grin. "She is."

The chatter of a few hundred kids filled the long house as Tristan, Kyle, and Matt entered its cool interior. The girl had disappeared. Finding chairs in the back, they sat down and Tristan surveyed the room, trying to catch a glimpse of her.

"Athletes, please find a seat." A tall, muscular man with dark hair stood at the front of the longhouse. He didn't use a mic because his authoritative voice let everyone know who was in charge. Within a few seconds, silence filled the place. Ross Stirling still looked as though he could go out on the ice and whip the butts of guys half his age. At one time he'd been one of the top scorers in the OHL, but an injury had kept him from pursuing his NHL dreams. Instead, he poured his life into helping youth achieve their dreams through coaching and this camp. Tristan admired the man.

"I'm Ross Stirling, and I am the director of this camp. Welcome, athletes." A cheer rose from the crowd, an electric charge igniting the campers. Tristan whooped and clapped, studying the kids who'd be his friends and competition over the next month. His eyes stopped when he saw her blonde hair. The girl, whoever she was, sat unmoving. Not even a smile. *Was that an eye roll? What's her problem?* He studied her a minute before shifting his attention to his buddies and the director, who had a big grin on his face as he waited for things to quiet down.

"Our Elite Athlete Camp is one of the best in the country, and I want to congratulate you for making the choice to better your skills. That being said, I need to remind you all that what you put into this camp—your hard work—is what you'll take from it. How hard you work and what kind of an attitude you have is what will make or break your camp experience. Good attitudes and work ethics produce results and a great experience. Our staff isn't here to babysit you this summer. It's their job to guide you, supervise you, and encourage you." He paced the front of the longhouse as he spoke, meeting the eyes of everyone he could. "So let's make this one of the best camps ever!"

The campers erupted in cheers filling the large building. Tristan couldn't resist eyeing the girl, whose bored expression and crossed arms hadn't changed in the last few minutes. Tristan's whooping quieted as he took her in. Her blue eyes locked with his, almost in a challenge. He shook his head and then turned to Matt, who was fist bumping everyone taller than himself. *He's such a joker.* Tristan tried to ignore the heat of the girl's stare boring into him. When he glanced over again, she quickly looked in the other direction.

Seriously, what's her problem?

* * *

The cheers of the athletes around her worsened the ache in her already throbbing head. All Shelby wanted was to curl up on her bunk and wish it all away. How had she got here? She'd gone over every reason her mother had given her, trying to understand why she'd send her to an athletic camp, but no matter how many times she went over them, it didn't make sense. A lump rose in her throat and she swallowed hard, hoping to dislodge it, but it kept getting bigger.

Casting a glance around the room, she noticed green eyes staring at her. *Auburn hockey guy.* Definitely gorgeous, but the heated stare he gave her wasn't the good kind of heat. Was he *scowling* at her? Why? Because she wasn't whooping it up? She locked eyes with him, a jolt jerking through her. She ignored it. Lifting her chin in a challenge, she frowned at him. *Who does this guy think he is?*

He turned away and Shelby forced herself to pay attention to the instructions. Once the meeting finished, she stalked out of the building and headed for the lake, wanting to get far away from everyone.

Tears fell as she hurried along the sandy path to the beach. *I don't fit in here. I'll have to prove myself worthy. Like always.* She had argued for going to Australia with her mother, but what she really wanted was her home. A deep-seated desire to have a normal summer hanging out with her friends, eating ice-cream, and splashing in the pool, made her throat ache.

Spotting a rock along the tree line, Shelby jogged to it and plopped down. She inhaled a shaky breath then let out a frustrated screech. *I hate my mother—she's ruining my life.* She'd been shoved off to this camp like an unwanted gift hidden away in a closet. Sniffing, she looked around. Alone. Thankfully, no one had followed her here. The beach sand was the color of toffee and the clear blue water beckoned. She breathed deeply, filling her lungs with clean air. A bird called from the trees overhead, another answering it. Maybe it wouldn't be so bad if she could come sit here every day. She didn't fit in at this camp, but she'd prove to them she was the better athlete. She'd outrun and outperform them all.

CHAPTER THREE

A HORN BLAST SHATTERED THE QUIET OF THE LATE AFTERNOON. BIRDS ROSE from the treetops, squawking their protests. *I totally agree.* Shelby rubbed her chest where her heart thundered, taking a breath. In and out. The horn summoned the athletes to their first contest, which the director had mentioned in his little pep talk. *You can do this.*

Sliding off the rock, her bottom numb from its hardness, Shelby trudged back to the main camp grounds. The birds returned to their trees, the horn now silent. Shelby glanced down at her reddening arms, frowning. *Need sunscreen.* Instead of the basketball court where the campers were to meet, Shelby hurried to her cabin.

"You're going the wrong way," someone shouted at her.

Waving them off, she jogged to her cabin. Yanking the door open, she almost took it off its hinges. Empty. She grabbed her cosmetic bag, zipped it open, and rummaged through it, tossing out mascara, blush, and finally landing on the smooth tin of the spray sunscreen. She doused her arms, neck, and legs then slapped some on her face before grabbing the baseball cap from her bed. After slamming the door, she ran to the courts.

Breathless, Shelby slipped into the midst of the fringe of kids standing on the blacktop. *Please don't see me.* Everyone appeared focused on one of the camp leaders, who was explaining the drill they were to do.

"Got it?" he asked the group.

Got what? The faces of the kids around her didn't give anything away, and her stomach nose-dived. She opened her mouth to ask what they were supposed to do, but hearing her name, she shut it. She peeked up from under her lashes at the counsellor who had called her out. *How'd he know her name?*

"It's Shelby, right? I'm reading your name tag correctly?" *Oh.* The guy waved her over. "Why don't you come up front and help us demonstrate the exercise?"

No. No. No. Heat burned her cheeks, her breath catching in her chest as she stumbled forward to the front of the group. She stared at the leader, swallowing the bile that threatened to bring up the lunch she'd had with her mother earlier.

"I, uh, I'm... I didn't hear the instructions."

The leader wasn't much older than herself, but he didn't cut her any slack. Instead, he lifted both hands. "It's hard to grasp the instructions when you're not around to hear them."

A sheen of sweat broke out over her body, but Shelby met the guy's dark eyes. "I needed sunscreen." She lifted her chin ever so slightly.

"That's what the ten minutes between Ross's talk and this exercise was for."

A bulldog, that's what he is. She didn't blink. "I'm sorry, I didn't realize."

Still staring her down, he called another name. "Tristan, come up and be Miss Wright's opponent."

A tall guy emerged from the group, and Shelby tore her eyes away from the counsellor, only to wish she could sink into the ground. *No, no, no.* Auburn Hockey guy. He smirked as he brushed past her and took the ball and the long stick the leader handed him. Shelby stared at the tiny ball and long, straight stick he held.

"Tristan, explain to Ms. Wright the instructions and then the two of you can give everyone a quick demo."

Auburn hockey guy—Tristan—dropped the stick on the ground and proceeded to do a series of bounces with the ball and his feet over the stick, explaining it to her as he demonstrated. It looked like hopscotch with ball handling. Heat flushed through her as she stared at him, incredulous. She hadn't handled a ball since kindergarten. She didn't have the kind of skill Tristan showed off. The footwork, once she figured it out, wouldn't be a problem, but she'd be too busy dropping the ball and chasing it to even get to that part. *I hate my mother.*

Tristan finished his instructions and handed her the ball and stick. Shelby stared at them blankly.

"Do you need to practice?"

Nostrils flaring, Shelby grabbed the equipment from him, keeping her back to the rest of the group. She dropped the stick to the ground.

"Wait. Tristan is facing off with you, and we'll time it. Fastest time wins." The leader handed another stick and ball to Tristan, who set up facing Shelby.

Shelby took her place, running through what Tristan had demonstrated to the group. She closed her eyes, taking a deep breath in and slowly letting it out. Thankfully, she picked up new choreography quickly which the footwork was—kinda, sorta. The ball posed the problem. She opened her eyes and watched Tristan, copying his starting stance. Knees and elbows bent, leaning forward slightly, the ball held loosely in his hand. *I can do this.* She met his eyes.

The leader blew his whistle. "Go!"

Tristan moved quickly and Shelby followed. She got the first few steps in without dropping the ball, but then she fumbled it, her fingers not quite catching hold. It bounced away from her and she lunged to grab it, but it rolled into the first row of the group. Tristan finished the drill and fist-bumped the air. Shelby's shoulders slumped as she reached for the ball from a girl holding it out to her.

"That was totally unfair to put Tristan against you." The girl, who had bright red hair braided in two plaits, shook her head. Her eyes were blue and kind. A warmth spread through Shelby's chest and she nodded, taking the ball and heading back to her stick.

"Okay everyone, grab a stick and time yourselves. Times under thirty seconds will compete against each other."

Shelby bent down and grabbed her stick, rising to find Tristan looming over her. She scowled. "What, didn't rub it in enough?"

"Don't take it personally. It's all about winning—you should know that." He eyed her. "What sport do you play? You can barely hang onto the ball."

Shelby's eyebrows hit her hairline. "Rude much?"

"Shelby, Tristan, get to work." The leader waved his hands at them.

Tristan's ears reddened. "I, no, I meant you must do something like gymnastics or..."

"Yeah, something *like* gymnastics." Shelby muttered as she stalked across the court, putting as much distance between herself and his arrogance as she could.

Setting down the stick, Shelby watched the other kids, memorizing their hand movements. *It's like choreography for your hands.*

The girl who'd given her the ball back walked over and dropped her stick on the ground. She smiled at Shelby. "I can help you with the ball-handling if you want. You've got the footwork down. I'm Renee, by the way."

Shelby smiled. "Shelby. And yeah, I could use some help with the ball."

Renee grinned and started to show her how to grip the ball so she wouldn't drop it. Shelby smiled to herself, glad for the show of kindness from this girl.

* * *

"What cabin are you in?" Renee dropped their balls into a wire mesh basket while Shelby shoved their sticks in the tall cylinder container. Dusting her hands off, Renee faced Shelby. "I'm in cabin twelve with a bunch of other basketball players and tennis players."

"You play basketball?"

"Yeah, made senior varsity in my junior year."

"Wow. That's impressive." Even with her limited sports knowledge, Shelby knew that was a great accomplishment.

"My dad was pretty stoked."

Shelby laughed. "What about you?"

Renee grinned. "Me too, but it was nerve-wracking at first. I worried I'd mess up a game or something."

"Did you?"

"No." Renee's grin grew wider. "My team-mates were awesome and made me feel like one of them, even though I was younger. After the first game, I stopped being nervous and focused on my skills."

"Sounds like a plan."

"So what's your sport?"

Shelby bit her lip. "I'm a dancer. A ballet dancer."

Renee stared blankly at her, as if she didn't understand what language Shelby had spoken. Shaking herself out of her stupor, she said, "Like the National Dance Company? I think that's their name. My mom's a big fan."

Shelby let out a breath she'd been holding since the words *National Dance Company* came out of Renee's mouth. *She doesn't know who your mom is.* "Yes, that kind of dancing."

Renee's brow furrowed. "Why are you at a sports camp?"

Shelby stepped back. "I'm every bit an athlete as any football player, basketball player, or baseball player. Or gymnast," she added remembering Tristan's words.

Renee held up her hand, palm facing Shelby. "Whoa. I'm not saying you aren't, but why not go to a dance camp? I'm assuming they have those, right?"

Shelby relaxed her shoulders. *Tone it down.* "Sorry. Yeah, they do. My mom thought I'd get different conditioning here that would help my ballet."

"I can see that. I think I've heard that football players take dance class. Is that right?"

"Some do, and they're better players for it."

"That's cool." Renee stepped onto the path that led to the longhouse and Shelby followed. "Obviously you don't use a ball much."

Shelby pointed to herself. "How could you tell?"

"I can help you with those skills."

"That'd be great. I hope I don't have to face Tristan anymore."

Renee smiled. "He's not so bad. I guess if you had as many scouts after you as he does, you'd get a big head too."

"He does seem to have some talent."

Renee held up her thumb and finger. "Just a little. He'd be in the NHL now, but he doesn't turn eighteen until next May."

"How long have you known him?"

"I've been coming to this camp for four years, and he's been here the last couple. He likes to win. At everything."

"I noticed."

"Don't pay him any attention."

They'd reached the longhouse, and loud shouts and the clanking of dishes drifted out to them. The smell of burgers on the grill filled the air and Shelby's stomach rumbled. She grabbed the door and held it open for Renee, leaning closer to whisper, "Believe me, I'll be too busy trying not to drop the ball in drills to worry about some hockey player."

* * *

From his table at the back of the large room, Tristan watched Shelby and Renee enter the longhouse. His buddies sat around him, joking and shoving each other. Like a male peacock parade, they showed off for the girls in the room. Personally, Tristan hadn't bothered noticing any of them over the years... until now.

An elbow shoved into his ribs. He pushed it away, rubbing at the tender spot. "What?" he growled at Matt.

"What's got your attention?" Matt followed Tristan's gaze to where Shelby stood with Renee at the food station. He slung his arm over Tristan's shoulders and grinned. "Or maybe I should say who?"

Shrugging away from Matt, Tristan muttered, "You're imagining things."

"Am I?"

"Yeah. For one, she totally sucks at ball handling. And two, she's got a bad attitude."

Matt cocked his head, rubbing his chin with his thumb. "So you haven't been paying attention."

Tristan opened his mouth then shut it. "It's hard not to notice how bad she did in that drill. She couldn't even coordinate bouncing the ball and moving her feet."

"True. But you seem to know more about her than I do, and I pride myself on knowing the opposite gender as well as my competition."

Tristan huffed. "Competition? You think she's competition for us? You're kidding."

"My friend, while you were obviously stuck on her good looks and bad ball handling, I noticed she was fast on her feet. She had no trouble maneuvering around that stick. I think we do footwork drills and she'll leave us all in the dust."

"How much would you like to wager?"

A slow grin spread over Matt's face. "You take over my dish duty if I win and I'll take over yours if you win. I pick the races that count towards the bet to make it fair."

"Deal." They shook hands.

Matt's eyes followed Shelby and Renee as they wandered to their seats. "I hope you brought lots of hand lotion, because doing all those dishes causes chapping and redness."

"We'll see." Tristan picked up his burger and took a huge bite, looking forward to getting out of dish duty, because no way was this girl beating him.

CHAPTER FOUR

THE CAMPFIRE LIT UP THE DARK NIGHT. SHELBY SAT BESIDE RENEE AND another girl, Brenda, from her cabin, whom she'd met after dinner when she had gone back to get a sweatshirt. Brenda had driven up from a city four hours away and arrived during supper, thanks to a back-up on the highway. The tall girl played hockey, which fascinated Shelby. "How do you not get hurt with all that crashing into each other hockey players do?" she asked.

Brenda smiled, the flames reflecting on her face. "It's called checking. Sometimes we get hurt, but if you do it correctly no one should get injured. Of course, there's always a thug or two who go after a person, especially if they're scoring goals."

"Ugh."

Brenda frowned and Renee nodded. "It happens in all sports. There are a few players in basketball who go for a cheap foul and end up hurting their opponents."

"Why do you play if you could get hurt?"

Brenda said, "Because it's fun. Don't you get hurt going up on your tippy-toes?"

Shelby cringed at the phrase. "It's called pointe, and no, you shouldn't ever get hurt doing pointe because you've spent years strengthening your ankles and building those muscles. Occasionally accidents happen, but no one hurts someone on purpose."

"I guess that's why it's called the arts, and what we do is sports." Renee held up her hand before Shelby could protest. "I'm not saying you're not an athlete, but I think our goals are different. We set out to score points, and you set out to achieve beauty."

"Agreed." Brenda smiled.

"It's true." Shelby pulled her sweater closer. A chilly breeze blew up from the water.

"What's true?"

Shelby's eyes narrowed as Tristan took a seat on the other side of Renee, his buddies squeezing in beside him. He knocked Renee's shoulder. "Hey, Renee." He glanced over at Shelby. "Shelby, right?"

Shelby glared at him. "Do you always barge into private conversations?"

"Only in public settings where the only seats available are next to the people having that conversation." His gaze travelled past Shelby to Brenda. "I'm Tristan, and this is Matt and Kyle."

"Brenda."

"She's a hockey player too, Tristan," Renee chimed in.

"Cool. What position?"

"Right wing." Brenda shifted over, making room on the log. Shelby moved closer to her new friend and away from Tristan.

Tristan stretched out his long legs. "Goalie."

Brenda poked her stick into the fire. "That's not a position I'd want to play. Takes a special person to guard the net."

Tristan shrugged. "I don't mind it."

Shelby tore open a bag of marshmallows, inhaling the sugary scent and ignoring Tristan. After tugging one out, she stuck it on the end of a stick the counsellors had handed to everyone as they arrived. The orange-red flames licked at her marshmallow, browning the end. As the conversation moved to who played what sports and positions, her chest tightened. *Please don't ask me about ballet.*

Shelby turned her stick in the flames and kept her gaze down. She didn't want to explain the athleticism of dance to dumb jocks. *Like you asked Brenda to explain checking?* She bit her lip. *Yeah, like that.*

"Hey, you're going to lose that to the flames." A hand reached over and moved Shelby's stick out of the fire. "I hope you like them well done."

Tristan's green eyes stared into hers as he held her stick aloft.

"As a matter of fact, I do." She gently pulled the stick away, afraid she'd lose her sweet treat.

"Okay then." He blinked and turned to his friend Kyle, sitting between him and Matt. "Got any chocolate over there?" Kyle handed him a big bar of dark chocolate and Tristan broke off a square, setting it carefully on the graham cracker he'd rested on his jean-clad knee. Sticking a marshmallow on a stick, he held it near the fire. The marshmallow turned golden brown as Tristan carefully turned the white blob over the flames. He carefully withdrew it from the flames then blew on it. "Perfection." He made up his s'more, white stickiness oozing out between the crackers. He licked it then took a bite.

The others were making up their own s'mores as Shelby stared at Tristan devouring his.

He winked at her and held out the rest of his treat. "Want a bite?"

Ignoring him, she turned to her blackened goo. She stuck it farther into the fire, letting the flames eat it. Someone strummed a guitar and a few people harmonized. The pretty music lulled Shelby and she sat silent, not wanting to join into the conversation about which sports were superior. *I just want to go home.*

* * *

The sound of clanging pots filled the air and Shelby ducked her head under the pillow, groaning. Six in the morning was too early to get up on summer vacation. Several other protests filled the room as her three bunkmates stirred from their sleep. Shelby peered over the side of the top bunk, watching her cabin mates come alive.

"I hate that sound. Every year after I leave this place, I hear it in my dreams for a month." A girl sat up, her dark curls flying everywhere as she stretched her arms over her head. Shelby thought her name was Jade, but the introductions yesterday were a jumble in her mind this early. Brenda shoved the covers back and sat up. She didn't have a lot of headroom, and needed to be careful not to hit her head on the ceiling. The other girl—Cecily?—hadn't even moved.

"Why are they making us get up so early?" Shelby cleared her throat, trying to get her words past the frog that sat there.

"Yoga, running, or swimming." Jade swung her long legs over the side of the lower bunk, feeling around with her toes for her flip flops.

Shelby sprawled on her back, staring at the ceiling. Could this camp get any worse?

A knock rattled the door. "Let's move it, girls."

"Moving!" Jade shouted back. Cecily groaned.

Each cabin had a counselor who supervised but didn't stay in the tiny hut with them. The camp wanted to promote self-motivation not nagging.

Shelby climbed off the top bunk and grabbed a pair of yoga pants out of her bag. Tugging on a pink tank top, she watched Cecily slowly yawn and stretch. At this rate, she'd maybe make lunch. Shelby stuffed her feet into her flip flops, yanked her toothbrush and paste out of her kit, and headed outside to the bathrooms, which were down the path. Brenda followed along with Jade.

Doors of cabins opened. "We want to get there before the hordes." Jade picked up her pace. "It can get gross if you're near the last."

Shelby grimaced and she caught a similar look on Brenda's face. The three girls ran for the bathroom.

* * *

Yoga on a sunny beach turned out better than Shelby anticipated. Watching the water lap the shore, she crossed her legs as they finished up. Leaning back, she let the sun warm her shoulders and face as she sighed contentedly. This kind of peace might make her believe in a God. She frowned. *Where did that thought come from?*

The yoga instructor bowed slightly in the direction of the group of twenty or so kids. "Great work-out, everyone. You have a half hour to get showered and dressed before breakfast."

Kids picked up yoga mats and chatted with each other, but Shelby didn't move. *I could sit here all day.* Unfortunately, that wasn't an option and she hauled herself upright, lifted her mat off the sand, and shook it out. She laid it on the pile for the instructor who was hosing them down and glanced down the beach. A couple of the athletes who had chosen to run this morning approached, panting and sweaty. Shelby recognized the tall guy even before the sun glinting off his auburn hair gave him away.

She started for her cabin, avoiding him. Her stomach betrayed her and somersaulted. *Weird. I must be hungry.* Tristan jogged over and stopped in front of her, blocking her path. He was still breathing hard.

She crossed her arms. "I don't think it's good for you to stop suddenly like that."

"I walked the last part, so no worries. Not going to drop dead on you."

"Too bad." Shelby tried to stop her lips from quirking upwards but failed. He was too charming for his own good.

Tristan picked up a clean towel from a pile and wiped his face. "C'mon, I know you'd be upset if that happened. You'd have no one to trounce you in all the drills."

"Right." She moved away from him. His clinging T-shirt showed off his muscular build, and she shifted her gaze to focus on his ear. *Do not look at his muscles.* "For your information, I don't plan on being "trounced" again. She used her fingers to air quote his word. "So you better watch out." She glared at his ear then turned and stalked up the path to the bathrooms, sure she'd be one of the last ones to use the shower. Gross.

* * *

Tristan grinned as he watched Shelby practically stomp all the way to the cabins. Feisty. Maybe she'd be competition, but he doubted it. Matt would be doing his dish duty, no problem. She could barely handle a ball, and her body shape told him she was either a runner or some kind of gymnast. But typically gymnasts weren't that tall or lean. What was the big secret, and why did it bug him so much, not knowing? He tried to remember if anyone had mentioned it but drew a blank. Tossing the dirty towel in the bin, he reviewed the conversations he'd had with her. She never mentioned her sport. In fact, she didn't talk about sports at all. *Number one on my priority list today is to find out Shelby Wright's sport. And why she's keeping it a big mystery.*

CHAPTER FIVE

"WHAT'S THE FIRST DRILL TODAY?" MATT ASKED. BREAKFAST WAS OVER AND they stood on the basketball court, waiting for the other campers. The past few days had been filled with contests that even the most accomplished athletes found challenging. The fifth day of camp wasn't going to be any different.

Tristan ran his finger down the sheet tacked to a bulletin board attached to the chain link fence. "Obstacle course then endurance, but it doesn't say what we're doing."

Matt tented his fingers and smiled widely. "Excellent."

Tristan glared at him.

Matt laughed. "Better go buy yourself some rubber gloves to protect your hands from that hot dish water. Today's races count toward the bet because I think she can handle the footwork and endurance, which levels the playing field. You're not going to have the advantage of ball drills, so I think she'll eat you alive."

Tristan raised his eyebrow and crossed his arms. "Is that right? Since when has anyone ever eaten me alive?"

"There's always a day of reckoning, my friend." Matt cracked his neck then stopped. A group of girls, including Shelby, were walking toward the courts. "Speak of the devil."

Tristan followed Matt's gaze. "Exactly." He turned to his friend. "Do you know what sport she plays? Her mother mumbled something about point, but I didn't catch the meaning."

"Nope, but maybe she's a baller. Pretty skinny for one, but she's tall enough."

"What's the big secret? I mean, if she's some pro that sneaked in here, all bets are off."

"I'm pretty sure she's not a pro but nice try."

Tristan elbowed Matt, but the guy stood his ground. His friend had bulked up over the spring, although Tristan didn't mention it— Matt's head was already the size of a blimp. "I'm not trying to get out of the bet. I want to know what I'm up against. Let's ask Renee or Brenda if we get a chance."

Matt bowed slightly as the girls passed by. "Ladies." He grinned, winking at them. A few giggled but Tristan shook his head. Shelby ignored Matt completely.

A lightness spread through Tristan's chest.

Ross stood at centre court waiting for them to circle round. "Good morning, athletes. I hope everyone is well rested. This morning's drill is footwork, so you're going to need all your mental and physical prowess. If you check out the field," he pointed, "you'll see an obstacle course laid out. You're competing against your own time. You'll have three attempts and your best time will be your entry into the competition. Josh," Ross inclined his head toward one of the counsellors, "will demonstrate, so let's make our way over there."

"Footwork," Matt mouthed to Tristan. Tristan wished he could wipe the smug smile off his friend's face. Instead, he clenched his fists. Agility ladders made up of hula hoops, sticks that formed a sort of hopscotch layout, a few steps that looked as though they were supposed to jump over them followed by pylons to race around, made up the course.

Tristan loved obstacle courses but found them tricky without skates on. His skating drills often involved a lot of footwork and on ice he didn't struggle. But dry ground always tripped him up. He'd stumble over his own feet, which felt light without the skates. He snuck a sideways glance at Shelby. She was eyeing the course, but she didn't appear nervous. A fierce expression covered her face. His stomach flip-flopped. *You got this. No way am I doing dish duty an extra week.*

Josh gave a demonstration and then they lined up in three lines, one for each course. Tristan stood in the middle line. Even though he was racing against himself, Tristan knew he'd perform better if he had an opponent hustling on either side. Shelby stood in the line on his right, not too far ahead of him. *Good.* He'd either watch her or compete with her, side by side.

The course was complicated—combining footwork and balance—and many athletes stumbled around like drunks rather than elite performers. The guy in front of Shelby had trouble with the course, so she'd be running at the same time as Tristan. *Excellent.* He stepped up to the head of the line, bending his knees slightly and breathing slowly. Next to him, Shelby did the same. The counsellor called out, "Set!" and then the green flag flew downward.

Keeping Shelby in his peripheral vision, he quick-stepped through the hula hoop ladder. Shelby stayed in sync with him, step for step. *Focus. You got this.*

Hopscotch next and Tristan increased his speed, using his strong legs to leap from block to block. Still, Shelby stayed stuck to him, breathing right beside him.

She flew over the steps, no longer in his peripheral vision but in front of him. They raced to the series of pylons, ran around them, then switched directions and did it all over again. He was good, but he had to keep his feet from getting too far ahead of his brain. Shelby, two steps in front of him, flew through the steps. *Work it, Kelly.* Urging his legs faster, he switched directions and ran the drill in the opposite direction until his legs burned. Cheers from the other athletes energized him, giving him an added spurt of adrenaline, but Shelby had him beat and crossed the finish line two seconds ahead of him. *Oh no.*

Bent over, gasping in air, Tristan felt a clap on his back. He glanced up to see Kyle and Matt laughing at him.

Kyle shook his head. "She smoked you, dude."

"I've got two more tries."

"You keep telling yourself that. Maybe you'll beat her." Tristan followed Matt's gaze to the board where the top ten times were posted. Shelby sat in second place with his time coming in fourth.

Tristan straightened. "I don't see your name up there, Matty-boy."

A shadow flickered over Matt's face. "Hey, it's not us you have to beat." He shot a look at Shelby before walking with Kyle to the end of the line. Tristan stood up and stretched his back, groaning.

Shelby clobbered all the other times in the next two attempts. Tristan had bettered his time but couldn't catch her and ended up in second. He stood scowling at the scoreboard as Matt sauntered up to him.

"I guess you're doing dishes."

"Na-uh. This is one race. She won this one, but I've beaten her in all the ball handling drills. We need a tie-breaker."

Matt furrowed his brow. "Okay, but it can't be something you're superior in."

"Deal." Tristan thought about the drills they'd done over the years. "Swimming? I don't think she's a swimmer, and that's not my strong event either. So that's fair."

Matt stared off at the tree line. "You're probably right, but I'm making sure just in case."

Tristan narrowed his eyes. "We need to find out what sport she does."

Making his way to the next training session, a hand-eye coordination drill, Tristan kept his eyes out for Renee or Brenda, but he didn't see either of them. Matt pumped his fist in the air when they arrived at the basketball courts. As he surveyed the basketballs lying on the ground, Tristan groaned. Along one side of the fence, tape marked out three different heights. Great. Hoops and verticals. Kyle came running up behind them, but as soon as he heard what the drill was, he slumped over.

Matt clapped his hand on Tristan's shoulder. "Yes! Guys... prepare to eat my dust."

"Consider it eaten," Tristan grumbled. "I hate verticals."

Kyle wiped a hand over his eyes. "I hear ya, bro. My body's not meant to fly."

Matt jumped, mimicking a jump off. "Like this?"

"Shut up." Tristan and Kyle spoke at the same time.

"What's the matter with you hockey and football players? All you know how to do is crash into each other. It's takes a real athlete to play basketball."

"Yeah, right. I dare you to come skate around a rink for five minutes."

"Or push back a two hundred pound body."

Matt cocked his head. "Guys, you're fooling yourselves as to who the real athletes are."

Renee ran up to them and draped an arm across Matt's shoulders. "Matty, the real athletes are the girls." She winked at Kyle and Tristan then turned to Shelby and Brenda, who had come up behind her. "Am I right, girls?"

"Absolutely." Brenda gave them a big smile.

Shelby didn't say anything. Tristan contemplated her. She looked uncomfortable. Hmmm.

"So, Shelby, what sport do you play?"

She stared at the basketball courts, her cheeks pinking.

"She's a dancer," Brenda chimed in.

Wait, what? Dancer? Why was she at an elite sports camp? Tristan stared at Shelby's pink face. Matt opened his mouth as though he wanted to ask her a question but couldn't get the words out. Kyle's brow furrowed and he rubbed his chin.

Tristan crossed his arms. "You're not an athlete. Why are you here?"

Shelby glared at him, lifting her chin slightly. "I am an athlete. I play a different style of sport, if you want to call it that. Obviously I trounced all of you at the footwork drill." She rested her hands on her hips. "Dancers are in way better shape than a lot of athletes."

He barked a laugh. "Yeah, right. You may be good at footwork, but you can't handle a ball. Can you keep up with us in other drills?"

She took a step toward him. "Endurance-wise, I could outlast you any day."

"Maybe you got lucky." He curled then flexed his fingers. "And it's not only footwork and endurance. It's about coordinating the whole body to move."

"You're such a jerk." She stomped away to where the rest of the kids were gathering. Brenda and Renee glared at him then followed Shelby.

Tristan turned to Matt. "Bet's off. She's not even an athlete."

Matt squinted. "Maybe."

"There's no maybe. It's an unfair contest."

"For her, since she's not an athlete as you so aptly pointed out. So why are you worried? You should beat her hands down, and I'll be stuck doing dishes."

"I'm not worried."

Matt studied him. "Sounds like you are." He opened his bottle of water and took a swig. "Bet's not off. Swimming sounds like a good equalizer."

Tristan shook his head and stalked off to centre court.

* * *

Brenda grabbed Shelby's arm as they stood around, waiting for the next session to start. "I'm sorry, was that a secret? I didn't know."

Shelby swallowed and tried to move her stiff lips upwards. "No, not a secret. I avoid telling people because, well, that's the kind of reaction I'm afraid of. People put dancers in a different box than athletes although we're in great shape. We just don't participate in a lot of sports to avoid injury."

"Aren't you afraid you'll get hurt?" Renee asked.

Shelby bit her lip. "Kinda. But my mother thought it would be good conditioning and help me be a better dancer. Besides, it's mostly drills and training—it's not like I'm going out playing in scrimmages of football and hockey."

Brenda kneeled down to tie her shoelace. "I guess. How does being here make you a better dancer?"

Her mother's words echoed in her mind. "Uses different muscle groups. Rounds out some areas where maybe I'm weak. Why are you here?"

Brenda stood up. "Same reasons, I guess."

Shelby watched Tristan walk over to the group of waiting athletes, his face hard. "What's Tristan's problem?"

Renee waved a hand through the air, dismissing him. "He likes being the best. He's probably threatened by your brilliance in the obstacle course. Don't pay any attention to him."

Shelby studied the hockey player, standing statue still, hands on hips, staring out at the trees. *Why do I care what he thinks? He's a jerk athlete.*

* * *

Not a basketball player. Never would be. Didn't care. Shelby threw her ball into the bin, her cheeks pink with exertion and humiliation. She didn't even know how to do a lay-up. Apparently everyone here had known how to do one by the time they were like five. *Mom, I could kill you right now.*

The kids were lining up against the wall where strips of red tape started above Shelby's head. They went up in increments of two feet to well past the tallest person there. The second part of the drill.

Ross stepped forward. "Verticals. Everyone know what they are?" He looked directly at Shelby. *Sheesh, nothing like singling me out.* Shelby nodded. *I think I know.* Verticals were a type of jump, like a soubresaut.

Ross clapped his hands. "Good. Line up in groups of five. You have three jumps to make your personal best."

Everyone lined up. Shelby made sure Tristan wasn't anywhere near her. He could stuff his ego and attitude.

She watched people jump. The basketball and volleyball players were by far the best vertical jumpers. Tristan took his turn and she smiled. She'd beat him by a mile. Her grin widened as she stalked to the wall. She leaped, hitting one of the higher markers. The coach smiled at her as he wrote down the height she'd achieved.

Her next jump took her even higher—on par with some of the better basketball and volleyball players. Her final jump took her to within the top jumpers. Only the really, really tall guys had her beat. She turned away from the wall, locking eyes with Tristan's blazing green ones. She cocked her head as she strutted up to him and said, "Beat that, super athlete."

His eyes narrowed and she smiled sweetly, brushing past him. Skipping over to Renee and Brenda, she curtsied with extremely bad form. Madame Clare would have a heart attack, but her new friends clapped and cheered.

* * *

Tristan avoided the smug expressions on Kyle's and Matt's faces. Matt had soundly beat them both, landing in the top ten jumps. Tristan had beat Kyle's jumps, but he figured Matt's smugness had to do with Shelby making the top ten. *Barely.* She was tenth. The only girl. And probably one of the shortest.

Matt burst out laughing.

Tristan swallowed the irritation threatening to spill out. "What's your problem?"

Matt doubled over, his hands on his knees. "Your face. You should... have seen it."

"Shut up."

Kyle grinned. "Yeah, I think incredulous would be a good word for it. Maybe she'll switch over to basketball."

"She couldn't do a lay-up," Tristan muttered.

Kyle nodded. "Oh yeah. Too bad. She's one heck of a jumper."

Matt straightened, wiping tears from his eyes. "I think that's what dancers do, jump a lot."

"Maybe so, but there's still the issue of her lack of hand-eye coordination."

Matt clapped his hand on Tristan's shoulder. "Don't be a sore loser, bro. It's not a good look for you. Let it go."

"Whatever." Tristan grabbed his water bottle and took a long drink. "I guess it comes down to swimming—then I'll be the one laughing as you wash dishes every night." Capping the water, he walked to the cabins, his friends following him. Matt and Kyle were giving each other noogies, so Tristan ignored them and sped up. He'd grab a shower and then eat. Hopefully by then the burn of losing to Shelby, *ballerina*, wouldn't hurt so much.

CHAPTER SIX

THE SMELL OF GARLIC AND ONIONS TEASED SHELBY'S NOSE AND THE
longhouse buzzed with the noise of the lunch crowd. Laughter, shouts,
and the clang of dishes all mixed together for a rousing camp melody.
Most of the tables were full as Shelby searched out her friends. She
wished she'd skipped the showers, since she'd had to wait because they
were busy. Swimming drills had been on the docket this ninth day at
camp—not that she was counting—and the lake water made a mess of
her hair. Conditioning her hair was not optional after a lake swim if she
had any hopes of getting a brush through it.

Renee waved to her from across the room. The weekend had provided time to get to know some of the other campers and relax their
bodies. Shelby had spent most of the days with Renee and Brenda. She
picked up a plate of garden salad with chicken and a container of yo-
gurt. The morning had been good. The drills went well and she'd had
fun. They hadn't raced the boys, which was a nice change. Still, she
smiled as she remembered Tristan's look when she creamed him in the
treading water drill.

Grabbing extra veggies and fruit, she walked to her friends in the
back but halted. Tristan, Kyle, and Matt sat there too. To her relief,
they'd been away for the weekend on a special hike and she didn't have
to deal with questions about dance or Tristan's ego. She forced herself
to move forward, set her tray down, and slid onto the bench beside
Renee, across from Tristan. "Come for more butt whooping?"

He scowled at her and then studied his chicken burger like it was
the most interesting thing he'd seen. Matt coughed behind his hand,
muttering something. Shelby narrowed her eyes at him. Did he say

something about dishes? What did that mean? She shook her head and turned to Renee, whispering, "Why are they here?"

Renee opened her mouth, but Matt chimed in, "We wanted to ask you about dancing."

Tristan kept chewing, as though he didn't really care. Shelby crossed her arms. "Riight."

Matt sipped from his soda. "Really. I want to know."

She stuck her straw in her drink. "I don't want to talk about it."

Tristan set his sandwich down. "Why not? Afraid?"

Everyone at the table stilled. She lowered her drink to the table with a thunk. "The only thing I'm afraid of is causing you embarrassment with my *athletic* prowess." Her stomach clenched. *Why did you say that?*

Tristan's eyes widened, but the rest of the table hooted and the guys pounded the table.

"Burn buddy."

"You go, girl!"

She smiled sweetly at Tristan. "And it's obvious you know nothing about ballet, so I'm not wasting my time talking about my *sport* to a bunch of buffoons who are only interested in making fun of it." *Shut up now.*

Leaning across the table, he said, "You're a snob. If I took that kind of attitude every time someone asked me about hockey, I'd have no friends or fans. I understand now why the arts are such an elite— not in a good way—thing. No normal person wants to hang out with such snobbery." He threw the last of his sandwich on his plate as he stood, then picked up his tray and strode away.

Shelby cringed. All eyes were on her and heat crawled up her neck. She sipped her drink and stared at her salad, her appetite gone.

"Don't listen to him. He must be going through puberty with all his mood swings." Matt's voice drew her out of her reverie. "Plus he's a sore loser."

Shelby picked up her fork, stabbing it into a piece of cucumber. "It doesn't matter. I told my mother the athletes wouldn't accept me when she signed me up to come here."

Brenda shoved her tray away. "Tristan did make a point, though. How are we supposed to understand ballet if you won't explain it?"

Good question. Shelby knew both Brenda and Tristan had made good points—maybe that's what made her want to slap Tristan so badly. She turned to Matt. "Okay, you want to know about dancing? This is how I train. I run every morning to build endurance. I attend a performing arts school, where I go to regular class in the mornings and then attend ballet class for the rest of the afternoon. When we're rehearsing for performances I can be in the studio for up to eight hours a day, and most of that time is spent dancing.

"Male dancers lift other dancers. Ballerinas dance en pointe, balancing all their weight on the pointe of their feet, sometimes only on one foot. You should Google a performance of Giselle, one of the most challenging roles for a ballerina. Then Google verticals that the male dancers jump."

Renee sipped her water. "Yeah, I've been to a few performances of the National Dance Company and whoa, those dancers are in top shape. Shane Tivoli, one of the main dancers, is unbelievable. She practically flies through the air."

Heart pounding at her mother's name, Shelby carefully set her fork down and clasped her hands in her lap. She needed to change the topic or get out of there.

"Shelby?"

Shelby blinked. "Uh sorry, spaced out there. What?"

"Have you ever seen Shane Tivoli dance?"

Ha! Have I ever seen her dance? Gulping in a breath, she smiled. "Sure, she's great."

Matt and Kyle stared at her. "You go to school for dancing?" Matt raised his eyebrows.

"Yeah, I mean, don't you go for football?"

"Yeah, but I don't take courses in it. It's extracurricular."

"What's wrong with your school then?" She grinned.

Kyle pointed a finger. "Good point. I'd say the dance world has got it right. I'd love to go to school half days and play football the rest."

"Well, it's not exactly like that. We have to fit all the requirements of our academic education into a smaller amount of time."

"Whatever. You get to do what you want to do the rest of the time."

Right. A quiver ran through her stomach. Did she get to do what she wanted to do the rest of the time? Like coming here to this camp? Spending every holiday at the theatre, watching her mother perform or rehearse? Not to mention the endless hours in the studio, the bleeding toes and aching muscles. She shoved away the unwanted thoughts. *Of course I love ballet. It's the only thing that matters... right? One day I'll prove to Mom I can be the best too.*

The bell rang, signalling free time for the afternoon. Shelby stood. "Uh, thanks for asking about dance. Sorry for being a snob." She stepped over the bench. "I've got to go." Grabbing her tray, she walked to the dirty dish deposit, biting her lip. She'd handled that all wrong.

* * *

Tristan stuffed his hands in his pockets as he strode down the path to the beach. After plopping onto the sand, he kicked off his shoes and stretched out on the warm ground. He closed his eyes. The girl was an elitist snob and no athlete. A prima donna—wasn't that what they called those demanding dancers? He sat up and threw a handful of sand. *Now I have to do dish duty for Matt too. Stupid treading water.* He hadn't realized it was the only drill he'd compete with Shelby in when they were swimming. The other lane races were boys against boys and girls against girls. Really? Rarely did Ross divide up the teams that way. Why start now?

The horn blew to signal free period and Tristan groaned. Matt was going to rub in the fact he'd lost the bet all afternoon. He stood and headed to the cabins and the full plate of crow he knew Matt would serve him.

* * *

The birds chirping in the trees outside sounded like a buzz saw in the still afternoon. Shelby sighed and rolled over on her side for the hundredth time. The hard bunk made it impossible to find a comfortable position. Finally, annoyed at herself, she grabbed her phone and quietly crawled down her ladder, not wanting to wake her bunkmates who were all enjoying naps.

When she closed the door softly behind her, the midday heat embraced her and she squinted in the bright sunlight. Shelby strolled to a shaded area and sat on an old stump. The scents of pine, earth, and newly-cut grass filled the air, and she breathed in deeply. The grounds were still and silent. Most kids chose to read, rest, or play a quiet game during this time. She scrolled through her contacts until she came to her mother's contact information and hit the call button.

One ring then her mother's voice shattered the silence. "Shelby darling, this is a surprise. Is anything wrong?"

"I'm fine, Mom. Thought I'd check in." She bit her lip. "People found out I'm a dancer, and of course they're asking why I'm at this camp." *Well, one person is anyway. That will change as word gets out.*

"Shelby, it's fine. You've only been there a little more than a week. Give them an education on how fit a dancer really is. I know you didn't want to go, but it's not like you to whine like this."

"I'm not whining, Mom." Shelby cringed. Maybe she did sound a little like a two year old. Didn't she deserve to? "Mom, this is a mistake. I need to come home now."

"Shelby." Frustration gave her mother's voice an edge. "We've already discussed it. I'm leaving for Australia tomorrow, and you can't stay by yourself. End of story."

Shelby groaned, her own frustration building. "Listen to me. I can take care of myself. I'm sixteen. I can't stay here."

"Yes, you can. We all do things we don't like or want to do, Shelby. That's life. You can do this. We don't quit. Besides, it will help with your dancing."

Hot pricks of liquid burned Shelby's eyes, and she wrenched the phone away from her ear, gulping air. "Please, Mom," she whispered into the air.

"Shelby? Are you still there?"

Bringing the phone to her ear, Shelby closed her eyes. "I'm still here." *Unfortunately.*

"Don't you want to improve your skills?"

She opened her eyes and stared at the waves lapping the shore but didn't say anything. *Why am I never enough?*

You are enough for me. The soft voice whispered like a breeze in Shelby's ear. She glanced around. *Who said that?* No one else was on the beach. Did she imagine that voice?

"Shelby?" Her mother's strained voice came through the phone. It definitely hadn't been her mother.

"Yes, Mom. Have a good trip." She clicked off, not caring that she'd hung up on her mother. Why did she expect her mom to behave differently? After dropping her phone into the pocket of her shorts, she leaned forward, propping her elbows on her knees and cradling her head. She was stuck here, and if she wanted to survive, she needed better hand-eye coordination. Dropping and chasing balls all over the place wasn't cutting it. She needed help and she had friends who'd assist her. *You are enough.* What a lie. She'd never be enough. Not for her mom. Not for ballet. Not for people like Tristan. But she wasn't going down without a fight. She'd show them. Hand-eye coordination and ball skills—she'd master both if it killed her.

CHAPTER SEVEN

THE EMPTY BASKETBALL COURT INTIMIDATED SHELBY. ON THE FLIP SIDE, NO one would witness her humiliation. She chuckled softly. *Who am I kidding? They've all witnessed my stellar ball handling skills.* Renee trotted over to the bin of balls and sorted through them.

Shelby stood next to the bin, watching. "Thanks for giving up your rest time to help me."

"No problem. I wasn't doing anything." Renee bent over and tugged out a tennis ball. "Okay, let's work on how to hold onto different ball widths. We'll work our way up from small to big."

Shelby raised her eyebrow. "I think I can hold onto a tennis ball."

"Really? Like you did with the hopscotch drill?"

She closed her eyes. *Oh.* "You're right."

Renee cupped her ear. "Wait, repeat that. *I'm* right?"

Shelby laughed, nudging Renee with the tennis ball. "Shut up and show me how to correctly hold it."

Renee examined Shelby's grip, moving her fingers around the fuzz. "Does that feel more secure?"

Shelby waved her hand around, then hopped up and down. "Amazing. It doesn't feel like it's going to fly out of my hand."

Renee grinned then made a zipping motion with her fingers over her lips.

Shelby rolled the ball between her palms, the fuzziness tickling them. "Okay, go ahead and say I told you so."

"I don't have to, you said it for me—soo much better." Renee handed her a basketball and showed her how to handle it. Shelby found it awkward and kept losing it as she dribbled. She let out a hiss of frustration.

Renee frowned then came over to her. "Okay stop. I'm not sure what the problem is."

"Coordination?"

"No, it's not that. Let's see your hands."

Holding the ball in place with the toe of her running shoe, Shelby stuck out her hands. "Why do you need to see my hands?"

"Hmm, that's what I thought. You've got small hands, which is why you're having difficulty with the ball. It's controlling you rather than the other way around. Keep practicing your dribble and feel the ball under your fingers."

Shelby tried to run up the court, dribbling, but ended up booting the ball across the blacktop. "Agh!" She chased the ball down and then dropped it into the bin. Basketball was like math—when would she ever use either?

"Let's move on. I'll practice dribbling later."

Renee picked up a football. "I find the football the weirdest to handle. I think it's the shape." She molded Shelby's fingers around the oblong ball.

"Yeah, this feels really awkward."

"Throw it."

Shelby attempted a toss, only to watch the ball nose-dive at her feet.

Chuckling, Renee bent over and picked up the ball. "You need to arc your arm way back and follow through."

"Huh?"

Renee demonstrated for her and then fixed Shelby's hand on the ball so her fingers gripped the laces. "Give it a try."

They spent the next few minutes throwing the football, then Renee drew out a hockey stick and handed it to Shelby.

"Why do I need this?" Thoughts of auburn-haired hockey players filled her head. *Stop it.*

"Because stick handling is as important as throwing in some sports. In hockey, for example, it takes the place of throwing the ball." She flicked the stick back and forth. "Besides, don't you want to at least try to compete with Tristan? If you can't handle the stick, he'll cream you and then rub it in."

Shelby grabbed the stick from Renee. "You're right. Show me all you've got."

"I can teach you basics, but you'll have to get Brenda to show you how to finesse it all."

* * *

Tristan watched Shelby try to stop the tennis ball with the hockey stick, only to have it roll away. She moved too slowly. His fingers itched to grab a stick and show her how to do it. Instead, he wandered over to where the canoes were stacked and dragged one down, then another.

"I hate this drill," Matt complained as he helped Tristan with the canoe. "My arms always kill afterwards."

"What? Your arms and shoulders are ripped. This should be a piece of cake." Reaching for a bright blue canoe, Tristan waited until Matt had a hold of the other end, then hauled it off the rack.

"I know, but there must be muscles I only use for canoeing, because I always hurt afterwards." He grunted as he yanked the canoe off the top rack. "I wonder how dancer girl will do."

"I don't care." Tristan spat out the words. "And why do you? You've won the bet."

"Just curious. She seems very passionate about proving herself as an athlete." His eyes narrowed. "And you? You protest too much."

Tristan dropped the canoe onto the grass. "What are you implying?"

Matt wiped his hands on his tie-dyed board shorts. "You're obstinate—you won't even give her a chance or acknowledge her athleticism."

Tristan tapped the side of his head. "All in your imagination. I don't like fakers, posers, whatever you want to call them. People who pretend to be something they're not."

"And that's what you think she's doing?"

He lifted his hands, palms up. "Isn't she? She comes here keeping it a secret that she's a *ballerina* until we force it out of her. Then she acts all high and mighty because we question whether she's an athlete. *Which she's not, by the way.* Dancing is an art form, not a sport."

"Doesn't make her any less fit than the rest of us."

"It's not the same."

Matt removed another canoe from the racks and set it by the others. "See? Obstinate. What's the big deal?"

Tristan ignored the question as he flipped over a yellow canoe that had been resting against the boathouse. After opening the door to the little hut, he strode in and gathered up a handful of paddles. Dropping two in each canoe, he thought about Matt's question.

"My dad's a poser."

Matt gathered a handful of lifejackets from the hut and tossed two into each boat. Tristan waited for him to say something. His friend knew his parents were divorced, but Tristan had never told him why.

"My dad pretended that he loved us. He pretended to be a good husband and father, but he lied. A total fake." Tristan stared through the trees to the lake as his heart pounded against his ribs. He'd never told anyone that. "I don't trust people pretending to be something they're not."

Matt's hazel eyes bored into him, but he remained silent for a change. Tristan shifted his weight, his cheeks burning. He was glad Matt didn't say anything, because he didn't want to hear any platitudes. He wouldn't be fooled again. By anyone. Especially Shelby Wright.

* * *

Shelby eyed the row of blue, yellow, and red canoes lining the beach. *Were they serious?* She bit her lip. *Shoot.* She had no idea how to canoe. Shane Tivoli hadn't thought it important enough to teach her daughter or, rather, have someone else teach her. Until now, apparently. Campers jostled for position around her, trying to get close enough to hear Ross. Shelby couldn't focus on his words because her stomach flipped back and forth, making her queasy.

I should be used to the humiliation. She hugged herself. Could she fake it? How hard could it be to swing the paddle back and forth in the water? Her stomach calmed. It couldn't be that hard. Yes, she'd fake it. She eyed the eager, tanned faces until her eyes were met by the piercing stare of Tristan's green ones. She tilted her head and raised her eyebrow in a challenge. *What are you doing? You don't even know how to canoe —why are you challenging him?* She knew why. Everything in her wanted to wipe the arrogance off his face. She'd show him that she was an athlete—as good as him.

He smirked.

Of all the nerve!

A jab to her ribs brought her back to the beach and canoes. Ross was reading names off a list and people were pairing up.

"You know how to canoe, right?" Renee hissed in her ear.

"Umm..."

Renee's eyes widened. "You don't? Did you hear who you're paired with?"

Shelby closed her eyes. Please no. *If there is a God, please don't let it be him.*

Renee uttered the dreaded word. "Tristan."

Panic clawed up her chest and into her throat.

Renee rubbed her back. "It's okay. Tell him you've never canoed."

She gently pushed Shelby forward, but she held her ground, resisting. "No, I can't..."

"Yes, you can. You don't have a choice."

Shelby stumbled over to Tristan, speechless.

He grabbed the paddles out of a green canoe. "C'mon, prima donna, let's go."

Shelby's eyes narrowed, her fear dissipating. "*What* did you call me?"

He threw her a life jacket that ended up ricocheting off her chest and falling to the ground. Huffing, she picked it up, slid her arms through the holes, and fastened the buckles. She stood, watching Tristan drop the paddles in the canoe, her chest tightening.

He shoved the boat into the water, then stood waiting for her. "Well?" He pointed to the front of the boat.

She took a step, halted, then took another step. Blowing out a breath, she forced her body forward. *You can do this. How hard can it be to paddle a canoe?*

The cool water licked her feet as she reached for the wobbling craft. Grabbing the sides with both hands, she swung her leg over and sat on the bench, yanking her other leg inside the boat. After shoving the canoe into deeper water, Tristan swung himself into the boat behind her, rocking it. She gripped the edge until the sound of his paddle knocking against the side of the boat alerted her to the fact that he'd picked it up, so she grasped hers. Her fingers ran over the smooth wood of the paddle. How did they do it in the movies?

"A little help, PD?"

"My name's not PD. What does that even mean?" Irritation made her voice rasp. *PD? What the heck? Ah.* PD for Prima Donna. Where had he picked up that term? Her mother was a prima donna. She wasn't. Judging by the tone of his voice, he knew what it meant. She clutched her paddle, fantasizing clobbering him with it. Enjoying the thought of smacking him, she forgot to paddle.

His voice brought her back to the present. "Are you going to help or not?"

She smiled broadly and glanced over her shoulder. "I don't know how to canoe." *Take that, you jerk.*

The boat started to turn in a circle. She dipped her paddle in the water.

"Wait!" He reached out and touched her shoulder, his fingers burning through the fabric of her T-shirt. He must have felt the heat too, as he yanked his hand away.

"Stop what you're doing."

Still watching him over her shoulder, she bit her lip to keep from laughing at his red face.

He glared at her. "Watch what I do and repeat it on the opposite side." He showed her how to work the paddle. She copied him.

"Keep doing that until I tell you to switch sides. I'm the one who steers, so all I need you to do is keep paddling. Got it?"

Shelby mock saluted and straightened on the bench as he let out a huff behind her. The corners of her lips lifted. Finally they moved out into the lake where a few other canoes waited by the buoy for the stragglers so they could begin the drill.

Tristan maneuvered them into place. His voice rumbled behind her and she turned sideways as he bent forward. "Paddle like I told you and follow any instructions I give you." She sent him a heated look before facing forward and watching the last boat float into place. She could feel irritation with her rolling off of him, and she wiped her sweaty palms on her jean shorts. *Why am I letting him get to me?*

The bull horn sounded and all the canoes lurched forward. Shelby kept her eyes on the buoy, moving her arms in the sweeping motion he'd shown her. In her peripheral vision, his paddle dug into the water like a shovel.

"Faster!" he yelled.

The paddle sliced through the water. In and out. In and out. Her arms and shoulders burned. She imagined her partner's muscles rippling as he paddled. She shook her head. *Focus.*

They approached the turn, and Shelby held her paddle steady as Tristan steered them around the buoy. Shelby peered over the side to watch for the buoy.

"Don't lean so far over the—"

Shelby jerked back, losing her balance. Grabbing wildly for something to hold on to, she tipped too far toward the water and fell headfirst into the cold lake. Her life jacket kept her afloat and she bobbed around, getting her bearings. The overturned canoe floated nearby with a scowling Tristan gripping its side.

"Hope you can swim, because it's impossible for us to get back into the canoe." His face was as red as his hair, which stuck up in all directions. Shelby giggled.

"It's not funny."

She covered her mouth with a dripping hand, but another chuckle escaped. He turned away, but she couldn't stop laughing.

One of the counsellors paddled alongside their canoe. With Tristan's help, he lifted it up and out of the water then flipped it right side up while it lay across his own canoe. Shelby was amazed at how efficiently he worked. He held it steady as the hockey player threw his paddle in the boat and then hauled himself out of the water and inside. The counsellor reached a hand out to Shelby.

"No, she's swimming to shore."

Her eyes jerked to Tristan. "No—"

"Yes, you are. It's not that far."

The counsellor glanced between them. "I'm going to let you two work this out." He rowed away.

Tristan picked up his paddle, reaching out with it, and sent her paddle drifting toward her. "See you on shore."

"Wait."

Tristan paddled away, and Shelby slapped the water, sending a loud splash toward the boat. "Jerk."

* * *

Tristan sipped his root beer as he watched Shelby emerge from the lake. Pieces of her hair clung to her scowling face. *Who's laughing now?* But the knot in his stomach tied his insides tighter. Making her swim was low. Her blue eyes, darker than he'd ever seen them, locked onto him. She flung her wet life jacket at him as she stomped by.

He forced his lips up. "Water a nice temp?"

"You are the biggest A-class jerk I've ever met."

His smile slipped from his lips. "Oh? Have you met yourself? Why didn't you admit before getting into the boat that you've never canoed? Were you going to try and fake it?"

Her cheeks and ears reddened.

She rubbed her upper arms with both hands. "I... I told you."

"Right. Once we were in the canoe and it was obvious you didn't know what you were doing. Can't ask for help or admit you don't know how to do something? Is that it? Is that how it works in the dance world?"

Don't admit your weakness. A lesson she'd learned early on in life. "It's not rocket science. Besides, we weren't the only ones who tipped."

"We didn't finish the race. My overall score, instead of being in first, is now third. Thanks to you."

She wrung water from her hair. "You'll make it up."

He stood and threw his soda can into the recycling bin, the clang of it ringing through the trees. She smelled like lake, coconut oil, and something all her. It teased his nostrils. He stepped away.

"Yeah, you bet I will. No thanks to you. You're a poser. How do I know you're telling the truth about being a dancer? Maybe you lied about that too."

Her eyes widened, then she shook her head and stalked away. He breathed deeply, in and out. He hated liars.

CHAPTER EIGHT

LIAR.

Tristan's words echoed in her mind as Shelby paced her cabin after dinner that night. She was no liar.

How do I know you're telling the truth about being a dancer? Maybe you lied about that too.

She walked over to her duffle bag and rummaged through her clothing, her fingers hitting soft satin. She plucked out her pointe shoes. The smell of sweat and rosin emerged with her shoes, and she ran her fingers over the glossy satin ribbons wrapped around them. Grabbing her phone off her bed, she hurried out of the cabin.

Ross had offered her space to practice, at her mother's insistence, in the basement of the longhouse. She'd stayed away, not wanting to draw attention to herself by slipping away every afternoon or night, but now the thought of practicing something familiar and routine drew her to the longhouse. *I'm no amateur dancer. How dare he!*

The quiet and solitude of the basement soothed Shelby's frayed nerves. The setting sun cast long shadows through the windows. After finding the room, she slipped inside and flicked on the lights. The room was bare with the exception of a counter along one wall, which was a perfect barre. Hardwood floors were buffed but not slippery. She fingered her shoes, along with the little bag of rosin stuffed inside them, as she kicked off her flip flops. Sitting on the floor, she stretched out her muscles, which groaned in protest. The camp provided lots of activity, but she hadn't practiced her ballet at all and her body knew it.

Shelby tugged on her slippers and tied the pink ribbons around her ankles, testing to make sure they were tight and would hold. Satisfied, she searched her phone for suitable music to do barre work to.

The sound filled the room and Shelby gripped the edge of the counter, losing herself in pliés.

* * *

Is that classical music? Tristan grinned, ready to mock whoever had such a poor choice in music. He crept to the door with light spilling from the window and peered in. His heart slammed into his ribcage as his jaw dropped. He ducked to one side of the door, out of sight, and ran a hand over his mouth.

Shelby. She was the one with the bad taste in music—only she wasn't listening, she was dancing. Hidden in shadows, he peered through the window. Not that she'd notice him. Clearly, she was lost in her own little world.

* * *

Moving to the centre of the room, her body limber after warming up at the barre, Shelby worked through her exercises. The music was gentle and breezy and her body became one with its rhythm. She was air and light. *This feels great.*

It'd been some time since she'd felt good about dance. Her mother's pressure and expectations for her to be top in her class and win all the lead parts in productions stole the joy Shelby had when she danced. Nothing was good enough for her mother, no matter how hard she worked. She always had a critique or comment on how Shelby could try harder, lift her leg higher, or simply be more. Pushing those thoughts away, she concentrated on the quick footwork of the pas dé chats and her body moving. *Just be.*

Shelby picked up her towel and wiped her forehead. Grabbing her water, she sipped then readied her body for piqué turns. As she rotated across the room, a shadow in the hall grabbed her attention. Losing her balance, she stepped out of the turn, hurried over, and flung the door open. Tristan stood in the hallway, looking like a kid who'd gotten caught with his hand in the cookie jar. He winced.

"Are you spying on me?"

He held his palms up. "Wait. No... I, uh, no!"

Shelby pursed her lips, waiting for him to calm down, enjoying the fact she had him flustered. Why was he here? How much had he seen? Why did his presence cause butterflies to erupt in her belly?

"I wasn't spying—not intentionally. I was putting away some equipment when I heard the classical music and wondered who had the bad taste in tunes."

Wow. This guy's arrogance zoomed off the charts.

His face softened. "But then I saw you... and I wanted to watch you dance." He cleared his throat. "You're definitely not an amateur— what I saw was incredible. You're an amazing dancer."

Heat crawled up her neck, making her already warm cheeks burn. "So not a liar?"

He hung his head. "No, not a liar. I'm sorry I said that. And I'm sorry I made you swim to shore too. That was mean."

"It was, but thanks." A warmth spread through her chest. She stepped back and moved to shut the door. "I need to practice."

"Wait." Tristan stuck his foot in the gap between the door and the frame.

She opened her mouth, but closed it without speaking. What more could he possibly want?

"Uh, do you mind if I watch? I've never really seen ballet up close." His cheeks flamed.

She stared at the ceiling. *Do I want him to watch?* Earlier comments about being a snob and not wanting to talk dance came back to her memory. *What could it hurt?* Maybe she'd convert him to agreeing that dancers were athletes too. Also, he looked cute standing there.

"Fine." She stepped back to let him in. "If you want to sit in the corner, I'll try not to step on you." Her lips lifted in a grin.

He bowed then hurried over to the far corner, settling himself against the wall.

She reset the music for the exercise and fanned herself. The room was a sauna. His presence filled the space, and his green eyes, the co-lour of sea glass tonight, bored into her. Goosebumps popped out on her skin and she rubbed them. *Focus on the turns, not him. Pretend he's not here. You've done this a million times.* Music swelled and Shelby lined her body up for the turns, channeling every ounce of her mother's confidence she'd ever seen displayed. *You can do this.*

* * *

Sweat dripped down Shelby's temples and back as she turned off the music. Tristan stood and shoved his hands in his pockets. Words eluded him. He'd witnessed a full body workout, not flitting around. Different from his hockey practices in how they worked, but no less in any way. He'd been so wrong about this girl and her "sport."

"How long have you been dancing?"

She chuckled. "Before I could walk."

Tristan laughed. "Really?"

"Pretty much." After picking up her phone, she shoved it in her pocket and rested her hip against the countertop. "My mom is a dancer too, and she took me into the studio when I was a baby. Once I could walk, she'd play dance with me. As soon as I was old enough, five or so, she enrolled me in lessons. I've been dancing ever since. You?"

"Since I was four. I'd skate around carrying a small hockey stick with me, and I was playing house league hockey by the time I was six or seven."

"I take it someone close to you played?"

"My dad." His chest hurt at the memory. "He'd make us a rink in our backyard every winter. We—my brothers and I—skated out there for hours, playing a pick-up game with our friends or shooting pucks at the net."

She smiled. "I guess we have that in common then—starting early."

"Yeah, I guess we do." His lips moved upwards too and he stared into her blue eyes longer than necessary. He shook himself out of the trance and toed the hardwood floor. *Get it together.* "Are you planning to dance after school?"

Her forehead creased.

Uh oh, wrong question.

Her shoulder lifted gracefully then fell. "Yeah, I mean, I guess I never really thought that I wouldn't. It's been sort of assumed. School is dancing, since it's a performing arts school, and from there I'll get scouted by dance companies."

"No college?"

"Not now. Can't waste my prime years sitting at a desk." She winced and muttered, "Oh my gosh, I sound like my mother."

"Your mother doesn't want you to go to college?" What mother or father didn't want their kids to go on to higher learning?

A sigh escaped those full pink lips that begged for a kiss. He frowned. Whoa, where had that thought come from? *Focus, man.*

"College has never really been a goal. One of my cousins got into an Ivy League school, and I asked a lot of questions. My mother didn't like it and dismissed the idea. She told me that I don't need to go to college until later—I need to use my prime years to dance, not sit at a desk and let my legs atrophy. End of discussion. I haven't brought it up since." She bit that full, lower lip. "You?"

Tristan forced his gaze away and studied his hands. "It's a little more complicated but also the same. I'm playing what is called major junior hockey right now in the Western Hockey League. NHL scouts are watching me, and if they decide they want to draft me, then I won't go to college right now."

"Do you want to play pro hockey?"

"Heck yeah. I can't imagine doing anything else. You don't want to dance?"

"I do, but I sometimes wish I had a choice instead of it being assumed." She studied her hands. "My mom's kind of a big deal in the dance world." She peered up at him from under long lashes. He didn't say anything. The words came rushing out of her like a dam breaking. "Ever heard of Shane Tivoli?"

He squinted at the ceiling. "Yeah, I think so. Prima ballerina with the National Dance Company? Renee mentioned her."

Shelby's mouth dropped open. He lifted a shoulder. "I'm not a total redneck." Heat infused his ears. "I might have Googled a few things."

She gave a shaky laugh.

"You know her or something? Is she your coach?"

Shelby crossed her arms over her chest. "No, she's my mother."

He sucked in a breath and her eyes flitted to his. "Oh."

She nodded, rocking her weight from one foot to the other. Side to side. Side to side. He stepped closer and said softly, "Wow, that's either really crazy good or really hard. Like having Wayne Gretzky for a father."

Her lips edged up. "My sports knowledge is limited, but I do know who Wayne Gretzky is—he's the G. O. A. T. in hockey, right?"

A warm sensation ran through Tristan's chest. "Exactly right. There's hope for you yet." The smile he was hoping to get with his little joke didn't materialize.

"Yeah." She swallowed. "Don't tell anyone, okay? No one knows she's my mother."

"Sure. I won't say anything."

Silence filled the room. Shelby lowered herself to the floor and began untying her shoe's ribbons.

He surveyed the now quiet, empty room. "Dancing must be a lonely pursuit."

She folded the ribbons around her shoes. "Why do you say that?"

"In hockey I have my teammates and it's like a second family, but dancing seems solitary. I like the company of a team. Do you have that in ballet?"

Shelby tucked her legs under her, crisscross fashion. "Yeah, there's bonding that happens when we put on productions and perform together. In class it can get competitive or at auditions. But isn't it the same in hockey? You compete for positions on the team or for ice time or for the little ball?"

"Puck."

"What?"

He laughed. "The little ball is called a puck."

"Whatever."

"Not whatever. Do you like it when someone says you dance on tippy-toes?"

"No."

"Same thing when you call it a little ball."

"Point taken." Shelby chuckled. "And speaking of pointe, danc-ing on your toes is called dancing en pointe." She made to stand up.

Tristan stuck his hand out, and she stared at it for a minute. "What? I don't have cooties."

She slipped her soft hand into his roughened one and an electric current jolted up his arm. *Did she feel that?* She withdrew her hand too quickly.

"Thanks for dancing for me tonight."

"I didn't dance for you. You spied on me and then I let you watch while I danced for myself."

"For the record, I wasn't spying. Blame it on the poor choice in music."

"Tchaikovsky is not a poor choice in music."

"I don't know about that, but I will admit that the dancing made it better."

That won him a grin and he smiled, enjoying the way her face lit up. They left the building together and he walked close beside her, their arms brushing against one another as they strolled to their cabins.

A shiver ran down his spine. *No distractions.*

CHAPTER NINE

THE CLIMBING WALL CAST ITS SHADOW OVER TRISTAN AND THE OTHER campers. A cold sweat covered his body, chilling him. He rubbed sweaty palms over the front of his long-sleeved T-shirt as he surveyed the twenty-foot wall. Day Eleven at Ross's was going to kill him. Campers lined up, excitedly chatting as they not-so-patiently waited their turns. He stared at the top of the wall as his stomach turned over. Suddenly he wished he hadn't eaten eggs for breakfast. The rope attached to his harness jerked him forward. He tugged it hard, and Matt, his partner today, stumbled toward him.

"Hey!" yelped Matt as he found his footing.

Tristan scowled at him. "Don't yank me then."

"I forgot you're mean when you're scared."

Heat burned his cheeks. He sighed. "Sorry, Matty. I was out of line."

His friend clapped a hand on Tristan's shoulder. "Keep moving. Don't look down. Your mission is to get to the top. That's it. Timer stops as soon as you're there. I'll make sure you get down in one piece. You know you can do this—you do it every year and live."

"But I have a heart attack every time."

Matt checked the clip on Tristan's harness, tugging it secure. He tilted his head to the left. "She's over there." His lips quirked up as he gave a final yank on Tristan's rope. "She's not sweating bullets either."

Tristan slid his glance sideways. Shelby was talking with her partner. Last week, he'd have crossed her off the list as a competitor in the climb, but after seeing her dance, he wasn't so sure. Yes, her ball and stick skills were brutal, but she had a strong core and legs, even though she looked like some kind of fairy rather than a warrior. A fairy warrior. The thought made his lips quirk up.

As if reading his mind, her eyes met his and a current passed between them. Did she notice it? Her partner said something, grabbing her attention. She took rosin from him, chalking up her hands. Even that mundane task, she managed to make look appealing. *Why couldn't he get this girl out of his head?* She drove him nuts, and he couldn't afford a distraction. Hockey was his focus—he couldn't let anything get in the way of his chance at the NHL.

Matt elbowed him. "Well, at least she helped you forget how scared you were for a moment."

Tristan opened his mouth then closed it.

Ross stood in front of the wall, clapping his hands to get everyone's attention. "Okay, athletes, this is a personal best as well as best time. Two climbs each. Best time overall wins, and best personal improvement also earns points. Are we ready?"

Shuffling closer to the wall, blood thrummed through Tristan's veins. *Don't pass out.* He drew in a deep breath and let it out slowly. He chalked up his hands a second time. The sweat wouldn't stop.

"Ready? One, two, climb!"

Tristan grabbed an outcropping over his head and hauled himself up, his feet grabbing the holds beneath him. His fingers trembled as he focused on the next step. Finding his rhythm, he climbed, listening to his own breathing and beating heart. If it wasn't for the height, he'd relish the burn of his arms and shoulders. He shoved through the pain and hit the top of the wall. Without turning around, he gave a thumbs up to Matt, who started the process of bringing him down. Once on firm ground, the surge of relief overwhelmed him. Kissing the ground briefly crossed his mind. Weak-kneed, he stumbled over to Matt. Once he caught his breath and equilibrium, he readied Matt to climb then waited, scoping out his competition. Kyle had hit the top of the wall, and Renee was past the three-quarter mark and moving fast.

His gaze shifted to the top where Shelby sat, gazing down at them. *I don't think she's afraid of heights.* In fact, she seemed happy to be on top of the world, looking down. She'd climbed fast too. Tristan studied the scoreboard, but they hadn't entered anyone's time yet, so he couldn't tell who was in the lead. He knew he had a good time, but was it fastest? Casting a glance at Shelby, doubt filled him. He had a feeling he'd underestimated Shelby Wright in a really big way.

* * *

Shelby dusted rosin off her fingers and palms. She was used to putting it on her pointe shoes, not her hands, and she didn't particularly like its stickiness. Renee sauntered up, a grimace on her face as she held out her palms. "I really need to get this guck off me."

"Me too."

Following campers with the same idea, Renee and Shelby meandered to the washrooms. Glancing behind them, Shelby asked, "Where's Brenda?"

"She's still climbing. It was her first time and she really enjoyed it. Ross said anyone who wanted to climb for fun could stay for a while."

Shelby held the bathroom door for Renee. "Good for her. It was fun—my first time too." Two girls stepped away from the sinks and Shelby and Renee took their spots. Shelby turned on the warm water and soaped up her hands. "I don't think my mother read the brochure when she signed me up. My dance teachers at school would freak if they knew some of the things I've been doing."

Renee rinsed the soap off her hands, then studied them to make sure she'd gotten all the white chalk off. "My coaches don't like us taking risks either. Sometimes they forbid us to do stuff. Trampolines are a no-no, for example, but Ross knows we can't get injured, so they try hard to make it as safe here at camp as possible. Of course, even walking sometimes poses a risk, right? Can't live in a bubble."

"Tell that to my mother," Shelby muttered, drying her hands with a paper towel.

Renee tossed her garbage into the trash can across the room. After making the basket, she pumped her fist, then grinned. "Your mom's really invested in your dancing, eh?"

"Um, yeah... that's one way of putting it."

They ambled along in silence for a minute, Shelby enjoying the warm sun on her face. Renee held out her arms.

"What are you doing?"

Renee giggled. "I'm trying to get a tan while we walk. I want as much vitamin D as possible."

"Why not take a pill?"

Renee dropped her arms. "Not the same." She turned to Shelby. "Did your mom dance too? Is that why she's such a stage mom, for lack of a better term? Or is she a teacher? I know a few parents who coach their kids and they're intense."

Shelby stared off in the distance. "Yes, she's a dancer."

"Like she still dances?"

"Um yeah. She dances with a company."

"Wow." Renee kicked a stone out of their path. "I can see where that would put pressure on you."

Shelby sighed. "I'm the best dancer in my class, but is that good enough for her?" She shook her head. "No, it's never enough. She always thinks I can be better, stronger, and more theatrical. And if she's not criticizing then I'm following her and her career around. I dream about a normal life where I go to school, come home, and we eat dinner together. Is that too much to ask?"

Renee bumped her shoulder. "I guess I take a lot for granted. That's my life. I go to school, play basketball, and then hang out with my family. It's boring sometimes."

"Well, I'd enjoy some of that boring."

"Where's your dad?"

"He's busy with his own work. He travels a lot now. I think he got sick of being the last person my mom thinks of, so once I got older, he pretty much checked out."

"Are they divorced?"

"No." *Not yet.*

They reached the cabins. Tristan stood talking to Kyle and Matt outside their bunk. His eyes locked on her as she and Renee passed by.

"Hi, guys." Renee waved cheerily. They boys smiled and called out to them, but Tristan's eyes never left Shelby.

"Hmm." Renee studied Tristan and Shelby. "Interesting."

Shelby furrowed her brow. "What?"

"I think someone's either got a crush or is intimidated."

"Me?" Shelby pointed to herself.

"No. Try the hockey dude who can't keep his beautiful green eyes off you. He hasn't stopped staring since we came into view."

"I'm pretty sure he doesn't have a crush on me, so he must be intimidated. Not."

"I don't know," Renee sing-songed.

Shelby shoved her hands in the pockets of her shorts, pretending nonchalance.

Renee nudged her. "Well, he should be intimidated by your ball and stick handling skills. I mean there's no one here who has skills like you."

Shelby burst out laughing and Renee joined her. "So true. I have no equal here in that department." The smile slid off her face. "But you're wrong about any kind of crush. He doesn't like me like that—in fact, he can't stand me. I mean, we have a kind of truce, but that doesn't mean he's crushing."

Renee held her finger in the air, her face serious. "What's that saying? It's a fine line between love and hate."

"Well, I think the line here is as big as the blue line on a hockey rink."

Renee stared at her.

"I Googled hockey so I'd be better informed when Brenda wanted to talk about the sport."

"Mmhmm. You keep telling yourself that." She pointed at Shelby as she backed toward their cabin then turned and ran inside, leaving Shelby alone with her half-truth.

* * *

A chilly breeze swirled around the campers and several of them tugged their light jackets and hoodies closer to their bodies. The bonfire's flames burned bright orange and yellow, but they didn't extinguish the bite in the air. Sparks jumped around the crackling flames but that didn't stop Shelby from holding her hands out in front of her in the hope that they'd absorb some heat. How could it be this cool in the summer?

Tristan plopped down beside her. "Anyone sitting here?"

"And if there were?"

"I guess it's their loss." His voice was low, relaxed.

She shook her head. "Your ego must be the size of Texas."

He extracted a beanie from his hoodie pocket tugged it on.

Shelby shifted to face him. "What, no comeback?"

"Nope. You've got me all figured out." His green eyes reflected the campfire as he studied her face.

She stuffed her hands into her jacket pockets and faced the fire, avoiding his intense gaze. How had she gone from freezing to scorching hot in a matter of seconds? She unzipped her jacket.

"Are you hot?" Renee, on the other side of her, sounded incredulous.

"I got too close to the fire."

Renee's glance flicked from Tristan to her. "Mmhmm." A smug smile formed on her lips before she turned to Brenda on her other side.

"You did well rock climbing." Tristan's voice drew Shelby's attention to him. He was still leaning against the rock. She bent her knee and rested her foot on the log.

"It was fun."

A shudder ran through Tristan.

"What? You don't like it? You were good. You placed in the top ten."

"It's a love-hate thing. I hate heights, but I love the physicality of climbing."

Shelby bit her cheek to keep from laughing. The guy was afraid of heights. *Seriously?* "No one would guess you didn't like heights by the way you climbed that wall."

"Show no fear. That's my motto. When I'm in net and a guy is barrelling toward me with the puck, I can't show any kind of fear or hesitation."

"Well, it worked."

He cracked his knuckles. "Do you climb much?"

"That was my first time. I'm not allowed to do that kind of stuff."

He tilted his head, studying her. "Why not?"

"The risk of injury is too great."

"All the time? I mean, I get it. We can't take risks when it's play-offs, but other than that, especially during the off-season, we can have some fun. Except trampolines. They're off limits year-round."

"No, I'm not allowed to climb. At least, it's frowned upon."

"Wow, your school is strict."

Shelby bit her lip. "That's not the school's rule. It's my mom's."

"I see."

The silence expanded between them. The fire crackled and snapped. Shelby followed the dancing flames.

"She's protecting me and my career."

Tristan's eyes bored into her, but she kept her gaze fixed on the fire.

"I guess that's legit." He grabbed a stick from the ground and poked at the logs.

Ross stood, attracting the campers' attention, and silence fell over the group.

"Good evening, athletes. Tonight we are announcing the teams for the Big Challenge, which starts next Monday. The rest of this week will be conditioning and brushing up on those skills that need practice. For those of you who don't know what the Big Challenge is, let me explain. All athletes will be paired off with one other camper to compete against the other teams in a series of drills over the week that will include all the skills we have practiced and then some." He gazed around the campfire. "Understand?"

Everyone shouted, "Yes, sir."

"Great. We've made up the teams." Groans filled the air, but Ross raised his hands. "Don't worry. We've tried to pair you up fairly and spread the talent around. We did not stack pairs. You can't ask for a trade. We all have teammates and schoolmates we don't get along with, and it's important to learn how to work alongside them in a productive manner, whether it be sports, school, or work. The teams will be posted after campfire. Activities start at seven am tomorrow. Breakfast is at six."

More protests filled the air. Ross cupped his ear with one hand. "I'm sorry, want to repeat that?"

The athletes clapped their hands, whooping it up. Shelby toed the dirt, ignoring the cheering. Tristan nudged her with his elbow. "Better find some enthusiasm—it's an endurance test."

"This is stupid. I don't even need to know how to handle a hockey stick or a basketball."

Tristan eyed her. "Afraid?"

"Of what?"

"Of getting your butt whooped is what."

Shelby stood. "Not at all."

He grinned. "We'll see."

She shook her head, turned to Renee, and said, "I'm heading back, I'm exhausted."

Renee got up. "I'll go with you. I think the lists were already posted because I saw Josh stapling sheets to the longhouse door on my way here."

* * *

Tristan glared at the white page. *What? No. Why her?* He ran his hand over his head.

"Hey, who'd you get partnered with?" Kyle ran a finger down the page and stopped at Tristan's name. "No way." He dropped his hand and stepped back.

"Right?" Tristan let out a short breath, then sucked in another gulp of air. Of course Shelby Wright was his partner for the Big Challenge.

"I guess it could be worse." Kyle slapped Tristan's back. A moth hit the light above the longhouse door with a dull thudding sound.

"I guess." Although he really couldn't fathom a worse partner.

"Her footwork is great, and she doesn't drop the ball as much anymore. And she's got great leg muscles—she's strong. That's something."

A groan escaped his lips as he thought about Shelby's poor ball handling. Half the drills were eye-hand coordination skills that Shelby had proven she was the worst at. Possibly in all the camp.

"Maybe you can use the next few days to help her with her ball handling skills and how to hold a hockey stick." Matt tapped the list with his fingers.

"Maybe," Tristan echoed. "Or maybe I should resign myself to losing."

"That doesn't sound like the Tristan Kelly I know."

"This is so not how I imagined this camp going." Tristan kicked a stray rock.

"It'll be fine, you'll see. Good luck." Matt saw his partner for the challenge and headed in her direction.

"I'm gonna need it," Tristan muttered, standing alone for a minute before trudging to his cabin, his doom hanging in the dark night air.

CHAPTER TEN

THE STARTING DAY OF THE BIG CHALLENGE DAWNED HAZY AND HUMID, WITH dark clouds threatening. Tristan slumped at the breakfast table staring down Shelby, who sat with her friends across the room. They were chatting and laughing, which only darkened Tristan's mood. He'd spent the last four days conditioning, practicing his weaker skills, and resting. But Shelby? She'd socialized with her friends more than worked on her eye-hand skills.

Matt dropped his plastic food tray, loaded with cereal, eggs, bacon, and toast onto the table. "Carb up bro—need to keep up your strength, since you're a one-man team today."

His gaze met his friend's then dropped to his bowl of oatmeal. "No kidding." He chewed, not really tasting his breakfast.

Matt picked up his fork and shovelled in a mouthful eggs. "It's not like you can't win this single-handedly. You can. We're all with partners who may or may not be a good match. Isn't that the point of the exercise?"

Tristan swallowed a bite of oatmeal. "Ross won't let me take over. It's a partnership, and the drills are designed to keep it that way. You know that."

"Okay, but I still think you can do most of it on your own. Remember Jason from last year? He had the worst partner and he managed to place a respectable third, all because he basically made sure he won his portion of the times."

"Third place is not winning. I need to *win* the Big Challenge."

"Why? Other than your humongous ego."

"Winning the Big Challenge at Ross's camp is a big deal to the coaches and scouts. Josh Snatch and Louis Gagne both won it and then got drafted into the NHL their senior year. Rogers won it and was drafted into the NBA after his first year of college. It makes you stand out. Competition is fierce, and I need the extra edge to stand out amongst all the other great athletes out there. I'm competing against four other guys for first draft pick. One of which is also a goalie."

Matt took a sip of his milk. "Then we all need to win. We've all got our careers or scholarships at stake."

Tristan scowled. "You know what I mean. I need to get drafted *now*." He lowered his voice and stared at his congealed oatmeal. "Mom's really struggling to make ends meet. We'll lose the house if I don't sign this year."

Matt stopped eating. "Wow. That's a lot of pressure for you. Can't she get a loan?"

Tristan shook his head. "She tried. I don't understand all the details, but they declined her request."

"Wow, that's tough. But you're only seventeen. Aren't there rules about being eighteen to play in the NHL?"

Tristan took another bite of his cold oatmeal. He grimaced and shoved the bowl away. "I can be drafted at seventeen as long as I'm eighteen by the time the season starts."

"You turn eighteen in May."

"Which means I can enter the draft this year." Tristan waved his spoon in the air. "So I need to rise above the competition now." His glanced at Shelby who had ignored him throughout the meal.

"That's a lot of pressure, but you guys are going to do fine."

Tristan crossed his arms on the table and rested his head on them. "Maybe so, but will we win? Anything less isn't going to work."

* * *

Shelby wiped her hands on her thighs as she strolled to the basketball courts, Renee on one side of her, Brenda on the other. A light wind blew her hair into her face. "Ugh, my hair is driving me crazy. The wind keeps taking it out of my ponytail."

Brenda handed her a thin, circular piece of material. "Try this. I find these headbands help with that sort of thing."

Shelby put it on and instantly the pieces of hair flying around her face were a thing of the past. "Thanks."

Now if she could only solve the problem of being Tristan's partner as easily. He came into view, his strong arms crossed and feet planted shoulder-width apart. Wind ruffled his hair, and a Greek god couldn't compete with Tristan's sculpted legs and arms. Her chest tightened. *Don't get sucked in by his looks. He doesn't want to be your partner.* She'd seen the glares coming from him at breakfast, even though she'd pretended she didn't. He'd tracked her activities all weekend too. At least it had felt like it. At one point, he'd even dropped a basketball on the ground beside her in an obvious hint. *Really?* Even two days later, the hair on her neck bristled. *Guess the truce is over.*

"Wow, someone is grumpy this morning." Brenda bobbed her head in Tristan's direction. "He must have gotten up on the wrong side of the bed."

Renee patted Shelby's arm. "It'll be okay. Ignore him."

"Easy for you to say—you're not his partner." Shelby headed in Tristan's direction. Channelling her mother's confidence once again, Shelby sashayed up to him. "Hey."

"Hey."

Okay, not the reaction I thought I'd get after those fiery glares this morning.

He stared at Ross and another guy standing on the edge of the treeline, not looking at her. "Here's the plan for today."

She held up her hand. "Why do you get to make the plan?"

Tristan opened his mouth then closed it. Finally he turned to her. "Because I've done this before. It's called experience."

Oh. She stepped back and studied her running shoe. He had a point. *I don't care about this stupid challenge. The goal is to survive today.* "Okay, go for it."

He eyed her then said, "For starters, I'm the leader. There are a lot of ball and stick handling drills. Let me coach you through those."

"I can do them."

He raised his eyebrows.

"You're insulting. I've been practicing with Renee. I can dribble and catch a ball."

"It's all about timing. I can't afford to have you take five minutes when the drill can be done in two."

She surveyed the growing crowd on the courts, clenching her fists then releasing them. *I don't care.* At least that was the mantra that kept playing in her head. But who was she kidding? She planted her feet with her hands on her hips. "I can do the drills. And I'll make up time on the footwork drills and obstacle course." Shelby wanted to win too, and she was sick of his condescending attitude.

His nostrils flared and he opened his mouth, but she cut him off. "You know what? I'm sick and tired of having to prove I'm good enough." Her arms flew in the air. "I am good enough. But whatever. You're stuck with me." They glared at each other in a face off worthy of any game rivalry.

A vein pounded in Tristan's neck. It gave Shelby an inordinate amount of satisfaction to see him irritated.

He gritted out, "I have a lot riding on this."

She pursed her lips. Rumours around the camp had already confirmed that he did indeed have more at stake than she did. A tiny part of her understood that kind of pressure. The tightness in her chest released. "I get it. So coach me, but don't talk down to me. I want to win too."

Tristan's face softened. "Okay, agreed." He stuck out his hand and she slipped hers into his warm, strong one. All too soon, he let it go. They stood in awkward silence, pretending to study the competition. Tension rolled off Tristan in waves, and Shelby took a step away, afraid she'd start to take it on. *I'm nervous enough already.*

"Kyle's and Renee's teams are our main competition, I think." He rolled his neck and shoulders.

"Agreed. Their partners round them out well from what I've seen. They're the whole package." She tightened her ponytail. "Bring it on."

He snorted.

"Thanks for the vote of confidence." Shelby let the sarcasm leak through.

"I hope you feel that way in two hours."

Taking a step closer to him, she jabbed her finger in his chest. "I'm used to competing, and even though you have doubts, I can keep up."

His green eyes locked on her. "Okay then." He strode over to the starting line-up, turning back to her. "Coming?"

Her heart banged against her ribcage. *What have you done?* Her breakfast threatened to come up as she trudged to the start line. She swallowed hard. *Breathe.*

* * *

Tristan yanked the green pinny identifying his team over his head. Shelby fingered hers as though it had the plague. She must have noticed him staring, because she quickly tugged the thing over her head. He turned away, his lips curving up. Oh boy, he was in trouble. *In more ways than one.*

He'd noticed a hockey scout standing with Ross as he and the other campers gathered on the courts after breakfast. His performance and the outcome were now under scrutiny, but he'd have to ignore that. He needed to focus on the day's challenges and make sure Shelby knew what she was doing. Kneeling down to tie his shoes in double knots, he asked, "Do you understand what we're supposed to do with this first drill?"

"I'm quite capable of understanding instructions," she sniped. *A little attitude was good.* That feistiness would fuel her today. He needed a partner willing to fight, not quit in defeat. He listened to her run through the drill.

"I run the ladder, then follow the light path—jumping to the spot that lights up—and then do a vertical to get the ball I've been carrying into the highest basket on the wall."

He squinted at the nets. "Right. Go for the highest basket. You can make that jump easily."

She ran her tongue over her top full lip. He cleared his throat, studying the obstacle course in an attempt to distract his wandering mind from her lips.

"Am I going first then?"

He inclined his head, not taking his eyes from the course. "Yeah."

Campers were lining up along the start line where three identical courses were laid out. Tristan directed Shelby to the middle line. He followed behind her, his stomach pitching around like a boat in a storm. *Why so nervous?* Not his usual MO. Winning was huge, though. He hadn't been exaggerating to Matt about his mom's struggles. Failing to stand out wasn't an option. Especially now that the scout was here. Maybe he was the cause of Tristan's haywire nerves, although it had never affected him when scouts came to his games. He'd treated the men like distractions, shut them out, and focused on his job.

The rolling of his stomach, that was new. Shelby hopped up and down, warming her legs and body, mere feet from him. He kicked a pebble deciding the ground was a safer spot to focus. This girl held him in the palm of her hand. *Great.* He'd had crushes before and been able to let them go. So what was different about Shelby Wright? *No distractions, like coach says.* He couldn't afford them.

Swinging his arms in circles, he hoped to dispel all thoughts of his partner and the butterflies making a home in his stomach. The two-minute whistle blew, and they moved closer to the white chalked line on the pavement.

His face inches from hers, he said, "You've got this."

She eyed him, crouching slightly. Tristan moved to the side. The whistle blew and she burst out into her lane. Her feet flew over the agility ladder, not missing a step even though she never looked down, focused on a point in front. She hit the squares as they lit up faster than anyone else. Now in the lead, she sprinted to the wall of baskets and jumped, hitting the highest basket and dropping the ball in. Making the hoop stopped the timer. One minute, fifty-nine seconds. *Yes!* Pumping his fists in the air, he crouched, ready to do his thing.

* * *

Shelby bent over, gasping in large breaths, hoping it would push air into her lungs. The shrill whistle signalled the start of the race. Renee's partner, a soccer player whose name Shelby couldn't remember, glided over the agility ladder ahead of Tristan until they hit the squares that lit up. Her partner seemed to know exactly what square was going to light up ahead of time. Reflexes of a goalie? She jumped up and down as Tristan surged past his competition and hit the highest basket, leaving everyone else in the dust. However nice it was to beat the competition, the real competitor was the clock.

She glanced over to where the times were posted. One minute, fifty-seconds. The number one lit up by their names on the scoreboard. Instead of relief filling her, her chest clenched at the sight. Could they keep this up? Could *she*? Even though he could be a royal jerk, Shelby didn't want to let Tristan down. He jogged over to her and she forced her lips upwards, hitting her knuckles to his.

"You're welcome."

He stared at her. "For what?"

"For winning that obstacle course for you." Perhaps an Oscar was in her future—her acting was getting so good.

"And yet I had the better time. How do you figure that?"

"I think you'd have lost the race without me. We had the top two times—any other partner and you'd be in second."

He opened his mouth to reply, but the whistle blew, announcing they had five minutes to get to the next drill. "Let's go." He took a couple of steps, then grabbed her hand and tugged her along, jogging down the path. She ran beside him, her hand tingling in his. *Focus. He's only trying to get you to the beach faster.*

A sideways glance confirmed her assessment of a man on a mission. His jaw was set and his eyes focused forward. A reddish tint to his cheeks confirmed that, although she'd seen him slather on the sunscreen, he was a true redhead. The muscles in his legs rippled as they ran and a warmth flooded through her. *Stop thinking about him.*

The grey lake water came into view as the path grew sandier under their feet. Tristan dropped her hand when they came out of the copse of trees onto the open stretch of sand and she missed its warmth. Spotting several badminton nets set up on the sand, she pointed to them. "Badminton?"

Tristan shook his head. "I don't like the looks of this," he muttered under his breath.

Shelby didn't either but remained silent. "What do you think this drill is?"

"In past years, it's an over-under jump thing. You do verticals and then lunge under the net."

"That doesn't sound hard."

He chuckled. "Try doing it for two minutes."

"Is that all there is to the drill?"

He studied the course and pointed. "See the rope lines behind the nets?"

Squinting, Shelby made out the lines he was talking about in the sand.

"My guess is we kick a soccer ball down the lane and back."

"Okay." The knot in Shelby's gut loosened. She could kick a soccer ball. Her feet were better at handling balls than her hands. "That doesn't sound too hard."

Tristan pressed a finger to her lips. "Don't jinx it."

She pushed his hand away. "Don't be ridiculous. You guys and your superstitions."

Many athletes, she'd noticed, had rituals or lucky socks, shoes, or some kind of charm that they believed gave them luck or a win. Renee had a lucky hairband that she wore to every game. Kyle had told her he wore the same T-shirt under his jersey every time. Meaning that, in a tournament, he'd wear it every single game. *So gross.* She shuddered, thinking how sweaty her dancing clothing got during class or rehearsal. Did Tristan have a ritual or lucky item he depended on?

"Let's come together!" bellowed Ross.

Shelby's curiosity about Tristan and rituals got side-tracked as Ross instructed the campers on the drill. She couldn't afford a mistake. Tristan had been right about most of the drill except the soccer balls. Listening, panic crawled up her throat. Not only did they have to kick a soccer ball, but also toss a tennis ball back and forth with their hands, while staying in their lane. Dropping the ball or moving out of your lane resulted in five seconds added to your time. Shelby dug her fingers into her waist but noticed Tristan watching her and dropped her hands to her sides. She avoided his eyes, not wanting to give him any reason to doubt her.

She searched the crowd and saw Renee, who gave her a thumbs up. "You've got this," she mouthed.

Shelby gave her a small smile. *I hope so.*

* * *

They were toast. Shelby couldn't handle two balls at once. He clenched his fists, trying not to let his frustration show on his face. "Just—"

She held up her hand. "I can do this. I don't need your lectures."

"I'm not lecturing. Coaching, remember?" He waited for her to acknowledge his words. "A couple of tips. The outcome of this drill affects both of us."

Her sapphire eyes met his. "Okay, what's your tip?"

He jerked his gaze to the left side of her head. *What had he been saying?* "Um, well," he stumbled. *Tips. Right.* "Concentrate on staying in your lane and not dropping the ball. Keep moving even if you're slower than everybody else—it's the five second penalties that will kill us."

She nodded, her ponytail bobbing. "Got it."

He seriously doubted it, but he kept his mouth shut. "You're first again. That way I can try and make up time if we need it." He waited for her retort but only a nod came from her.

The whistle blew, signaling the campers to the start line. The wind flapped the netting of the badminton nets. Small waves were now cresting the beach. Tristan hoped they wouldn't have any swim drills today. He spotted the scout sitting with one or two counsellors along the sidelines. He shifted his gaze away from the man. *Keep your mind on this task. Forget him.* His partner studied the course. Hopping from one foot to the other, he bit back the list of instructions he wanted to drill into her and settled for, "No time penalties."

She didn't answer, only got in her starting crouch.

"Campers, ready, set, go!" The whistle blew.

Shelby burst out of the starting line and hit her first vertical, then lunged under the net. She repeated until her timer went off then lunged under the net for the last time and ran to the ropes where both a soccer and tennis ball sat on the ground. She picked up the tennis ball and kicked the soccer ball into place. She'd nailed the lunges and verticals but a couple of the campers were right on her heels, picking up their balls. Tristan willed her forward.

Shelby tossed the ball back and forth and kicked the ball forward. She wasn't moving super fast but as long as she didn't drop—

Ugh. The ball fell to the ground, and Shelby scrambled to pick it up. A red flag went up signaling a five second penalty.

C'mon, c'mon. You're almost there. The yellow ball went back and forth as the soccer ball crawled forward. The finish line was only a few feet away when the soccer ball went out of her lane. A second red flag went up and Tristan groaned. Shelby got the ball back and crossed the finish line. At least two other competitors also had red flags, so Tristan reined in his panic. They might be okay.

The whistle blew and he lunged for the nets. The vertical and lunge combo was a difficult drill, especially since he was so tall. He could easily get tripped up, so he kept himself tucked as he went under the small nets. The clock beeped, ending the lunges, and he flew to the ropes and balls. The ten seconds of penalties Shelby incurred had to be made up. A sense of urgency filled him, but he forced himself to slow down and concentrate on the drill—on the ball in his hand and the one at his feet.

At last the finish beckoned him and he spotted the clock as he crossed the line. No penalties—meaning he had one of the fastest times—but with Shelby's penalties and slow time he had no idea where they now stood in the competition. He stared at the scoreboard, waiting for the results. He felt rather than saw Shelby's presence beside him. She didn't say anything—no apology for dropping the ball. She stood waiting to see the final times.

They were in second spot overall. The tension rolled off his shoulders, and he let out a slow breath.

She patted his shoulder. "Good job."

"Um, thanks?" She turned and jogged over to Renee. *Good job?* Try amazing since he'd had to make up for her shortfall. He ran his hand over the back of his neck. Irritating didn't even begin to describe that girl.

Matt gave him a thumbs up. "Nice piece of work there. Too bad your partner has a close relationship with the red flag."

Tristan shoved his friend in the shoulder. "Not funny."

"Lighten up. You'll do fine. She's got enough skill to not totally embarrass you. Also, you're a sports god. You'll make it up."

"I hope so." He cast a long gaze at his partner, who ignored him. He scowled. It was going to be a long day.

CHAPTER ELEVEN

SHELBY LAY ON HER BACK, STARING AT THE SKY BUT SEEING NOTHING. *I couldn't move if a team of horses were threatening a stampede.* A dull ache throbbed through her body and exhaustion threatened to overtake her. The combination of the challenging drills and Tristan's intense monitoring of her every move had her shoulders stuck to her ears. He expected perfection while waiting for her to fail. Ridiculous. She couldn't take another day of it.

"Need a hand up?" The voice summoned Shelby from her ruminating. She opened one eye. Renee stood, casting a shadow over Shelby. Her friend grinned and wiggled her hand in Shelby's face.

"You bet I do. I can't move." Shelby grabbed Renee's wrist and let her friend pull her to her feet. "I'm so sore."

"Yeah, the Big Challenge is a killer."

"Who'd have thought a lot of little drills would hurt so much?"

"Right?" Renee massaged her shoulder. "Well, that and the fact that Tristan is breathing down your neck. What's up with that?"

"You noticed, huh? I think that's my problem. It's stressing me out. He needs to place first so scouts notice him."

"What? He already has practically the whole NHL after him."

"I don't know. He said he needs to rise above his competition."

Renee guffawed. "That guy has a huge ego. He stands out already."

Shelby threw her hands up. "That's all he would say and I don't understand how the draft—is that what they call it?—works. I get what it's like to have to prove yourself, but I can't deal with his control-freakishness another day."

Renee snickered. "He really is a control freak."

Shelby groaned. "It's not funny."

"Tell him to lighten up. His ego needs to be edged down a notch or two. Or twenty."

"I don't know. It's like his career is resting on me. It's not fair."

Renee grabbed her elbow. "Hey, his future doesn't depend on you. It's all on him, and one little competition at camp won't make or break his NHL career, regardless of what he thinks or says." She gently squeezed Shelby's arm. "You did amazing today. Keep doing your thing and let him worry about his junk."

Shelby grabbed her friend's hand and squeezed. "Thanks. I needed to hear that. I have enough pressure from my mom. I don't need it from Tristan on summer vacation too."

As they approached the longhouse, tantalizing smells of barbecue and spices filled the air.

Next to her, Renee's stomach rumbled. Her friend patted her mid-section. "I'm so famished. I could eat a horse."

Shelby inhaled the delicious smells. "Yeah, me too. Lunch seems like days ago."

They trotted into the longhouse, which was crowded with laughing, chatting kids. Music blasted out of a sound system making the din louder. They found the end of the long food line and waited.

"I guess everyone else feels the same way," Shelby said. Spying Tristan at a table, she turned her back to him. He was the last person she wanted to see—she might clobber him.

As they filled their plates with the spicy pulled pork, coleslaw, and green beans, Shelby noticed other campers moving stiffly. She nudged Renee and nodded to a girl limping. "I'm not the only one hurting."

Renee lifted her tray off the buffet table. "I'll bet we all are, but most of us have too much pride to show it."

"Ah." Shelby felt her cheeks grow warm. *Don't show weakness.* Her mother's words echoed over the years. She threw her shoulders back, following Renee to the table where Brenda and her cabin mates were sitting. As she passed Tristan, their eyes locked. She lifted her chin slightly and strutted by. Did he think he could intimidate her? *Show no weakness.* Not to him.

* * *

The next morning dawned an exact replica as the previous day—humid, with dark clouds in the distance. Shelby rubbed her eyes, then stretched, trying to wake up her mind and very sore body. The other campers didn't seem too enthusiastic about the early start either as everyone appeared to be in a zombie-like trance. Gripping a hockey stick, she stared at the pylons lined up. The stick felt like a foreign object attached to her hand.

"Do you need me to throw cold water over your head?" Tristan jiggled his water bottle.

She scowled. "What?"

"You seem tired, like you could nod off standing here."

"It's six am. Leave me alone."

"I practice every day at six in the morning. Don't give me that."

Brushing past him, she picked up her water bottle and took a swig "Well, I guess that makes you superior to the rest of us because you play a dumb sport that practices at six in the morning." She set the bottle down.

"It's not dumb."

Shelby banged the stick lightly against the pavement. "Whatever." His presence wasn't improving her mood. "Don't you have something to check or someone else to boss?"

Tristan's face hardened, but he didn't pursue their argument.

Ross called for everyone to gather. His huge grin welcomed everyone. "Good morning, athletes. Welcome back to the Big Challenge. We hope you have a great day. Today we are starting off with a stick handling drill."

No, no, no. The pit in her stomach bottomed out as she avoided Tristan's stare. Ross's instructions seemed simple enough—stick handle the ball around the pylons to the end of the pavement. Then the catch. Do it all in reverse, literally. Walk backwards around the pylons while maneuvering the ball the with the stick. Shelby suppressed a moan. *What's the point? To break our necks?*

After Ross finished the instructions, Shelby stepped up to the line, the stick loose in her hands. Tristan stepped closer and reached for the stick.

She jerked back. "What are—"

His strong arms came around her, his hands placing hers down along the stick handle. The beat, beat, of his heart drummed against her back. "Hold the stick like this, as it gives you better control. Keep a firm grip at all times or you'll lose the stick or the ball or worse, both."

Shelby nodded, but his warm breath tickling her ear and the smell of soap and citrus wrapping around her turned her knees weak. He moved away, a whoosh of air filling the spot where he'd been. She steeled her legs and studied her hands. *What did he say again?*

The whistle blew and she surged into her lane of pylons. The stick felt awkward and had a mind of its own. The ball, instead of being in her control, fought her, and she struggled to keep it close to the stick. She moved slowly around the first pylon, noticing in her peripheral vision that many competitors were ahead of her. Quickening her pace, she made up time, but then the ball rolled into her neighbour's lane. She reached out with the stick to halt it, but it was too late. The red flag went up.

Groaning, she concentrated on holding the stick like Tristan had shown her through the rest of pylons. No more penalties but she finished last. Surprised Tristan wasn't yelling at her, she shot him a glance. He'd already moved to the start line. His eyes were focused and his jaw set.

Hockey was foreign to her, and she'd never seen him play. Nor had she paid attention to the drills that involved hockey because she'd been concentrating on not humiliating herself. Now she stood mesmerized. He moved with the grace of a dancer down the lane, controlling the ball with a flick of his wrist. *Wow.* The stick, instead of being a foreign object attached to him, was an extension of his arm. His muscled legs moved with precision, and his eyes focused on the finish line. He never looked at his arms or legs. *I'd love to see him do that on skates.*

She shut her open mouth as he passed a number of other athletes but couldn't rally to win. Still, his time was impressive. He halted beside her, barely out of breath.

"Wow." Her brain had nothing else to offer.

He dipped his chin. "Thanks."

They turned to the scoreboard, and her heart sank. They'd dropped to fourth place overall. *Shoot.* She didn't want to be the reason Tristan didn't win. Running a hand over her eyes, she considered her options. If she dropped out, would he forfeit? Could he still win? She shook her head—she wasn't dropping out. She had too much pride to do that. Plus, her mother would kill her if she found out, and she always did. Nothing got past Shane Tivoli where her daughter was concerned. Shelby sighed. She'd have to keep her fingers crossed that she could rock the next challenges.

* * *

After the hockey stick race, they did a water obstacle and Frisbee combo drill at which, Tristan had to admit, Shelby excelled. Apparently, catching a Frisbee was easier for her than a ball. With two days to go, he and Shelby were ranked third.

Today was a new day. The tightness in Tristan's shoulders had loosened after the scout left last night to visit another camp. He'd spoken briefly to the man after dinner and Tristan had been encouraged by the man's words. But that was last night and today was an opportunity to face another hurdle. Tristan sipped his water, scanning the rock climbing wall. This drill was fairly straightforward. Climb the wall fast. Don't fall. Blood rushed into his head at the thought. He swallowed his water then set his bottle down and reached for the bag of rosin. Rubbing the white chalk into his hands, he rehearsed the climb in his head, hoping it would calm him. He clapped his hands together, sending a white puff into the air. "Ready?"

Shelby held his gaze. "You can do this."

A warmth flooded his chest, and the fear clawing his throat receded somewhat. He didn't feel as though he was going to throw up now. Shelby gave him a thumbs up, and he faced the wall. *Don't look down.*

The whistle pierced the air and Tristan grasped the hand hold and lifted himself up, his feet finding purchase under him. He climbed rapidly, one hand after the other. Since he couldn't see anyone on either side of him, he knew he led the rest of the climbers. He hit the top of the wall, clicked the timer button, then rappelled down, his shoulders loosening as he got closer to the ground.

Below him, Shelby stood still, waiting for the counsellor to check her ropes. After getting the go ahead, she signalled to Tristan that she was ready to start. As he watched, she found her footing and hiked herself up, her arm and leg muscles working. She moved like a cat—strong and agile. *Stop staring.* Hitting the top, she whooped and he grinned. She rappelled down and ran over to him, her white teeth gleaming with her big grin.

He held up his hand to high-five her. She smacked it, still beaming.

"Nice job, Shelby."

"Do you think it will help us move into first?"

"We have to win by twenty seconds at least. That's my calculation."

"Did we make it?"

Tristan started to unclip her. "Possibly." Once they were free of the ropes, they moved to the back of the group of climbers, watching the make-shift scoreboard in the room. As the times for the other teams came in, Tristan calculated they'd be tied for second. He nudged Shelby. "Another chance after lunch."

She stretched her arms over her head and bent to one side. Tristan stared at his feet, deciding it was safer to look there than at her.

She waved her hand in his face. "Hey, did you hear me?"

"Uh, sorry. I spaced out. What did you say?" Heat crawled up his neck. *Darn his red hair.*

"Do you know what this afternoon's drill is?"

Tristan focused on the scoreboard. That was safe. "I think it might be a speed drill like a beat test."

"Okay, that might not be too bad."

"It's all about endurance and speed." He studied her. "I'm sure you have the endurance."

She snorted. "Uh, yeah."

He laughed and held up his hands. "Okay. We should be fine and hopefully get closer to first place."

"And tomorrow?"

"Last day of the Big Challenge."

"What's the final drill?"

"I don't know. It's always a surprise—something completely different."

She furrowed her brow. "That could be good. Or bad." She studied him.

"I guess we'll see." His stomach lurched. They had to be in first place by the end tomorrow. He had to win so he'd get drafted and his mom could pay the bills.

CHAPTER TWELVE

THE FINAL DRILL OF THE BIG CHALLENGE COMBINED ALL THE SKILLS THEY'D worked on since they arrived at camp—footwork, hand-eye coordination, strength, and balance. Shelby hopped from one foot to the other, trying to stay warm. Tristan stood in a huddle with Matt and Kyle. Everyone waited with bated breath to hear the instructions and details of the final challenge. Tristan locked eyes with her and gave her the thumbs up.

She rubbed her sweaty palms on her shorts. He was playing nice now, but what if they lost it all because of her? *Don't think like that.* Her mom's voice echoed in her head. *Show no weakness.*

She tugged her ponytail. *I could really handle a few pliés and grand jetés right now.* She could win with those but with balls and sticks? The whistle blew the five-minute warning and Tristan trotted over to her. "Ready?"

She cracked her neck and saluted. "You bet." *Fake it 'til you make it.* Schooling her face into blankness, she hopped from foot to foot.

Ross appeared, the campers quieting down. "Okay, athletes, this last drill starts with a swim out to the buoy and back, then an agility ladder, followed by five verticals at the net. Shoot five baskets, adding ten points for every hoop hit. Then pick up a stick, shoot five pucks at the net, adding ten points for every goal. Finally, kick the soccer ball all the way to the finish line. Besides points for goals and baskets, this is also a timed drill. Go fast. Got it?"

Everyone shouted, "Got it!"

Tristan clapped his hands and whooped with the rest of the campers. He nudged her arm and smiled. "Not so bad."

For you, maybe. "Riight." Shelby willed her lips into a smile, but her stomach clenched so tightly she worried she might vomit. Instead, she followed her partner out to the beach.

* * *

The cool water felt good on Tristan's skin as he tore through it to the buoy. Shelby had made good time on her turn but hadn't scored many extra points at the nets. They were still within reach of winning, motivating Tristan forward as he used every muscle to the max. He turned at the buoy and pushed his body. Hitting shallow water, he stood and ran up the beach, water dripping down his torso. The agility ladder was next and he let his feet feel their way from square to square. After sprinting to the volleyball nets, he completed five verticals.

He ducked under the net, sprinting to the basketball court and making three of five baskets. *Keep going. Don't think about it.* Hockey skills were next, and he could make up any lost ground there. He picked up a stick, which felt at home in his hands, and neatly drove all five pucks into the net. Catching the soccer ball, he set it on the ground then maneuvered it with his bare feet toward the finish line. The ball slipped against his sandy feet, and he kicked too hard. It rolled away and out of bounds. *No, no, no.* A red flag waved at the end of his lane, signalling a ten-second penalty.

He ran after the ball, kicking it back into the lane, rushing to the finish. Crossing the white line, he checked the clock on a white board set up on the beach. He had the best time, but the ten-second penalty was going to cost them. He ran his hands over his damp hair. Closing his eyes, he bent over.

A choking sound came from behind him as one of his competitors sauntered by. "What's up with the choke, Kelly?"

Tristan straightened, glaring at him. "I didn't choke. It was a simple mistake."

"Call it what you want but ..." the guy made the gagging sound again, then laughed loudly as he strolled off.

Tristan clenched his fists and bit his tongue. *Not worth it.*

"He's jealous."

Tristan turned to see Shelby at his side. He frowned. "No, he's right. I choked. I can't believe it."

"You're human. We all make mistakes, and it's the first one you've made all week long."

"It's going to cost us. Maybe the win."

Shelby placed her hand on his arm, her touch like a hot coal on his skin. He sucked in a breath but didn't move his arm away. "I know it's important to you that you win, make yourself stand out, but I don't think it matters today. You handled that hockey stick in the drill this morning like it was a second appendage, and then you sent all five pucks into the net. You're a star already. No one else moves like you do with a hockey stick."

His jaw dropped at her unexpected words. A joke about him blowing the competition or a heated exchange—that he expected, but a compliment? He swallowed, his throat constricting. "Thanks," he whispered. He'd made a costly mistake, so he appreciated the unexpected praise. She turned to walk away, but he laid his hand on her arm, holding her in place. "You did great these past days."

She smiled at him, lifting her chin. "I have a thing about humiliation." She sauntered away.

He stared after her. He had a thing about humiliation too, and now it was his turn to endure it.

* * *

Shelby held the silver medal in her hand, its cool metal a contrast to her warm palm. Normally second place would be catastrophic, but today, at *this* camp, it felt like a win. *Would mom think so?*

The warm afternoon sunshine reflected off the medal and she pocketed it. The cool breeze off the lake cooled Shelby after the medal ceremony in the hot longhouse.

"Congratulations, Shelby." Renee and Brenda ran to her, lifting their hands for a high-five.

"Thanks. This is nice. I don't think I've ever won anything for sports, ever."

Brenda pointed to the medal. "You earned it in more ways than one. You should win gold for patience, with Tristan for a partner. Talk about hard to get along with."

"He's eating humble pie now." Renee discreetly pointed to him. Shelby followed her finger. Several of the guys were miming choking gestures and laughing. Tristan wore a grim smile.

"He's taking it better than I thought," Shelby agreed. "Congratulations to you too, Renee! First place—that's got to feel good."

Her friend grinned. "So good." She rubbed her gold medal and they laughed. "How'd you do, Brenda?"

"We placed sixth overall."

Shelby fist bumped her. "That's awesome."

Brenda's eyes lit up. "I'm pleased. Not bad for my first year, and I had fun."

Renee wrapped her arms around Shelby and Brenda. "We need to celebrate—we all placed in the top ten. We rule!"

They laughed and headed to the buffet table laden down with burgers, baked potatoes, and Caesar salad.

The smell of beef and garlic filled her nose, and Shelby's stomach growled. Renee and Brenda chatted beside her. She smiled at them. "I've really enjoyed hanging out with you guys this summer. It's been a long time since I had close friends."

"We are fierce together!" Renee brought their hands up in the air, and they laughed.

Shelby's stomach rumbled again. "Let's get something to eat before it's all gone."

CHAPTER THIRTEEN

SHELBY YAWNED AS SHE HEADED OUT OF THE GREAT ROOM OF THE longhouse. *All I want is my bed.* Passing the entrance to the kitchen, she noticed Tristan in an ugly green plastic apron, scraping leftover food from dirty dishes into the garbage. He glanced up from the chore, his eyes meeting hers. She stumbled.

A look crossed his face, but before Shelby could read it, his features relaxed. He held up a dirty plate and grinned. "Want to help?"

Ew. "Gross." Shelby pretended to gag.

He laughed. "Afraid of leftovers?"

"Yes, yes I am." She stepped into the kitchen. The clatter of dishes and silverware filled the space as hot, humid air hit her like a wave.

"I've never been back here." She stopped in front of him.

"What duties were you assigned?" He made a face as he dumped a pile of unappetizing scraps into the garbage. "You didn't get cleaning bathrooms, did you?"

"No, thank goodness. I had to clean up the waterfront the first of camp."

"Nice. I think they go easy on first-time campers."

"Believe what you want." She toed the brown-tiled floor. "Are you upset about coming second?"

He stilled then stared her straight in the eyes. "I'm not mad at you, Shelby. We could have won if I hadn't messed up. I have no one to blame but myself."

"I think you're too hard on yourself."

He scoffed. "You're telling me you wouldn't be beating yourself up if you were in my position at a dance camp?"

He had a point. "Maybe. Okay yes, but standing on the other side gives me a new perspective. You made a mistake. That's all."

"A costly one."

"Why do you need to stand out? Aren't the scouts already knocking on your door?"

He wiped the tip of his nose with his wrist. "Yes, but it all helps. And I... there's stuff at home." He sighed. "It's complicated."

It was none of her business, so she kept her million questions to herself. "I hope it still works out for you." She turned to go but stopped. Something niggled in her mind. Facing him, she asked, "Didn't you already do your time in here? I thought I heard you mention doing dishes a couple of weeks ago."

He cleared his throat. "I lost a bet," he muttered.

She raised her eyebrow. "A bet?"

"Yep." His cheeks had gone a deep shade of beet, and he shifted from foot to foot.

Was he embarrassed? Why?

"Matt bet me that you'd beat me in a few of the drills."

Her eyebrows hit her hairline. "What?"

"It was stupid. I'm sorry."

"You lost?"

"Yeah. I have to do his week of dish duty." He stared at the stack of dirty dishes. "I'm really sorry. I didn't know you, and I thought you were hiding something. I was dumb." He picked up the stack of dishes.

A roar rushed through her ears and heat crawled up her neck. "Yeah, you were. Serves you right." She spun on her heel and stomped out, afraid she'd dump dirty dish water over him. *I hope you have chapped hands so bad you can't hold a hockey stick. What an ego!*

* * *

Tristan slumped beside Matt at the campfire. Only a few people sat on the logs, since it was still early. They waited for the others to arrive.

Matt shot him a smug smile. "How are those dishpan hands?"

"Shut up." He clenched his fists, desperately wanting to wipe that look off Matt's face.

"Whoa. You're done dish duty for the day. Why are you so grouchy?"

"Shelby saw me tonight in the kitchen."

"So?"

"I told her about the bet."

Matt stilled. "Why would you do that?"

Tristan ran a hand over his face. "Because I felt like a schmuck— like I lied or something."

"Wow." Matt crossed his arms. "I didn't realize you had it this bad."

"What are you talking about?" Tristan scowled.

"You're a lovesick fool."

"What? No!"

Matt poked him in the ribs. "Yeah, you are. She's been under your skin since the first day I caught you looking around the longhouse."

"No."

"Deny it all you want. I know you." Matt grabbed a bag of marshmallows and a stick off the seat beside him. "What happened to no distractions?" He jammed the sugary treat onto the stick.

"That's still firmly in place."

"Is it?"

"Yes, it is. No worries." He elbowed Matt. "You're imagining it. I felt bad when she caught me doing time. The right thing was to come clean."

Matt turned the stick so the white glob turned a golden brown. "And her reaction?"

Tristan winced. "She's mad at me. What else is new?"

"Good." Matt yanked the stick out of the fire and blew on the marshmallow.

"What?"

Matt gingerly pulled the sticky goodness off the stick. "If she's mad, she can't be a distraction. The Big Challenge may be over, but you still have to get drafted. Don't lose your focus now." He popped it into his mouth and chewed.

Tristan snagged a marshmallow and jammed it on a stick. Matt was right, so why did his chest weigh a hundred pounds?

CHAPTER FOURTEEN

THE END OF SUMMER SPED TOWARD THEM LIKE A JUGGERNAUT. SHELBY HAD mixed feelings about that. The freedom she'd gained at camp was something she could get used to, and Renee and Brenda had become good friends. What would happen when she went back to Spencer School of the Performing Arts?

She yanked her hoodie on then grabbed the can of bug repellant. Holding her breath, she sprayed herself with the stinky stuff before stepping away from the spot and coughing.

Brenda came out from the cabin and swatted the air. "That stuff reeks."

"Yes, it does, but it works." Shelby held the can out to Brenda. "Want to save yourself from itchy bites?"

Brenda shook her head. "No, I'm bundled up in a hoodie and jeans."

"Your funeral." Shelby set the can on a small wooden table by the cabin door. The two of them strolled arm in arm to the campfire. Renee joined them and the three huddled together.

Renee shivered. "I can't believe it's this cold—it's still summer."

Shelby burrowed into her hoodie, her mouth and chin hidden. "I know. It must the northern climate. I bet the city isn't this cold."

Matt and Kyle sat beside them. Matt rubbed Renee's shoulders. "You guys are so wimpy."

"I'd pop you, Matt, but I'm too cold." Renee let him continue to warm her arms. "Where's Tristan?"

Kyle shrugged, and Matt shook his head. "No idea. He took off after supper and I haven't seen him since."

Shelby stared at the fire. *I don't care where he is.* It had been a day since she'd learned about the bet, and she hadn't talked to him.

Someone nudged her aside. Tristan squeezed his long, muscular body between her and Renee, crowding her space. She glared at him, but he ignored her. One of the counsellors stood and started the evening program. Tristan's shoulder brushed hers, his body heat warming her. She shifted, but Tristan edged closer.

"Do you mind?" she hissed.

He turned his green eyes on her. "What? I can't move over."

"Why did you sit here? There are lots of other seats."

He grinned and turned to listen the counsellor, ignoring her subtle hint. She palmed her forehead. *So infuriating.*

* * *

Games. He hated these stupid campfire games. Of course they'd paired them up with their Big Challenge partners, so he stood by a scowling Shelby. Nice. He stared at the egg and spoon—he'd done this game so many times he could do it in his sleep, but the daggers coming from his partner's gorgeous blue eyes hurt his chest. She stomped over to her place for the race.

How did he make things better with her? He didn't want to leave camp with her mad at him.

The whistle blew, and he ran with the egg and spoon to Shelby who took it and ran it to the next person. It would go to one more camper before coming back down the line and finishing with him. It looked easy. It wasn't. Someone always dropped the egg. Shelby jiggled the egg as she hustled to him. It swayed from side to side on the spoon. She was so close—then the egg slipped from the spoon and slime slid between his toes, sloshing around in his sandals. *Yuck.*

Her hand flew to her mouth, but not before he thought he saw her lips curve up. "I'm so sorry."

"Yeah, right."

"I didn't do it on purpose."

He shook his head. "Doesn't matter. I probably deserve it." He toed off his shoes and picked them up. "I've got to clean up." He motioned to the counsellor, who waved him to the water. He jogged to the beach and stepped into the cool shallow waves. He squatted and scrubbed his feet. A pair of jeans and pink Chucks came into view. He slowly stood, running his eyes from her toes to her head. Man, she was gorgeous. Swirling the water with his foot, he gazed at the setting sun.

"Tristan, I'm sorry."

"It's fine." He picked up his sandals, glad they weren't leather, and swished them through the water. "I should be the one apologizing. I've been a jerk. I'm sorry."

Shelby swung her arms at her side. "You have been. You know, it's hard enough coming here as an outsider, but to know you bet against me is so humiliating."

He tossed his shoes onto the wet sand. "I know I hurt you. For that I am so sorry."

She met his eyes. Her face softened, and she nodded. "I forgive you."

"You do?"

"Yeah. Truce?" She held out her hand to him.

He clasped it and squeezed gently, enjoying the sensation of her soft skin against his calloused fingers. "Truce." His lips turned up, and he couldn't have wiped the smile off his face had he tried.

* * *

"Shelby."

She turned to see Tristan jogging to her. "Hi, what's up?" The last night of camp seemed an eternity away a month ago. Now all she wanted was for time to stand still. The final week had been full of team competitions—beach volleyball, field hockey, and ultimate Frisbee. It had been fun being part of a team and competing against her friends, who were on opposing teams. She'd had the time of her life. Now, against all her expectations at the start of camp, she wished she could freeze time as Tristan caught up to her.

"I, uh, wondered if you wanted to go for a walk along the beach."

Her eyes widened. *Um, yeah.* Unable to get her vocal cords to work, she nodded.

His smile softened his face. She followed him down the path that led to the water, deserted since most people were still celebrating the team competition in the longhouse. Shelby kicked off her flip flops and squished her toes in the warm sand. The clouds from earlier had disappeared. Tristan kicked off his sandals too then faced her. His auburn hair had threads of gold running through it in the light of the setting sun, and his sunburn had deepened to a tan that turned his green eyes the colour of emeralds. She licked her dry lips. "Race ya to the water."

She took off, but he soon caught up to her, his powerful long legs making short work of the distance. He ran into the surf, beating her by a foot. She waded in, stopping when the water reached her ankles.

He splashed water her way. "Don't be a chicken. Come farther in."

She placed her hands on her hips. "I'm not a chicken. I'm smart. I know exactly what you plan to do."

He waded over to her. "And what's that?"

She leapt back. "Don't even think about it.'

He feigned innocence. "What?"

She took another step back, but he hit the top of the water with his hand, drenching her legs and the hem of her shorts. A squeal left her lips as she turned and ran out of the water. "You're a brat." Laughing, she shook off the water.

He smirked. "You looked hot."

"I'm sure."

They strolled down the beach, his closeness jumbling her senses. His fingers knocked against hers, sending a jolt up electricity up her arm. Blood rushed through her veins as her heart slammed against her ribcage. *Can I die from too many feelings?*

"Shelby?"

She jumped. "Sorry, what was that?"

"Am I boring you?"

"No, lost in thought."

He smiled, his grin crooked. "About what?"

Ignoring his question, she attempted to redirect him. "You were saying?"

He crouched to pick up a round stone. Tristan rolled it around in his hand then threw it into the lake. It skipped over the water not once but three times."What are your plans for the rest of summer?"

"I only have a week left before I start summer ballet classes. After that, we go back to regular classes earlier than other schools."

"Wow, so summer's pretty much over for you."

Shelby grimaced, her chest tightening. "I'm usually counting down the days to the start of school..." Leaving the sentence unfinished, Shelby met Tristan's eyes. A warm breeze had picked up, and it swirled around them, blowing strands of hair from her ponytail. Tristan lifted a piece off her face, twirling it around his finger before tucking it behind her ear.

"What changed this year?" His voice was husky and low.

"I had a normal summer."

His chuckled. "You call this normal?"

"Yeah. I've only been to dance camps, which are very competitive. I never made friends."

"But this was a competitive camp."

"It wasn't the same, though. Maybe because I didn't have to win here." *Nor did I have my mother breathing down my neck.* "I made friends and had fun."

"You don't have fun at the dance camps?"

"Sometimes. I guess."

"Why dance if you don't like it?"

Shelby whipped her head toward him. "I didn't say I didn't like it. Why would you say that?"

Tristan lifted his hands, palms facing up. "I don't know. You never seem too enthusiastic. Actually, that's not true. The day you let me watch I saw your passion. The rest of the time you try to hide it. You don't talk like you love it. Did you practice anymore after that one time?"

Shelby stared out at the water. "I did practice, but I didn't advertise it. And I do enjoy dancing—but the pressure of being the best takes away the joy."

"I get that. But don't you want to be the best in your sport?" He finger quoted the last word.

"I guess. Maybe. My mother wants me to be the best of the best, but I don't think I'll ever be good enough for her."

"Ah."

The sound of the waves hitting the shore serenaded them as they meandered to the end of the sandy beach then turned and headed back to camp.

They reached the path that led to the cabins. Shelby slipped her flip flops on. "What are you doing for the rest of summer?"

"I'm helping my uncle in his shop."

"What kind of shop?"

"He's a mechanic. I help out when I'm not playing hockey."

"You like cars?"

He cracked his knuckles. "Yeah, and my uncle is a great guy."

"And your dad? Does he work there too?"

A shadow passed over Tristan's face, and he gave a curt shake of his head. "My dad left a long time ago."

"I'm so sorry."

He picked up his sandals and held them in his fingers. "It's old news." Whatever truce or peace had been between them on their walk vanished. Shelby felt the prickles he'd put up around himself. Tristan strode up the path, and Shelby scrambled to follow him. She reached to touch his arm. "Hey, I'm sorry I didn't know. But don't take off on me."

He whirled around to face her, his green eyes scrutinizing her face. His body sagged. After dropping his sandals, he shoved his feet into them. "Sorry, I don't like talking about my dad. He left my mom and me and my two brothers for another woman. He's barely kept in touch. Or provided any kind of support." He exhaled loudly. "He's the reason I need a contract with the NHL—my mom works hard, but sometimes it's not enough."

Shelby winced. Her dad worked a lot, and her mother wasn't around much either. At least they all cared for each other, even though her mother could be annoying and pushy.

"Let's talk about something else. Tell me about your school—what do you like most?"

Shelby pursed her lips. "Hmmm. I go to Spencer School of the Performing Arts in Reinholt, and I'll be a junior there this year. I think one of my favourite things is the Benefit we do every year. The whole school is involved—from the orchestra, to the dancers and art students who design the costumes and sets. It's a chance for students to strut their stuff, and a lot of scouts from dance companies attend."

"Sounds like a lot of work."

"It is, especially when you have rehearsals every night plus schoolwork. But I love performing." *At least I used to.*

"That's what hockey is like for me—school, practice, games. But I love playing."

Tristan stopped in the middle of the path leading in opposite directions to their cabins. His green eyes seemed to see right to the depths of her soul, and Shelby shivered.

He took her hand. "Sorry about earlier. I don't have a very good relationship with my dad, and I generally try to forget him."

"I understand. There are days I feel the same about my mom."

"Yeah." He stared at their intertwined fingers, squeezed them slightly, then let go.

Shelby pressed her lips together, her hand missing his touch already. He cleared his throat. "Thanks for the walk."

She started for her cabin. "See you later," she called over her shoulder. A prick of disappointment made her frown. *What's going on?* A group of kids strolled by and waved. *I wanted him to kiss me.* She halted. What? Where had that thought come from? She didn't need a hockey player to come and interfere with her dance career. If he was a dancer, things would be different—they'd have the same goals and schedules. But Tristan? No, he was definitely off limits. She didn't do long-distance relationships either. She'd witnessed her parents try to do one, and it didn't appeal. No, she had to get Tristan Kelly out of her mind. Right. Now.

* * *

Idiot. He'd gone and ruined it. He'd been alone on a beach with Shelby and he had wanted to get closer to her but he'd chickened out. To make matters worse, he'd become irritated when she mentioned his dad. When would he stop letting that cheater ruin his life?

Why hadn't he kissed her? *Because you're a coward.* Fear had paralyzed him, and he'd let the moment pass. He ran his hand over his head before scratching his neck. He sighed. It wasn't as though he hadn't kissed a girl before or even had a girlfriend. Why was she so different?

He opened the door to his cabin, glad to see it empty. He slumped on his bottom bunk, resting his head in his hands. *Forget her. Girls are distractions, and you can't afford that. This is the year that could make or break your chance at the NFL.* Besides, she lived far away. With his travel schedule, he'd never see her. *It's for the best.* His head told him yes, but why did his heart still pound at the memory of her touch?

CHAPTER FIFTEEN

THE LAST DAY OF CAMP DAWNED BRIGHT AND SUNNY, WITH NOT A CLOUD IN the sky. Shelby sat up on her bunk and stretched her arms, careful not to hit the ceiling.

She climbed down and grabbed her towel hanging on a makeshift rope clothesline outside. Hurrying to the showers, she caught up to Renee on the pathway.

Renee grinned. "I see I'm not the only one trying to avoid the shower rush."

Shelby nudged the door open with her hip. "I can't wait to be in my own bathroom. Is that weird?"

Renee set her bathroom bag on the counter then slung her towel over a stall. "Not at all." She breathed in deeply then coughed. "The eau de mildew versus rose petals and cleanliness—not much of a competition."

Shelby smiled as she entered the stall and stripped down. The water thrummed against her sore muscles and she sighed, enjoying the brief respite. The door to the washroom banged, and laughter and chatter filled the hut. Quickly soaping herself, Shelby rinsed then shut off the water. While towelling dry, she could hear more girls entering the room. *Glad I got here early.* After wrapping the towel around her, she stepped out of the stall. "All yours," she said to the redhead waiting next in line.

Walking over to her toiletry bag, she extracted a brush and started to comb out the tangles. Renee set up beside her and smeared toothpaste on her brush.

"What's happening today?"

"That's right, you've never had the pleasure of the last day of camp." She pointed her toothbrush at Shelby. "It's Get Back at the Counsellors Day."

Shelby's eyebrows hiked. "What does that mean?"

Renee turned on the sink tap. "It means we get to devise drills and make the counsellors suffer for the pain they inflicted on us this summer." She brushed her teeth.

"Sounds like fun."

"Ict sith," Renee mumbled through a mouthful of foam.

Shelby laughed. "I'm taking that as an affirmative."

* * *

Laugher filled the longhouse as Matt handed out the prizes for the counsellors, who'd been good sports during the morning drills. They had good-naturedly run more ladders and jumped more high verticals than necessary. Jolene, a university student, curtsied as the campers cheered. The counsellor had won the prestigious award for Best Face Plant. Tristan grinned, remembering her expression as she pitched forward into a sand pit earlier. He stood next to Matt, helping his friend who lapped up the attention like a dog that hadn't seen water in days. The guy loved the spotlight.

Tristan's gaze swept the room and rested on Shelby sitting off to the side, laughing at the antics of everyone. Her smile dazzled. Better than the scowl she'd worn the first day here. Her blue eyes met his. He winked then turned his attention to Matt. He liked her. Too much. Matt called on another counsellor who had, amazingly, juggled five tennis balls. Tristan handed him the homemade "trophy"—a tennis ball wrapped in tin foil. A wooden sign stuck to it displayed the winner's name.

The back door opening caught his attention. Ross strode in along with the scout from the other day. Tristan's mouth went dry. *What's he doing here? I didn't know he was coming back.*

Matt finished handing out the awards, but Tristan barely heard the announcements. The scout from the NHL, sitting next to Ross at one of the tables, had no doubt been informed of his loss in the Big Challenge. As the crowd dispersed to the dining area for the final meal of camp, Tristan made his way through them, toward what he hoped was still his future.

The scout noticed him and held out his hand. "Tristan, good to see you."

Tristan shook his hand and forced his lips upwards. "Sir."

Ross excused himself, and the scout smiled. "Ross told me about the outcome of the Big Challenge." His grey eyes grew serious as the smile was replaced with a thin line.

Tristan swallowed. "Yes, sir."

"The silver medal overall is impressive."

"Thank you, sir."

"I hear you had a unique partner. You didn't mention that when I was here before."

"She's an elite dancer and a fine athlete. It's my mistake that cost us the gold." Tristan swallowed. "Sir, can I ask you a question? No disrespect, but I don't understand how winning a competition at a skills camp is so important to the NHL draft."

The scout perched on the edge of the table behind him and crossed his arms. "As you know, Tristan, competition is fierce. This camp and others like it showcase how well-rounded you are as athletes. It lets us see teamwork and skills other than shooting a puck and stick handling. I know it seems silly, but having other skills can help you be a better athlete. Ever heard of football players taking ballet class?"

Tristan's lips quirked up. "Yes, sir, I have."

"Skills that seem unrelated can be very advantageous, not to mention the leadership training this camp provides. We are looking for qualities such as leadership, a good attitude, and a teachable spirit. Athletes who have those skills plus the hockey talent are invaluable to coaches. These types of competitions give us insight into what type of character and integrity you have beyond the ice. I'm not saying we haven't seen that in you, but winning the gold here would have put you that much further ahead."

Tristan bit his cheek. Over his years of hockey he'd seen players and coaches whose attitudes and leadership were questionable. Coaches taking it too far with players, punishing rather than disciplining them. He'd had teammates who had used their popularity for their own selfish advantage. He checked himself and remained silent. Now wasn't the time to voice any grievances. He shoved his hands into his pockets. "What does it mean then—for me?"

The scout clapped his hand on Tristan's shoulder. "It means you work hard and give one hundred and ten percent, like you always do."

"Yes, sir. Thank you."

Tristan noticed Shelby watching him and the scout. After saying goodbye to the man, Tristan hurried out of the longhouse, not wanting to talk to Shelby or anyone.

* * *

Shelby threw a stray pair of socks into her duffle bag, scanning the room for any more items. Spying her running shoes in a corner, she trotted over to retrieve them and tossed them into the bag too. Running her hands through her hair, she sighed. She needed to focus on packing, but Tristan's face as he spoke to the scout played on repeat in her mind. His red face and thin lips weren't good signs. Then he'd left, and when he returned to eat later, he sat with Matt and his bunkmates, ignoring Shelby.

Did I cost him? He'd mentioned that he needed the gold to stand out. Her head pounded. She shoved her pj's into her duffel bag. Shouting outside brought Shelby out of her musings. She searched around one last time for any missed items then exited the cabin, wandering in the direction of the beach.

As she emerged from the copse of trees, she saw a lone figure standing near the water. Tristan.

She jogged to him. Wind blew her hair, so Shelby used the elastic she kept around her wrist to tie her hair back, away from her face. "Hey."

Tristan eyed her. "Hey."

They stood silently, watching the hypnotic water crash onto the shore.

Finally Shelby broke the silence. "Was that a scout I saw you talking to earlier?"

"Yep."

She turned and studied him. His green eyes were dark today, like a storm coming in off the water. He slouched and kicked sand. The dancer in her wanted to correct his posture, but she resisted. Although she waited, he didn't say anything else.

"Not good news?"

"Not the greatest. Nothing I didn't already know. Winning is everything. Now I work harder." He sighed. "Like I haven't been busting my butt all these years?"

Shelby blew out a breath. "I'm sorry, Tristan. Especially if I held you back."

He swallowed. "It's not your fault."

She scratched her chin. "I don't understand why this is such a big deal. It's a sports camp, not even a hockey one. Plus, it's not like we were fairly paired. It was random."

He shook his head. "Doesn't matter. Everyone has handicaps, so the idea is to work with it and through it. They're not only looking for hockey skills but also leadership and all-round skills, the scout said." He smiled at her. "Like football players taking ballet. He mentioned that."

"Hmm." She couldn't hold back and her lips widened in a big smile.

He chuckled then grew serious. "Do you ever wonder if it's worth it? All the sacrifices, all the practices and early mornings? Or, I guess in your case, late nights? I mean, I've spent over half my life on ice rinks. Have I missed out?"

"Do you think you've missed out?"

He stared out at the water, watching the waves roll in. She waited patiently and was rewarded with a soft, "No, I don't."

"Then you haven't." The waves beat a rhythmic song. "But yes, I have wondered if it's worth it. I guess we won't know until we make it."

He frowned. "What if we don't make it?"

"Do you doubt you will?"

"No."

"Well, then."

"What time is your mom picking you up?"

Glancing at her watch, Shelby calculated how long until her mother showed up. "An hour. You?"

"I'm taking the bus to the airport. We leave in forty-five minutes."

A pang went through Shelby's chest. *Will I ever see you again?*

Tristan turned to face her and grabbed her hand, lacing his fingers through hers. Tingles travelled up her arm.

His eyes met hers. "I know we didn't always see eye-to-eye and I was a jerk at times."

"At times?" Shelby teased.

"Ha. You're so funny." He stared at their entwined fingers. "You know, this is one of those times I'm asking myself if it's worth it."

Shelby stilled, not sure where he was going with this but hoping.

"I like you, Shelby. You're fierce and have major skills, although the ball and stick handling need work." He grinned. "But if I went to your school or lived in your town or wasn't on track for an NHL career, I'd totally ask you out." He shifted his weight.

He's nervous. I make the great Tristan Kelly nervous.

"But I can't afford the distraction of a girl." His eyes took on a longing. "Also, long-distance relationships are the worst."

All the air left Shelby, leaving her deflated like an abandoned balloon on a beach.

"And I'm thinking the same is true for you. Am I right?"

Shelby bit the inside of her cheek, not trusting her voice to make it over the lump that had taken residence there. She cleared her throat. "Yeah. My mother would kill me if I got distracted by a boy. And a jock at that."

He stared into her eyes, lifting a hand to cradle her cheek. His lips brushed ever so softly against hers.

"See ya later, Shelby Wright. My wish is that all our dreams come true. I hope in the end we believe it was worth it." His breath caressed her cheek. Then he stepped back, letting go of her hand and trudging away from her along the path leading to the cabins.

Shelby stood staring after him, unable to breathe. *What just happened? Did he start and end something with me with that kiss?* She brought her fingers to her lips, still tingling from his touch. Even though it had been brief, it had been awesome. His lips were soft and gentle but confident. That wasn't his first kiss. He definitely had skills other than hockey. She stared at the waves, feeling his absence. Euphoria from the kiss mingled with regret that whatever had been between them was over before it started. "I sure hope it's worth it too, Tristan Kelly," she whispered to the waves.

CHAPTER SIXTEEN

Eleven Years Later

THE BEAN BUZZED WITH ACTIVITY, THE FRONT DOOR CHIMING AS PEOPLE steadily poured into the café. The smell of apples, spices, and coffee blended together, and Shelby's mouth watered. A huge fireplace in the middle of the room provided warmth to the tables nearby, but Shelby sat too far away to benefit from its flames. Her toes were frozen under the table, and she wished she'd worn her boots. She drew her knit shawl closer and lifted the ceramic coffee mug to her lips, hiding her smile as her friends, Coco and her husband Mike, competed with each other in the trivia game spread out between them. Neither was giving up, and it was hilarious to watch.

Shelby shook her head. She'd been on the other end of Coco's competitive drive in the ballet studio—intense was an understatement. She studied her friend's dark hair and brown eyes. How she'd hated her when they were roommates at Spencer School of the Performing Arts their senior year. Coco was a talented dancer, and she had threatened Shelby's dreams like no one else. Shelby had fought back the only way she knew how—she'd made Coco enemy number one. Her cheeks heated at the thought.

The fact that they were friends now proved miracles did happen. They'd left school as enemies but, years later, after Shelby had left dancing, Coco had been a patient at the physical therapy clinic where Shelby worked. Maybe they'd matured or the different set of circumstances made it easier, she didn't know, but they'd made an effort at friendship and it stuck.

Coco's triumphant whoop brought Shelby back to the present. Mike hung his head then broke out chuckling as he leaned in for a kiss from his wife. Watching the pair, Shelby's chest tightened as she forked the remnants of her apple crumble pie. *Hate being the third wheel.* "Well, guys, this was fun, but I have to go. Early start tomorrow." She slid off her tall stool to retrieve her heavy winter jacket and leather gloves.

Coco studied her friend. "Oh all right, but next time, at least try to compete in the trivia. I think you lose on purpose."

"What, and steal all your fun?" Shelby laughed.

Coco rested a hand on Shelby's shoulder, waylaying her. "Hey, um, would you be interested in meeting one of my co-workers?"

"Sure."

"Don't agree too quickly." Mike waved his hand. "Coco's playing matchmaker and wants to set you up on a blind date. Or, in this case, a double date with us."

A loud "oof" came out of Mike as Coco belted him in the chest and glared at him. "Ouch." He rubbed at the spot.

All the air went out of Shelby. "Oh."

Coco shook her head vigorously. "It's not like that. He's a great guy, and he's single, and I think you'd get along really well. I wouldn't set you up with a dud—you know that, right?"

"I'm really not interested, Coco. Work is busy and I don't have time for dating or a relationship."

Coco opened her mouth, but her words faded into background noise as the TV at the far end of the café caught Shelby's attention. A goalie in a Reinholt Renegades jersey, stopping pucks like a superhero stopping bullets, filled the screen. *Tristan Kelly is one of the best goalies in the NHL,* the headline read. Shelby stared at the television until a hand waved in front of her face.

"Shelby!"

Shelby jerked her eyes to Coco. "I'm sorry. What did you say?"

Coco's eyes narrowed as she shifted her attention to the bar. "Is someone over there? Who's got your attention?"

"I was just... watching the TV."

Mike stared at the big screen on the wall. The story about Tristan finished, and Shelby fisted her hands, hoping he didn't put two and two together.

Coco braced herself with her palms on the table, waiting for Shelby to answer whatever question she'd asked. When she didn't, Coco sighed. "Will you let me set you up? It'll be a double date with us, and we'd maybe go to a movie, take the pressure off."

"I don't know. Let me think about it, okay?"

Coco muttered, "Okay, but I'm not letting you off easy. I will hound you."

Mike turned his gaze from the sports show on TV to study Shelby. "Feel free to say no."

Coco nudged him in the ribs with her elbow. "He's a nice guy," she huffed.

"I'll talk to you on Sunday." Shelby waved before hurrying out the wooden door of The Bean. Somehow she had to come up with a good excuse between now and Sunday to get out of this blind date.

* * *

The frosty rink air wove around Tristan and seeped between his bulky pads and jersey. A shiver ran down his spine and he swung his arms, trying to keep warm. Ottawa was frigid this year, and the arena colder than usual. He needed to keep moving, but the game was starting and he needed to stay in the crease. Hopefully the adrenaline would keep him warm and limber.

The two centres faced off and the puck raced toward him. Tristan readied himself, because this right winger clearly wasn't backing down—he'd take the shot. He'd already scored a goal on Tristan earlier in the pre-season, and no way he'd let that guy do it twice.

The forward passed the puck to his centre, who skated around the back of the net. Tristan kept his eyes on the puck, noting the pass that returned to the right winger. He took a slap shot at the net, but Tristan lunged and caught it in his glove, his heart hammering against his chest. *It's gonna be a long game.*

* * *

They were down 2-1 with two minutes to go until the end of the third period. Tristan crouched in front of the net, waiting for the assault to continue. One of the Reinholt Renegades forwards shoved his opponent. Gloves came off and the two players wrangled in the middle of the ice. *C'mon, guys. Let's play the game.*

Tristan sighed as he skated out to the middle of the ice, deciding whether to get involved. Reynolds fought the opponent's goon. Tristan stayed behind. Reynolds was the unofficial enforcer for the Reinholt Renegades. Ottawa had been scrappy all night, going after Reinholt's star player on a couple of plays. Reynolds' job was to let them know that wasn't cool. The refs skated over and broke up the tussle. Reynolds headed to the penalty box along with his fighting partner.

Tristan returned to his net, yanking his mask over his face and settling into his spot in the crease. The whistle blew, signalling the puck was in play. The black disc flew up the ice in the opposite direction of his net. His eyes followed the action, knowing it would soon be coming his way and he couldn't be caught napping. One of his teammates took a shot—missed—and Ottawa headed his way. He bent his knees, his full attention on the puck and player, trying to read where and when he'd shoot the puck. The player faked a pass and kept coming at him. Tristan stared down the black orb flying toward his face. Scooping it out of mid-air, he gathered it to his chest so it wouldn't get knocked out of his glove.

Suddenly his face mask was grinding against the ice as he lay sprawled on his stomach, two hundred plus pounds of solid muscle weighing him down. The guy shoved himself off Tristan. He groaned as he rolled onto his back. Where did he hurt? Could he sit or stand? Hauling himself to his elbows, he panted as his teammates skated to him. One of the team docs picked his way across the ice to Tristan, his gaze on the blood pooling by Tristan's skate. His opponent's blade had found a slit between his skate and padding at the back of his leg and had sliced his calf. The doc applied a pressure bandage.

"Did you hit your head?"

Tristan blinked. "I don't think so."

"Can you stand?"

"Maybe." Tristan slowly rose to his feet, but winced as heat spread through his ankle. "I'm not sure I can put any weight on it." The doctor grimaced, which Tristan took as a bad sign. He swallowed the bile rising in his throat.

"Okay, let's get you off the ice and into the locker room. I need to see what's going on with your leg and follow concussion protocol."

Two teammates helped Tristan off the ice and into the locker room. The crowd cheered, but Tristan seriously doubted there was anything to cheer about.

CHAPTER SEVENTEEN

THE HAIRLINE FRACTURE ABOVE HIS ANKLE DIDN'T HURT AS MUCH AS THE gash the skate had carved in Tristan's skin. Gingerly ripping off the bandage, Tristan hissed as the fabric stuck to the stitches and the scab that had started to form.

He tossed the bandage into the garbage can and reached for the antibacterial cream the doctor had prescribed. He smeared a little onto the cut, swallowing a few unsavoury words. *Man, that hurts.* After wrapping the wound with a new bandage, he picked up his crutches, hobbled over to the couch, and sank down. Grabbing the remote off the coffee table, he switched on the TV and turned to the hockey game. He moaned at the score.

The phone ringing interrupted further groanings about his team.

"Hi, Mom."

"Sweetie, how's the ankle? Do you need me to come out there?"

Tristan closed his eyes. "Mom, I'm a big boy. I can take care of myself."

"Okay. You'll let me know if you do need help?" She sounded disappointed.

"I will, Mom." He swallowed. She'd always been there for him. *Maybe you should let her come out.* "How are you doing?"

"I'm good, sweetie. Stop worrying. What's going on with you? I'm concerned. I know an injury is disappointing. How long are you out for?"

"Probably a couple of months. Hopefully not more or I may miss the rest of the regular season."

"You're young and healthy and in great shape—you'll heal quickly. When do you start physical therapy?"

"Once the gash and the fracture heal. The docs thought a month."

"Is the team therapist taking care of it?"

Tristan tossed the remote onto the couch beside him. "No, I have to drive an hour to Wyattsville. There's an excellent physical therapy office there, and my doctor and the team doctor highly recommended it. Said it was worth the trip."

"Are you able to drive?"

"Yeah, it's my left foot."

"Well, I guess if they're good, it's worth it."

Tristan stared at the blank TV. "I hope so."

* * *

One Month Later

Shelby sat at her desk, scribbling furiously as she tried to remember the details of her last patient's visit. Her watch buzzed, notifying her that her next appointment was due any minute. Closing the file, she reclined in her desk chair, wondering for the hundredth time who the mystery patient was and why all the secrecy.

Technically he wasn't her patient, but the physical therapist assigned to work on him had to go out of town for a family emergency, and since Shelby specialized in sports injuries, whoever he was had become her patient. No name came with the file, but she'd needed to sign a non-disclosure agreement. She shook her head. Didn't they realize patient confidentially was a thing?

Jessica, the administrative assistant, stuck her head into the room. "Shelby, Mystery Guy is here."

Shelby straightened. "Who is it?"

Jessica shook her head. "I don't recognize him, but he's gorgeous."

Shelby chuckled. "You think every guy is gorgeous."

The young woman giggled. "I'm not exaggerating with this one." She waggled her brows then disappeared down the hall, her heels clicking on the wooden floors. Shelby stuck the folder in the Done basket and stood, stretching her arms over her head and bending slightly from side to side. Curiosity piqued, she stepped out of the office into the hall. The muffled sounds of Jessica laughing and a deep male voice drifted through the closed door to the reception area. She sighed, hoping he wasn't a prima donna of the sports world. She'd had enough of that with her mother and with dance companies. She didn't miss it at all.

Pushing open the door, she halted, staring in disbelief at the person sitting in the waiting room.

Green eyes met hers and a shiver went down her spine. She shut her gaping mouth and willed her brain to think. *Say something. And stay cool.* His eyes widened, the shock on his face mirroring how she felt.

"Tristan?" *Clever.*

"Sh-Shelby? What are you doing here?"

Jessica pointed a pen at Tristan and then Shelby. "You two know each other?"

Shelby couldn't find any words.

Tristan stared at Shelby. "We did. A long time ago."

"That's so cool!" Jessica gushed.

Shelby forced herself to walk to Tristan and take the forms he held out to her. She cleared her throat. "I'll be working with you today."

His head jerked. "You're a physical therapist?"

She nodded, holding up the forms. "Why all the secrecy?"

Jessica rested her elbows on the counter, not-so-subtly revealing cleavage. Shelby suppressed the urge to roll her eyes, but Tristan wasn't paying attention to Jessica. He still stared at her.

Finally, a sheepish smile crossed his face. "My agent didn't want anyone to find out and harass your clinic or me. We didn't think you'd appreciate a horde of press coming down on you."

Jessica said, "Are you famous?"

He laughed. "I play for the NHL. I'm a goalie for the Reinholt Renegades."

She clapped her hands. "Oh, I *do* know you. The sports channel did a big exposé on you not long ago. You have one of the most winningest records for goalies in like twenty-five years." She snapped her fingers. "That's why I didn't recognize you—the goalie mask hides your face."

His face turned a nice shade of beet. *Okay, I'll rescue you.* Shelby motioned for him to follow her, studying his hobbling gait as he limped across the room.

"When did this happen?" As if she didn't know, since she'd watched most of his games.

"A month ago. Someone slammed into me, cutting me with his blade and hitting me hard enough to cause a hairline fracture."

Shelby opened the door to the exam room, letting him pass her. "Sit down and let's see what we're dealing with." He situated himself on the low padded bench. She discreetly wiped her sweating palms on her pants then examined his ankle and foot, hoping he didn't also notice her trembling fingers. How on earth had he ended up in her clinic?

* * *

Stop staring or she'll think you've turned into a creep. The posters of skeletons and anatomy that hung on the wall in front of him blurred. His eyes strayed to the woman sitting in the end of the bench, her strong fingers deftly feeling along his ankle, sending electric bolts up his leg that had nothing to do with the injury. She was stunning, which didn't surprise him because at sixteen she'd been a beauty. Her long blonde hair was combed back in a low bun at the nape of her neck. Several long sections hung loose, framing her face. Her eyes were still a startling blue, the color of sapphires. Obviously she continued to work out, but she had grown into a woman, and he enjoyed the curvier version of her. A little too much. He jerked his eyes from her to the boring pictures of bones. *Much safer.*

How did he get here? How had the past waltzed back into his life? He hadn't thought about Shelby Wright in ages. Sure, he'd pined for her after leaving Ross's camp, but he'd been so busy trying to make it to the NHL he didn't have time for anything or anyone. On rare occasions when he needed a mental break from the grind of hockey, he'd remember that summer. Trace her image in his mind. And wonder. *Stop it—not cool.*

She set his foot gently on the bench. "It's healing nicely. How long did you have the boot?"

He cleared his throat. "A few weeks."

"How does it feel if you put weight on it?"

"It's weak."

She chewed those full lips he remembered well and asked him a question, but his brain failed him. Was he dreaming? He moved his foot. Ouch. Nope, not a dream.

"Lie back."

He focused on her. "What?"

She furrowed her brows. "Lie back on the bench. I want to show you a few strengthening exercises."

He let out a breath. "Right." He rested on his elbows as she examined his ankle. "We need to get your foot mobile and your leg strengthened."

As she worked on his ankle, he ground his teeth and clutched the sides of the bench. This was going to be hard work. Whenever he'd imagined meeting Shelby again, this wasn't how the dream had gone.

CHAPTER EIGHTEEN

SHELBY STUDIED TRISTAN, WHOSE SWEAT POURED DOWN HIS TEMPLES. THE damp shirt clinging to his torso emphasized his athleticism. He was in great shape with a surprisingly good attitude. The first appointment was never easy. *Not the guy I knew from camp.* Was this his first major injury? She searched her memory but came up with nothing.

"How did you end up at this clinic? I mean, why not get treated in Reinholt?" Shelby handed him a clean, white towel. He took it and wiped away the perspiration.

After swinging the towel around his neck, he tugged on the ends. "I could ask you the same question. What are you doing here in Wyattsville?"

She gestured with her hand. "You first."

"Dr. Shapiro and the team doctor recommended coming here for physical therapy because this clinic is the best."

Pleased that the clinic had been so highly recommended, Shelby smiled. "That's nice to hear. Our physical therapists work hard and we have a high standard when it comes to education. Many of us are athletes too, so we understand where our clients are coming from."

"How did you end up here? I thought you were dancing all over the world."

Shelby picked up a towel that had fallen off the shelf and folded it. Pressing it to her stomach, she stared at him. *Would he think her a failure because she'd quit?* She had never doubted her decision, but standing in front of him, knowing he had gone after his dreams and succeeded, she wondered how it would look from his perspective.

She set the towel on the shelf. "I did for a few years, but I wanted something else. Something more."

"Like what?"

She curled her toes in her running shoes and stared at the stack of towels. "I wanted more from life. I wanted to make a difference, give back rather than take all the time."

"Ookaay. And dancing didn't do that?"

"Don't get me wrong, I love dancing. In the end, though, it wasn't worth it to me." The words echoed as she remembered their conversation on the beach that last day at camp. Did he remember? "The pressure from my mom never let up, and I wanted a normal life. Every holiday growing up we traipsed around after my mom's ballet company. I wanted Christmas at home without attending endless performances of *The Nutcracker* and relaxing summer vacations where we swam or read all day. Ross's camp was the most normal experience I had as a kid. My life hardly changed after I became a professional dancer. The only difference was that, instead of traipsing after my mom, I was the one dancing all the time. I wanted a different life."

She bit her lip. "Here," she motioned around the room, "I make people feel better. They're able to go back to their lives and careers with our help. I love that."

He stood slowly, shifting his weight. His ankle was still weak and he favoured his left, injured side. The road to health was going to take hard work. Her gaze ran the length of him. He towered over her and she figured he'd grown a couple more inches after that summer.

"I'm glad it's worked out for you, Shelby. You're good at what you do." Tristan's words brought her back to the moment.

"Thanks, but you may not be so generous about my talents tomorrow."

He chuckled as he moved his body. "You might be right."

"Physical therapy is as intense as a workout." After handing him her business card, she said, "Make an appointment with Jessica on the way out. Those are my numbers in case of an emergency. "

He took the card, his long fingers touching hers for a moment. She let go and stepped out of the way to let him pass. His gaze lingered on her then he tossed the towel in the bin. "Thanks." He limped out of the room, leaving an emptiness behind him. She frowned. *I'm imagining things.*

* * *

Tristan sat in his idling pickup, his hands grasping the leather steering wheel. Thankfully it was his left ankle that was injured so he could drive. Good thing, because he didn't feel like talking to a cab or uber driver.

Shelby Wright—a ghost from his past.

In the end, it wasn't worth it to me. Her words bounced around the cab of the truck, taking him back to the beach at Ross's Elite Athletic Camp. He'd asked her that question before they said good-bye. He still didn't have a satisfactory answer for himself, but she did. She appeared happy. Contented. It suited her. Really well.

Could she say the same about him? Probably not. Contentment. What did that even look like? He's spent his life going after something more—breaking the next record, capturing another shut-out, or the Stanley Cup. Nothing was ever enough.

Don't go down that rabbit hole. He reclined his head against the dark leather seat, his arms straight out in front of him, fingers still gripping the steering wheel. His thoughts betrayed him, and his dad popped into his mind. The man was a ghost too. Tristan had barely seen him over the years. After he had turned eighteen, he'd written his dad off. By then his father had remarried and had a second family.

Tristan squeezed his eyes shut and swallowed. Willing the thoughts away, he shook his head, but the tape in his mind kept playing. After Tristan had been drafted second in the NHL, his dad managed a phone call to the son he'd taught to skate on the backyard rink. It had lasted all of two seconds, because he was out with his new wife. Pain shot through Tristan's chest and he rubbed the spot. *Forget him.*

He turned the key in the ignition, the roar of the engine rumbling through his body. He blinked, remembering where he was. Soft light slid through the cracks of the blinds in the window of the clinic and the weight on his chest lightened. His lips curved up. A few weeks of rehab suddenly didn't seem so bad.

CHAPTER NINETEEN

SHELBY GLANCED UP FROM HER COMPUTER SCREEN AT THE SOUND OF someone clearing her throat in the hall. Jessica stood with one hand on her hip. "I believe you have somewhere to go."

Shelby squinted at the woman, trying to focus on what she said, but the words made no sense. "Hmm?" The last patient's visit still held her mind captive.

"Earth to Shelby. Don't you have a date to get ready for?" Jessica stepped into the office and stuck a hand in front of the computer. "Or are you still thinking of a gorgeous hockey player?" She studied Shelby. "Can't say I blame you."

Date. A groan escaped Shelby's lips. She'd totally forgotten. Perhaps a certain auburn haired hockey player from her past had played havoc with her brain, making it mushy goo and good for nothing. Or maybe the fact that she'd reluctantly agreed to go out with Coco's friend then promptly put it out of her mind had something to do with it. *Possibly both.*

She clicked out of the program. "Thanks, Jessica. I lost track of time." She stood and stretched before grabbing her change of clothes from the hook on the wall. Jessica stood in the doorway blocking Shelby's exit. "Excuse me." Shelby tried to shoulder past the administrative assistant.

"You're not going to tell me anything?"

"There's nothing to tell, and if you don't let me past, I'll be late."

Jessica huffed out a "Fine" and moved back a step so Shelby could get by. "I'll lock up out front while you change. We're the last ones here."

"Great idea." Shelby hurried to the staff bathroom and shut the door, wishing she could shut out a certain date—and a certain hockey player—from her mind.

* * *

Fifteen minutes later, Shelby checked the lock on the front door to the clinic, and she and Jessica strode to their cars. The clear night highlighted the moon, which shone brightly in spite of the cold. Little puffs of fog formed around their mouths when they spoke. "See you tomorrow. Have a great night."

"Have fun." Jessica winked.

Shelby wiggled her fingers then opened her car door, sliding down into the driver's seat. After closing the door on the frigid temps, she checked the time while starting the engine. It took twenty minutes to drive to the restaurant where she was meeting Coco, Mike, and their friend. "This better be worth it."

Her hand stilled as she remembered what she'd said to Tristan a couple of days earlier. *Stop.* That pesky goalie had taken up way too much real estate in her mind since she'd first laid eyes on him in the waiting room. She merged into traffic. *Focus on your "date" and driving.* It wasn't a date though. She'd agreed mainly to get Coco off her back and hoped the evening wouldn't be a total waste of time.

Fifteen minutes later, she drove into the full restaurant parking lot. She searched and found a spot quickly, smiling at her luck. Opening the large wooden door of the restaurant, she stepped into the warm space and breathed in the smell of garlic and tomatoes. Her mouth watered. Several people stood waiting in the foyer, chatting and sneaking glances at their watches. The hostess smiled at her, but Shelby spotted Coco weaving around tables toward her.

"I'm with her." Shelby pointed to her friend. "Hey, Coco." She slid her arm through the crook of her friend's elbow and squeezed.

"Hi there. Thanks for doing this. How was work?"

"Good." She left it at that. Coco knew she couldn't talk about her clients.

They made their way into the dining room. Coco whispered, "Ryan's here too. Just give him a chance, Shelby—he's a really great guy."

Shelby forced her lips up. Mike and another dark haired guy in a blue button-up sat chatting easily. Mike stood as they approached and hugged Shelby then held out a chair for her.

Shelby acknowledged Coco's friend, who also had risen from his seat. He was tall, at least six four, and handsome with a strong jaw and dark eyes. Shelby smiled for real this time. He extended his hand, "I'm Ryan."

She shook it, his strong grip confident but not threatening. "Shelby."

He took her coat, and she slid into her seat. At least he had good manners—a step up from her dates lately. "It smells delicious in here."

Coco picked up her menu. "I'm so hungry I might faint if I don't get food soon. I think I had a tuna sandwich for lunch and that's it."

Mike peered over the large burgundy vinyl menu. "Did you find a parking spot? It's getting pretty busy here."

"Yeah, I lucked out." Shelby ran her sweaty palms over her denim skirt, glad for the covering of the table. Her mind blanked and she sipped her water. *Say something.*

She turned to face Ryan who sat on her other side. "So Coco tells me you're a teacher at Spencer. What subject do you teach?"

"Science."

Oh. "Any specialities?"

"Chemistry."

Could he string a couple of words together? He was killing her. "I was horrible at chemistry, but I liked biology."

Coco groaned. "I survived the academic courses so I could get to the good stuff—dancing."

Mike lifted a hand, palm facing them. "Hey, math and science are good stuff."

"Speak for yourself." Coco tapped Mike's menu. "What are you ordering?"

"I'm thinking lasagna. Do you want to share?"

"I'm thinking fettuccine, and yes, we could split." She grinned at her husband.

Shelby scanned the printed words, the tantalizing descriptions making the choice hard. "I'm having the veal parm." She turned to Ryan. "Have you been here before?"

"Yeah, a couple of times. Their vegetarian pasta is good."

"You're a vegetarian?"

"Yes. I haven't eaten meat in years."

Her eyes widened. "Really?"

He laughed. "It's not that bad. I eat a lot of tofu and plant-based meat substitutes. You can't even tell the difference."

"I'll take your word for it." Ryan's vegetarianism surprised her. "I'm not sure I could survive without meat." Her diet included lots of veggies but always meat and fish.

"You'd be fine. They've come a long way in the food industry over the last decade."

Shelby forced a small smile. Did it look as fake as it felt?

Coco narrowed her eyes. *Be nice.*

Their server approached, carrying a tray full of glasses of ice water. *Thank goodness.*

"Hi there, my name is Tracey, and I'll be your server tonight." After setting down their waters, she opened her tablet. "What can I get for you?"

They placed their orders and Shelby folded her napkin, creasing it with her fingers. Wait staff rushed back and forth from the kitchen and bar to the various tables. Every table was full or had *Reserved* signs on them. People laughed and chatted as they ate and drank. An open partition of the kitchen showed off a stone oven where they cooked the pizzas. "Wow, this place is really hopping."

Coco tapped her temple. "Whoever though of building a restaurant halfway between Wyattsville and Reinholt was brilliant. I've heard it does really well. And it doesn't hurt that the food is amazing."

"Wyattsville has certainly grown and improved since you grew up here, Coco." Shelby took a sip of her icy water.

"It certainly has."

Mike elbowed his wife. "It wasn't that bad."

Coco made a face. "You don't know what you're talking about. One movie theatre where you saw everyone you knew—not an ideal situation if you're the pastor's daughter and you're trying to get in to see a movie your parents think is questionable. I don't know how many times Brent and I got tattled on because someone saw the preacher's kids doing something they weren't supposed to do."

"That must have been hard." Shelby couldn't imagine being under that kind of scrutiny all the time. She'd experienced it in ballet class with her mother, but outside of dancing her mother didn't care what she did.

Coco tilted her head. "Everyone has their thing growing up."

Mike grinned. "Not me. I was perfect."

Ryan tossed a rolled-up straw wrapper at his friend. "Yeah, right."

"Just stating it like it is, right babe?" Mike slung his arm around Coco's shoulders.

She patted his arm. "You keep living in that fantasy world there."

He winked at his wife. "Real life is way better than fantasy." His voice was low and intimate. A pang ran through Shelby's chest. Her eyes met Ryan's dark ones.

He smiled. "These two need constant supervision."

She laughed, the tension in her shoulders easing. "I know."

Balancing a large tray filled with salads, their server moved like a dancer around the tables and diners. She deposited the plates in front of them, the aroma of herbs and garlic wafting under Shelby's nose. "Mmm, this smells delicious." She forked a piece to her mouth, savouring the cool crispness of the lettuce and the tang of the dressing. They ate in silence for a few minutes, until Shelby set down her fork.

"How did you end up at Spencer, Ryan?"

"Mike. We went to teacher's college together. I recently finished a maternity leave contract and needed a job."

"So no dance or drama background. Music?"

Ryan grimaced. "I have two left feet and am tone deaf. I can draw a very good stick figure though."

Mike snorted, and Coca and Shelby giggled.

Okay, this might not be so bad. She liked a guy who didn't take himself too seriously. Unlike other people she knew. Heat infused her chest and neck, and she quickly took a sip of her water. *Stop thinking about him. You're on a date with someone else.*

Coco gazed at her a little too long. Had she noticed Shelby's flushed skin? "You okay, Shelby?"

She waved a hand in front of her face. "It's warm in here and the hot food. You know."

Ryan set his fork down. "Coco told me you were a dancer and went to Spencer. I saw a few photos of you in one of the showcases in the hallway."

"Oh my. Why do they have those old photos up?" She was now officially on fire. Could they talk about something else?

Coco wiped her lips with her white napkin. "They like to promote past dancers to help keep the students focused on their dreams."

"But I'm not dancing anymore."

Coco's smile was warm. "No, but you're making a difference in the lives of dancers who get injured, athletes too. It's not only showcasing performance careers."

Shelby smiled at her friend. "Let me guess—you had a say in that decision."

Coco lifted a shoulder. Mike kissed her cheek.

Turning to face Ryan, Shelby said, "I graduated from dance at Spencer and then I performed with a professional dance company, but I didn't get a lot of satisfaction from it. I also wanted to go to college, which a career in dance doesn't make room for." She sipped her water. "So I quit dancing and went to school to study to be a physical therapist."

"Wow. That's quite a commitment. It takes a long time to become a physical therapist, doesn't it?"

"A few years."

Coco laid her hand on her friend's arm. "She's amazing at it."

"Did Shelby work on your knee, Coco?"

"Not at first, but since then, she's worked with me. I'd highly recommend her."

Shelby pushed her plate away. "That was delish."

"I'm stuffed." Mike rubbed his flat abdomen.

Coco lifted her eyebrows. "Really? So you don't have room for dessert?"

Mike grabbed her hand, "I always have room for dessert."

Shelby laughed. "You two."

"What?" Mike laughed while Coco's face flamed.

Coco, Mike, and Ryan discussed dessert. Shelby was too full to eat another bite. A few men had gathered around someone sitting at the bar, and a couple of women eyed them as if they were the main course. One of the men shifted his position and auburn hair became visible. Shelby stilled.

A low whistle came from Mike. "Hey, check out who's at the bar. I can't believe it."

Ryan and Coco turned to see who had caught Mike's attention, craning their necks slightly.

Coco rose in her seat. "Who is it?"

"Tristan Kelly," Shelby whispered.

Mike gave her a sharp glance. "I'm surprised you know that." His gaze narrowed. "*How* do you know that? I didn't think you liked hockey."

Shelby kept her face blank. "I watch hockey... once in a while." Could her friends hear her pounding heart?

Mike's eyes bored into her, scanning her like an x-ray. She shifted in her seat.

Ryan turned his attention to the dessert menus but kept the conversation going. "Doesn't he play for the Renegades?"

Mike's gaze shifted from Shelby to the bar and then back to Shelby. "Yeah, but he's injured." He dragged the last word out.

Shelby lifted the dessert menu higher so it covered her face. "I think the chocolate cheesecake pie sounds great."

Lowering the menu slightly, her eyes met Mike's. *I can't talk about it, Mike. Non-disclosure and patient confidentiality.* After setting the menu on the table, Shelby pushed her chair back. "If you'll excuse me, I need to use the ladies room." Her shaking legs carried her to the washrooms. She skirted wide, avoiding the bar area like it had the bubonic plague.

* * *

Tristan shook the guy's hand, then stepped back, but the bar stool behind him blocked his way. No escape. He enjoyed his fans, but his ankle throbbed and all he wanted was to get his food and get out of here. His gaze drifted to the table of four in the far left corner. Shelby sat with a couple who were obviously together and another guy. A date? The guy leaned close to Shelby, and Tristan clenched his teeth. *Why do I care?*

Two more men sauntered over, obstructing Tristan's view of the table. He forced himself to pay attention. Fans bought the tickets that paid his salary. He shook their hands and focused on them rather than the woman he'd let go of a long time ago.

At least he tried to. His eye caught the movement when she left the table. *Is she leaving?* She walked in the direction of the restrooms and the tension building in his shoulders eased. The fans around him chatted, and he focused on their words, trying to make sense of them. Nodding at something one of them said, he hoped the hostess would come to seat him soon.

"Mr. Kelly?"

Thank goodness. He excused himself to follow her to the table in the back corner. Shelby's table was still visible. Not glancing at the menu, he ordered and requested the meal be boxed up for take-out. The combination of a sore ankle, Shelby, and exuberant fans had tired him out and he felt unable to deal with anything. He just wanted to leave.

Ten tortuous minutes later, the server finally delivered his order. Clutching the bag, Tristan made his way through the restaurant, shooting glances at Shelby with her date—was he a date? He shook his head. Not his business.

The second guy at Shelby's table was eyeing him. *You can't talk, Shelby, you signed the non-disclosure agreement.* She wouldn't talk—the guy was probably a hockey fan. As he glanced over his shoulder, Shelby laid her hand on her date's arm and laughed. A scowl formed on his lips, and he yanked open the heavy wooden door and traipsed into the dark cold night.

CHAPTER TWENTY

SHELBY SLUMPED DOWN ON THE COMFORTABLE MICROFIBRE SOFA IN HER living room, tucking her feet up under her. After picking up the remote, she clicked on the TV, hoping to distract herself from the day's events. Dinner had been nice, but no spark had ignited between her and Ryan, only fizzle. A nice guy but she had little interest in him. What was wrong with her? *Guess I really am horrible at real-life chemistry.* Once Tristan had appeared, she hadn't been able to concentrate on her companions. She'd tried to play it off as exhaustion, but she knew Mike hadn't been fooled. Ryan had been oblivious, which helped. She didn't want to be the date attracted to someone else. But the truth was, she had been.

The last few days played through her mind like a slideshow. Tristan showing up at the clinic had scrambled her brains. Had she been in a time warp? That's what it felt like. But he definitely wasn't a teenager anymore. He was all man. Seeing him at the restaurant messed with her further. Surrounded by adoring fans, he'd reminded her of her mother. Then there were the drooling women. Was that a typical outing for him? To his credit, he hadn't appeared to engage the women in much other than a greeting. He'd primarily spoken with the men. A warmth spread through her chest. *That's good, right?* She frowned. *Why do you even care?*

"I don't," she muttered to her empty apartment. She stared at the TV, which was failing to distract her. Hitting the off button, she tossed the remote on the coffee table and hugged her knees to her chest. She'd known the guy for one summer a long time ago. Sure, he'd gone from cute to gorgeous. And sure, she followed his career, keeping tabs where he played and if he won, but she wasn't a crazed stalker. So why after all these years did seeing him make her a basket case?

A buzzing sound went off beside her. She picked up her phone. Coco.

Dancergirl: What'd you think of Ryan?

Healer2athletes: Nice.

Dancergirl: Puppies are nice. Pie is nice. I need more pls.

Healer2athletes: Cute, friendly, a little quiet.

Dancergirl: Not a great endorsement.

Healer2athletes: I'm 2 tired to think.

Dancergirl: K. Sweet dreams

Ryan was sweet, but Shelby didn't have time for a relationship right now. A handsome goalie flashed through her mind, but she blinked him away. *Not going there.* She didn't need the aggravation of what would surely be a complicated relationship. Images of Ross's camp filtered through her mind. They had been focused on their futures, and neither she nor Tristan had been willing to let anything or anyone interfere with their dreams. She still lived that way to a degree. Her work came first. She didn't have time for a social life beyond Coco and Mike and a few friends from work. And a love life? *Pffft. Who needs one? Especially with a certain hockey star.*

* * *

Tristan couldn't decide if physical therapy was more grueling than conditioning for hockey or the other way round. Treatment pushed him physically, and his tight muscles protested. Adding to his discomfort were the electrical currents leaping through his body as Shelby touched his ankle and leg. *Physical and mental torture.* He gritted his teeth as he followed Shelby's instructions.

Sweat trickled down his back and underarms. How could he be this wiped out? She must think him an out-of-shape wuss.

At last, she stepped back and threw a towel at him. He grabbed it and covered his face. After a minute, he wiped the sweat away and glanced at her warily. "Are you done?"

A wicked smile lit her face. "For today. But there's always tomorrow." She let out a maniacal laugh.

Tristan stared at her, then chuckled. "You're pure evil."

"When you're back on the ice, in your glory, you'll be praising my name."

He rubbed his chin, then shook his head. "I don't know. I can't see it happening that way."

"Oh it'll happen all right. But in the meantime, rehab is hard work. Those muscles are tight and weak, but it'll get better." She pulled open the door. "See you next time," she called over her shoulder as she left the room.

He lay on the bench, staring at the ceiling, his lips curving up slightly. She was as feisty as he remembered.

"Tristan Kelly?"

Tristan slid his gaze sideways, spying a guy his age standing in the doorway. Sitting up, he signaled the man over.

The guy stepped into the room, extending his hand. "Hi, I'm Jason Albright and I'm a phys-ed teacher at the high school in Wyattsville. I work part-time here at the clinic too."

Tristan shook his hand. "Nice to meet you."

"I'm sorry to bother you, but I wasn't sure I'd get to see you again." He coughed into his arm then stumbled on. "Our high school team is in desperate need of a coach—someone who knows what they're doing. The team is going to fold after this season if they don't start racking up a few wins. I've been filling in, but I need back-up. I wondered if there was any chance you'd help me out?"

"I'm not retired. I'm only out with an injury for a couple of months."

"I know. But we really need the help, so even if you could give us a couple of weeks to help with drills and encourage the guys, I'd appreciate it."

Tristan scratched his head, his damp hair reminding him he needed to get home and shower. "Who was the old coach?" No way did he want to walk into a high school drama.

"Scott McFarlane."

The name rang a bell in Tristan's memory. "He's coaching in the OHL now, right?"

"Yeah. We haven't been able to replace him with anyone who has his kind of knowledge of the game."

Tristan pointed to himself. "You think I have that?"

Jason lifted both hands. "You're playing in the NHL."

"Doesn't make me automatic coach material."

Jason's smile turned into a thin line. "I realize that, but I'm betting you'd be great. It'd only be practices. School staff have to coach, so I'm it. No one else wanted the job." He ran his hand over his chin. "You probably get all kinds of demands on your time and other resources, but I'm desperate. It's a couple of mornings a week and two afternoons. I need someone who can help me get the team in both physical and mental shape. Even if you're not coach material, I think you'd inspire the guys."

Tristan gazed out the window then stood. "I'll think about it."

"Awesome."

"I'll get back to you in the next couple of days. Does that work for you?"

"Yeah. Thank you." Jason slapped the doorframe once then disappeared down the hall, whistling as he went.

Tristan tossed the white towel into the bin. *What are you doing?* Rehab was supposed to be a time of rest and rejuvenation. Instead, it was getting more complicated by the minute. First Shelby and now coaching? Did he want to coach? Did he have time? He swallowed. Unfortunately, he had all the time in the world. He'd miss at least another month to six weeks of the season. He hobbled to the door. Tending goal was much easier than navigating the complexities of life. He missed hockey and his life in the NHL. Maybe helping out the high school team would fill the time until he could go back to that life.

CHAPTER TWENTY-ONE

TRISTAN STIFLED A YAWN AND STARED AT HIS WATCH. THE WHITE LED lights glowed brightly in the dark. Five-thirty am. He groaned softly. His fingers were frozen in the lined leather gloves, and he rubbed his hands together, willing the blood to flow. Closing his eyes, he thought about his warm bed.

"Morning."

Tristan opened one eye. Jason stood in front of him, holding out a steaming beverage.

"Thought I'd better bring you some fuel this early in the morning."

Tristan gratefully took the steaming cup, the boldness of the blend tickling his nose. "Thanks." He popped the top open and took a long drink. *Better.* "I think I can put two thoughts together now."

The players trickled onto the ice, skating around the rink, warming up. They didn't look awake either.

"Why do you practice so early?"

"It's only this early twice a week." Jason lifted his cup in Tristan's direction. "Take an educated guess why."

"Ice time."

"Bingo." Jason drank a deep swallow of the hot coffee. "Never used to have a problem getting the ice in the afternoon until last year. All of sudden there are things more important than the high school hockey team. I had to fight to get two afternoons."

Tristan sat on the cold bench. "I think I'll watch today and see what's what."

"Sounds good. I'll introduce you then you can observe."

Jason tossed his cup in the garbage can before opening the door to the ice. He blew his whistle, and Tristan winced at the shrill sound.

"Okay guys, c'mon over. I want to introduce to you someone."

Tristan filled up the notepad quickly as he observed the hockey practice. He tapped his pen against the page. What had he signed up for? The players filed off the ice, a few of them casting furtive glances his way. His presence had created a buzz, and he was glad he'd sat it out today. He stuffed the notepad into his backpack and zipped it up.

Jason skated over to the boards, stopping in front of him. "Well, do I want to know?"

Tristan flipped through pages of his notebook. "Give me time to mull things over. There's a lot of work to do, but you've got talent."

"Okay. We'll see you tomorrow after school?"

"Three o'clock?"

"See you then." Jason patted the top of the boards with a gloved hand. "Thanks, Tristan. I really appreciate it."

"No problem." Tristan grabbed his backpack and limped up the stairs to the exit. He wasn't sure he could do a whole lot to help out. In fact, he'd kind of hoped his contract might forbid him to work with the team—but his agent, coaches, and GM had been cool with it. No doubt they hoped it would give the Renegades good press. He'd be coaching from the sidelines, though, until Shelby gave him the okay to lace up a pair of skates.

The thought of her made his heart skip a beat then pound furiously in his chest. He rubbed at the spot. Carefully climbing into the cab of his truck, he turned the ignition and waited while the vehicle warmed up. The dashboard clock told him he'd be early for his appointment. Pressing the gas pedal, he headed to the local diner to grab a quick bite. Then it was on to the clinic for his dose of healing and Shelby.

* * *

Shelby followed Tristan, observing how he maneuvered his ankle. "I'm hearing rumours you're coaching the high school hockey team."

"Wow, that was fast." Tristan stopped and turned to her. "For the record, I'm not really coaching, only helping out until I can get back to my own hockey career."

Shelby motioned him onward. "Stop stalling and keep walking."

"You're a task master today." He stole a glance over his shoulder, a slow smile curving his lips, which made her breath catch. "Wait, you're always cracking the whip."

"Move it, Kelly."

He chuckled but hobbled into the physical therapy room, chose a bench at the side, and sat down. "How long until I can rejoin the Renegades?" A hopeful expression crossed his face.

"Takes time. It's up to your body and every body is unique."

The hope in his eyes dimmed, and he hunched his shoulders.

She perched on the edge of the bench. "You're making great progress, especially since you're healthy and were in peak physical form before your injury. Still, your ankle will be ready to go in its own time. We can't rush it or you could be back here with a worse injury."

"Okay. Then let's get going."

Shelby set his folder down on a nearby stool. "Tell me about the hockey team. I thought it folded."

"Not yet, but if we can't come up with a few wins this season it will."

We? "What happens when you return to the NHL?"

"That's why I'm not being named as a coach. I'm assisting, sharing my knowledge of the game."

Shelby furrowed her brow. "You're not actually going out on the ice, right?"

"Uh, no."

"Good to see you have a little sense in there." She pointed to her temple.

"The goal is to get back to the NHL fast, so I'm doing everything you're instructing me to do. I'm not on the ice, but I'm teaching Jason drills and conditioning routines. The players need to put the hours in at the gym and on the track to build endurance, which will help their skills."

"True." She winked. "They also need to take ballet lessons."

Tristan laughed. "You can't be serious."

Shelby jutted out a hip and crossed her arms. "Why not? It helps in so many ways—balance, agility, posture." She listed them off on her fingers.

"Okay, okay. I believe you, but I don't think I can convince the higher ups. It's been tough enough for Jason to get ice time."

"Hmmm. Lots of challenges for you as a coach."

"That's why they pay me the big bucks."

"Right. Let's get to work."

* * *

Shelby's cell phone was blowing up in her cargo pants pocket. Trying to ignore it, she continued to work with her patient, but the constant buzz annoyed her. *Someone's impatient.* Unfortunately, she knew who. Glancing at the screen only confirmed her suspicions. Her mother.

"Let's take a break, okay, Julie?"

The woman sighed heavily and sprawled on the mat. Her burned leg and arm were still angry looking months after the accident. Shelby bit her lip.

Julie closed her eyes. "Thank whoever it is who's so desperate to get a hold of you. I need the break." One eye popped open. "Is it a hot man wanting your attention?"

"Ha. Nope, far from it. It's my mother."

"Rats."

Shelby chuckled as she strode to the door. "Sorry for the interruption. Rest for a minute."

"You don't have to tell me twice."

Leaning against the wall in the hall, Shelby hit her mom's name. "Mom, what is it? I'm working."

"Shelby, don't be rude. Didn't I teach you better manners?"

"Mom, I'm with a patient and I can't talk right now. Is there an emergency?"

"None other than I need to talk to my girl."

"Then call me tonight. I gotta go."

"Okay but—"

Shelby clicked off the phone and shoved it into her pocket. Her mother would go weeks without speaking to her, but when she got bored or lonely Shelby couldn't get rid of her. She blew a stray wisp of hair out of her face and bent over, inhaling deeply. Guilt prodded her as she replayed her curt words. The great Shane Tivoli drove her daughter nuts. She barked out a laugh as she imagined that headline. After years of wishing her mom would have time for her, when it happened Shelby no longer cared. She had travelled the world chasing her mother. She had taken a position with a great dance company after graduation from Spencer, and still it wasn't enough. Shane Tivoli had been too busy to notice her daughter. Until she wasn't.

Shane didn't care about Shelby's career or the fact her daughter couldn't talk because she had patients. Her mother's needs always came first. Shelby would never measure up. *I don't care.* Pleasing her mother was a fantasy, and she didn't have time for fantasies. Or her mother. *See how you like it, Mom.*

Shelby straightened and shook out her hands. Taking calming breaths, she paced in a circle. Julie waited for her in the next room but, unlike her mother, Julie didn't require Shelby to flip over backwards to please her. She only had to do her job. She opened the door to the treatment room. *Focus on Julie and forget Mom.*

And anyone else who might distract you from your job.

CHAPTER TWENTY-TWO

TRISTAN LIMPED DOWN THE SHORT FLIGHT OF STAIRS TO THE BOARDS surrounding the rink and propped himself against them, watching the players skate around the pylons, maneuvering the puck with their sticks. Jason had a staff meeting, so Tristan was on his own this morning during their second week of practice. Pieces of conversations drifted over to him. He didn't like what he was hearing.

A big guy muttered, "Why are we doing these lame drills?"

His friend, who stood slightly shorter and stockier, banged his stick on the ice. "Right?"

"What are we—in beginner hockey?"

The whining went on, and a few other players joined in. Tristan frowned. *Coach would have our butts if we'd complained like this. We'd be skating laps.*

He banged his hand on the boards, signalling the guys to come over to him.

His lips formed a thin line and his brows furrowed. They slowly skated over to where he stood. "When your coach tells you to get over here, it means get over here. Now." He glared at them, his jaw tightening. "I think we are experiencing a miscommunication here. Coach Jason asked me to come and help get you all in shape. These drills are to build endurance, improve hand-eye coordination, and assist you to skate faster. I don't care if you're a beginner or have played most of your lives. I expect you to go out there and give it one hundred and fifty percent. No one is too good for these drills." He stared them down. "I do them every day at practice for the Renegades. So if you're going to complain, then the exit is over there." He jabbed his thumb at the red digital sign. "Are we clear?"

The boys mumbled, and Tristan shouted, "Are we clear?"

"Yes, sir." That came from the team's captain, Ian. The rest followed suit. *Good. Someone is showing leadership. I can work with that.*

"Now get out there and do it again until I tell you to stop."

* * *

The arena parking lot had emptied out after the kids left for school. Tristan stood beside his truck, hot coffee in hand, while he waited for Jason. He sipped the hot liquid, relishing the slightly bitter taste. A light dusting of snow had drifted down since he'd arrived a couple of hours ago, and the city of Wyattsville looked as if it had been dusted with icing sugar. *Pretty but dangerous.*

A beat-up, red compact drove up and parked in the spot next to Tristan's truck. Jason jumped out and picked his way over the icy surface to where Tristan stood. "How'd it go?"

"They gave me a little attitude, but I called them on it."

Jason's shoulders slumped. "Sorry."

"They're teens, but it's something you'll have to keep on. Hockey is more than the plays and physicality—it's up here too." Tristan tapped his temple. "That includes respect for the coaches, each other, and the game."

Jason ran his hand over his toque. "I know."

Tristan gulped the last drop of his coffee and crushed his cup. "Why don't they respect you on the ice?"

"I never played hockey past ten years old. I injured my shoulder in a car accident, and it's never been quite right. I can predict the weather pretty good though." He smiled wanly, rubbing his right shoulder.

"Did you tell them?"

"No, but one of the mothers remembered and told her son. Of course, by the end of the day everyone knew. So they think I don't know what I'm doing, which doesn't help with leading a team. That and the fact that the alumni are withholding funds. They want to win, so they won't hand over any cash until we put up more than a couple of W's. Or find a new coach."

Tristan stared out at the road, which had few cars on it yet. The lightening sky woke the world around them. "From what I've seen, you know the game."

"Yeah, I've studied it. I still play, but it's recreational not competitive. I took a course on coaching when I got my teaching degree. I know what I'm doing."

"They have to believe it too. And the only way you're going to convince them is if you win. Keep doing what you're doing, but don't let them disrespect you. You need to believe in yourself first and then they'll follow."

Jason opened his car door. "Thanks, and sorry they gave you a hard time."

Tristan smiled. "Nothing I can't handle." Jason drove away. As Tristan started for his pick-up, his foot caught the edge of an icy patch and he lost his balance, jerking his injured foot. Grabbing the truck to keep himself from going down, he felt a sharp pain shoot up his injured ankle. *No, no, no.*

Steadying himself, he opened the truck door and hauled himself in, trying not to put any weight on his foot. After slamming the door, he rested his head on the steering wheel and squeezed his eyes shut, his breath coming in short pants. *Not good.*

* * *

Shelby stared at the man in front of her, trying not to notice the broad shoulders and thick arm muscles that peeked out below the sleeve of Tristan's T-shirt. "What happened?"

Tristan sat on a hospital bed, his ankle covered in ice packs. His pinched face was not a good sign. "I hit a slippery patch in the parking lot. I wasn't doing anything but getting into my truck."

Shelby sat in the chair by the bed. "How bad is it?"

"It's a setback, but I didn't re-fracture." He stared at his foot. "Thanks for coming. They won't let me drive since they had to give me pain meds."

"No problem. When are they releasing you?"

"I can go now. I've already seen the doctor."

"Already? Wow, the NHL star gets a few privileges."

"I didn't ask for them."

"But you didn't refuse them either." Her tone came out flat.

He glared at her. "I was in pain, and I'm not even sure I jumped the line. Why does it matter?"

Because my mother has used her fame for selfish reasons all my life. She shook her head. "It doesn't."

The sheet bunched up in his closed fists, but Tristan didn't say anything more.

Shelby pushed a wheelchair over to him. He held his hand up. "No."

She rattled the chair. "Yes. Or you stay here and I go home."

His jaw tightened for a few seconds before relaxing. "Fine," he huffed.

She locked the chair and held out her hand. Brushing it aside, he growled, "I can do it."

She handed him the crutches the doctor had given him, which he laid across his lap. "You are the most stubborn man I've ever met," she groused, giving the chair a jerk as she pushed it forward. He grunted.

They exited the hospital, and she pushed him over to her car parked in one of two spots close to the exit doors.

"Where's my truck?"

"I'm not driving your truck. You'll have to arrange for someone to come get it."

He threw his hands up. Her lips lifted slightly. *Why do I enjoy irritating him so much?*

"Sit in the back where you can elevate your ankle on the seat." Shelby held the chair steady as he crammed his large body into the seat of her very small car. She laid the crutches on the floor behind the driver's seat. A porter took the chair from her, and she ran around the vehicle to the driver's side. Sliding onto her seat, she tried not to notice how his presence filled the small space.

"What is this, a toy car?" he grumbled.

She bit her lip, holding in the snicker that itched to escape.

"Stop complaining." She glanced at him through the rear-view mirror, his green eyes meeting hers.

His eyes narrowed. "You're laughing. I can see it."

She chuckled softly, her shoulders shaking.

"Stop laughing."

But she could hear the smile in his voice. "You should see yourself stuffed in back there—it's like a clown car with one person." She shifted the car into reverse and backed out of the parking space. "What's your address?"

"I'm staying at the apartments on Wellington Street. My coach knew of someone who's away for a few months on business and needed someone to stay in their place."

"Convenient."

"It is." His voice sounded thick, as if he'd started to drift off. How much pain medication had they given him? "How long will this set me back?"

"I'll have to check the x-ray and your foot. I'm not making any guesses before then." She parked in front of the only apartment building on the street, a red brick, six-story structure. "Here we are. Is there an elevator?"

"Yes." Tristan hauled himself out of the car. Shelby stood watching, ready to help if he lost his balance. His pale face accentuated the dark shadows under his green eyes, and his usually full lips were a thin line. His hands trembled slightly as he grabbed hold of the door to steady himself.

"I'm going to need extra physical therapy from riding in that car of yours. Is that how you manage to keep a steady stream of patients?"

"Ha ha, very funny." She closed the car door.

He jiggled the apartment key in his hand. "Thanks for coming to get me."

"You're welcome. I'll see you at the clinic."

He saluted, then shook the crutches the nurse had given him. "I'd thought I'd seen the last of these."

"Sorry, but it's better to keep the weight off that ankle for now." She took a step back to let him pass, but her heel caught the curb and she stumbled into the car door. Tristan reached out his right hand to steady her, still clutching the crutches with his left. They stood so close she could feel the heat radiating off him.

"We don't need you injuring yourself." His low voice whispered against her cheek. When she raised her face a fraction, his green eyes searched hers. He moved closer and her heart beat a staccato rhythm against her rib cage. *This can't happen.* She dropped her head, avoiding his eyes, and eased out of his grasp.

"All good." She clasped her hands tightly. "Do you need help upstairs?"

He studied her, then shook his head. "I'm fine. See you later." He hobbled up the walk and into his building.

Shelby slid onto the driver's seat and stared out the front window. *What just happened? Did he almost kiss me?* What did that mean? Did he feel the same swoop of butterflies every time she smiled at him or touched him? *Of course not.* He had to have women falling all over him. Beautiful women. Rich women. Famous women. She'd seen pictures in the gossip rags of him attending movie premiers and awards shows with famous actresses and heiresses. Why would he want to have anything to do with her? *He doesn't. You're his ticket to health and returning to the NHL. If anything, what he felt for a moment there was gratitude. Yes, that was all.* She turned the key in the ignition and drove away from the curb, heat building behind her eyes. She didn't want grateful, and maybe it was for the best.

Because she'd already lived with one famous person, and she didn't want a repeat of that life, did she?

CHAPTER TWENTY-THREE

"I HAVE GOOD NEWS AND BAD NEWS. YOUR STAY IN WYATTSVILLE MAY BE longer than anticipated." Shelby slid the X-ray into Tristan's folder and then set it on the bench. Sitting on her stool, she ran her fingers over his ankle. "The good news is you didn't cause any major damage, you only knocked back your return to the ice by a couple of weeks."

He ran his fingers through his auburn locks, which were longer than she'd ever seen them. The green pullover he wore brought out the colour of his eyes. He should be arrested for being that gorgeous. She cleared her throat and shoved away the thoughts. At least the news of his extended stay distracted him from their almost kiss. Or had that been her imagination?

He groaned and tipped back his head, staring at the ceiling.

"You're young and healthy. You've made an amazing recovery. Give your ankle the time it needs and you'll be playing at your best before you know it."

"Will I catch any of the regular season?"

Shelby shrugged—how long did the hockey season run? From the forlorn look on his face, even two weeks wasn't good news. She set the clipboard on her desk and covered his hand with hers. "I'm sorry."

"Coach will be ticked off. Especially since I'm at fault for this."

"Accidents happen. My practice is made up of accidents. You didn't slip on purpose—surely he'll understand?"

"Doesn't matter. I need to be in the net. Now. Our back-up doesn't have the experience I have."

Or talent. She'd watched a couple of games on TV in the last few weeks. Tristan's absence left a gaping hole in their defence. She removed her hand from his. He sat with his hands clasped in his lap.

Shelby had no idea how to lift his spirits. "I'm not working on you today, because you need to rest your ankle and body. Go home, ice it, and rest."

He stood and moved slowly to the door, the crutches making a scrunching sound on the hardwood of the office floor. Pausing at the door, he smiled. "Thanks."

She grinned and he left. She exhaled a puff of air and sank onto her desk chair. Tristan staying longer than originally planned was problematic and not only for him. He needed to rejoin the Renegades so she could forget him and move on.

* * *

His fists clenched, it took all Tristan's willpower not to slam the back of the cab driver's seat. He inhaled, counted to four, then let out his breath. *Stupid, stupid, stupid.* The word summed up the whole situation. He knew it was slippery, yet he'd let his guard down. Added to that humiliation was the almost kiss. *He'd lost his head and all common sense being that close to her.* Had she noticed he'd leaned in? Heat burned his cheeks thinking about it. Of course she had—she'd looked away. And if she hadn't, he would have looked an even bigger fool. *Stupid.*

Staring blindly out the window of the taxi, Tristan wished he could have a dozen do-overs.

* * *

Shelby smoothly maneuvered her small car into the tight parking spot, thankful for compact cars. Jostling the take-out container of Thai food—the scent of spicy garlic and peanut filling the tiny space—her mouth watered. After carefully easing the bag of food out first, she followed, squeezing herself between her car and the mammoth black SUV beside her. She dragged herself up the four flights of stairs to her apartment. The lure of the couch and a good novel beckoned her. When she rounded the corner, she halted mid-step. *What is she doing here?* The tall, willowy figure in a white coat paced in front of her blue apartment door, arms crossed.

"I thought you were in Europe." Shelby winced at the harshness in her tone.

The woman spun to face her. "Darling, is that any way to greet your mother?"

Shelby kissed her mother on both cheeks, European-style like she preferred, then fit the key into the lock. Ushering her unexpected guest inside her apartment, Shelby mentally went down the list of why her mother would be in Wyattsville.

Shane dropped her white wool coat onto a wing chair near the door and proceeded to walk around the small living area, running her hand along a blanket or glancing at pictures. *Taking stock* was how Shelby liked to describe it. She glanced around, trying to see her living space through her mother's eyes. The furniture was comfortable but not leather, which her mother preferred. Most of it was second-hand, bought at a thrift store. Her mother didn't need to know that, though. A favourite blue knitted blanket draped across the back of the charcoal couch and a colourful rug added a cheery welcome to the room. Her spotless kitchen didn't appear used. She didn't cook much, so no need for all the gadgets, which reminded Shelby of the take-out bag in her hand.

"I brought Thai food—do you want any?"

"No thanks, I can't eat all those carbs." Her mother turned from the photograph she held of Coco and Shelby laughing last Christmas. She tapped the glass. "This is your old roommate from Spencer right? Coco—after Chanel?"

And that's the reason she loves you so much, because you never forget her namesake. "Yes, that's Coco."

"How's she doing? Her injury was such a tragedy."

"She's doing great, Mom. I'm not sure she'd classify it as a tragedy—maybe a long time ago, but she's very happy teaching at Spencer. She's married and enjoying life."

"Well, at least she didn't purposely throw her career away." Her mother set the photo on the side table, her comment dropping like a rock.

Shelby's fingers clenched the bag she still held and she bit her cheek. There was no point in addressing the comment. *She will never understand.* Her appetite gone, she dropped the bag of food on the counter. After extracting a plate from the cupboard, she scooped a spoonful of food on it, anything to keep her hands busy. The smell of peanut sauce and chicken rose with the steam as she filled her plate. She turned on the faucet and held a glass under it. "Do you want water, Mom?"

Her mother sat down on the couch, her spine straight and hands clasped in her lap. "Thank you."

Shelby filled a second glass with water and set it on the coffee table in front of her mother before retrieving her dinner and sinking onto a chair.

"What brings you to town?" Her heart pounded, but Shelby kept her voice calm and even.

Her mother smiled. "I wanted to see my girl. Do I need any other reason?"

Shelby balanced her plate on her lap and picked up the fork. She narrowed her eyes as she studied her mother. "No, only you don't usually have that kind of time."

Her mother sank against the couch's pillows and tilted her head. "No, I suppose I don't. Which is what I want to speak to you about."

There it is.

Shane held her hands out, inspecting them. Warning bells clanged in Shelby's ears.

"I'm retiring, dear."

What? The plate of food tipped dangerously in her lap, and Shelby hastily set it on the coffee table. "You... you want to retire? What brought this on?"

"I'm not getting any younger, and I don't want to be one of those old bats who doesn't know enough to realize when her time's done."

"I don't think that is an accurate description of you or your career, Mom. Everyone still seeks you out as a teacher and choreographer. You're what—in your fifties? That's not old."

"It's ancient in the dance world."

"You're exaggerating."

Her mother lifted her shoulders. "Maybe, but I feel like it's time."

Shelby swallowed. "And Dave?" She didn't know her mother's second husband well, but surely he factored into this somehow.

"I think that's over—we had a couple of good years, but he doesn't understand my career." Shane waved her hand in dismissal. "Anyway, enough about my marriage troubles."

Of course. "So what are you going to do?" Dread clawed its way up her throat. *Do I really want to know the answer to that question?*

"I'm weighing my options. I do want to spend more time with you. I know I haven't always been available."

Haven't always been available? Try never. "I see. What are you thinking?" She drew a pattern on the surface of the chair, avoiding her mother's gaze.

"Well, I thought about moving here. To Wyattsville."

No, no, no. "I think you need to reconsider. Wyattsville is small town—none of the restaurants you're used to and very little theatre. You'll be bored."

Her mother stared at her. "Well, if not here, what about Reinholt? Spencer is looking for a new director of dance. Madame Clare has been asked to take on the directorship of the school."

Shelby met her mother's gaze. "Madame Clare is the new school director? That's a brilliant move."

"Yes, but it's not known yet, so keep that to yourself."

"How did you find out?"

"They approached me to take her spot."

Drawing a throw pillow across her lap, Shelby asked, "Are you sure you want to settle down?"

Her mother picked up her glass of water, her finger circling the rim. "Possibly." A wrinkle formed between her perfect eyebrows. Her tongue ran over her top lip. "I know that my career kept you on the run as a child. But I thought the travel would be good for you—provide you with an education that school couldn't. I might have been wrong. I know you wanted to stay home holidays and summers."

Shelby tried to make sense of the words coming out of her mother's mouth. *Wait. Is that an apology? Am I in a kind of alternate dimension?*

"Uh, this is unexpected, Mom. I could say it's fine, but it did hurt me that you never listened. "

"I know. I thought I knew best. I was wrong."

Shelby stared at the alien who had to be possessing her mother. Never in her wildest dreams did she expect to hear her mom apologize. "Thanks for that." Silence filled the room, and Shelby jerked from her seat, the cushion tumbling to the floor. "Do you want tea?" She'd like something a lot stronger than tea, but since she didn't drink alcohol, caffeine would have to do. The doorbell buzzed.

Her mother popped off the couch. "I'll get the door, you go make the tea."

The sound of her mother speaking into the security system followed Shelby into the kitchen. "Mom, don't let in a stranger. I wasn't expecting anyone," she called over her shoulder. After filling the kettle, she snagged two cups and the tea from the cupboard. Her thoughts tumbled one after another like acrobats at the circus, and she ran her hand over her face and hair. Her mom apologizing? What did that mean? Was she sincere? The whistle of the kettle brought Shelby back to the task at hand. As she poured hot water over the tea bags, her mother's words ran through her mind. Retirement, move, Spencer, apology. The spicy scent of the black tea revived her, and she carried the two cups into the living room, halting at the sight of Ryan standing there talking to her mom.

"Ryan, what are you doing here?"

Both her mother and Ryan turned. "Hi, Shelby." He smiled sheepishly. "I, uh, I wondered if you wanted to go to a movie tonight and thought I'd chance it. I didn't realize you had company."

Her mother picked up her coat, "I'm leaving. You two go out and have fun. Shelby, we'll talk soon." She winked at them and then gracefully glided out of the apartment, leaving only the scent of her perfume behind.

Shelby stared down at the two steaming mugs. "Tea?" she lifted a cup to Ryan.

CHAPTER
TWENTY-FOUR

"SHELBY, YOUR NEXT PATIENT HAS BEEN WAITING FOR OVER TWENTY MINUTES. Are you ready for him?" Jessica hissed.

Shelby lifted her pounding head from her desk, where it had been resting for too long. "I don't have a patient right now."

"You didn't get my memo."

Shelby propped her elbow on the desk and rested her head on her hand, pushing down the sigh that threatened to leak out. "What memo?"

"Tristan Kelly is here for a therapy session. He had to reschedule tomorrow's appointment. I wrote it down *and* sent you an email."

The groan escaped Shelby's lips, and Jessica came into the room and shut the door.

"What's going on with you? The last few days, you've been in a fog."

"My mother."

"Ah."

"It's too much to go into right now." She stood, stretching her arms over her head.

"Well, you've got the hockey hottie to cheer you up for the next forty-five minutes," she whispered.

"Jessica, that is so unprofessional." She bopped her friend in the shoulder, but couldn't stop the flutter of her heart. She didn't need this today. Why was her life so complicated?

She followed Jessica out to the waiting area. Tristan sat on a hard vinyl chair reading a magazine, but he somehow managed to look as if he were doing a model shoot. How could he make grey sweats and a navy T-shirt look so good? Jessica smiled broadly at Tristan as she sat at her desk. A thin film of sweat broke out on Shelby's forehead and she glared at Jessica from the shadows of the doorway. After stepping into the waiting room, she cleared her throat. "Tristan, sorry for the wait. Come on back."

He set the magazine down and stood, his height making the room feel suddenly small. Grabbing the crutches from where he had left them against a chair, he hobbled to where Shelby stood waiting for him. He moved slowly but didn't wince in pain. *That's a good sign.*

When he passed her in the narrow hall, the scent of citrus and soap tickled her nose. He looked and smelled good. *Be professional, girl. What is wrong with you?*

She directed Tristan over to the bench in the far corner. "How are you feeling today?"

He sat down, tucking the crutches under the bench. "Much better. I've rested my ankle, slept."

She wrote in her notes. "Good. No hockey rinks?"

"No, I called Jason and gave him a game plan but told him I couldn't be there this week."

"You're doing all the right things." She wrote a few more notes, avoiding his eyes.

"Aren't we formal today." It wasn't a question.

She set her chart down on a chair. "I'm thinking."

He crossed his arms, his biceps bulging. "Riight."

"You know, it's too late in the day for you to annoy me this much." Rubbing her hands together, she sat down. "Let's get to work."

"How long until I can return?"

There it was, the dreaded question. She closed her eyes then opened them, locking her gaze on his. "I'm hoping you'll only be delayed a week or two. But as I've already told you, every body is different."

His green eyes narrowed and a slight frown creased his brow, but he didn't say anything. Shelby appreciated that. Between her mother and Ryan, she didn't want to deal with a temperamental auburn-haired hockey player too.

* * *

Tristan felt the burn. Sweat tricked down his temples and armpits. This wasn't therapy, it was a workout. Shelby's full lips quirked up as he grunted the last repetition. "I don't think it's very professional for the therapist to enjoy her client's suffering," he panted.

"Probably not." She didn't give an inch, which was part of the reason he was attracted to her. Not just attracted but liked her. He wiped his forehead on his sleeve. *No distractions, remember?* He had to get back to the NHL as soon as possible.

"Have dinner with me." The words popped out. Apparently his mouth and brain weren't communicating.

She stilled, her blue eyes glued to his chart. *Look at me.* Finally, her gaze locked with his.

"What?" she whispered.

He couldn't take it back now. Might as well run with it. "Have dinner with me."

"Like a date?"

"Why not?" NHL, distraction, no time for relationships—all reasons why not. He could see her ticking her own reasons off in her head. Did he want this? Or should he let the idea die with all their excuses beating the life out of it. A warmth filled his chest. *I want this.*

"Um, you're my patient. It would be unethical."

Oh. Right. "I could switch physical therapists."

"I don't think that's—"

"It's just a meal. You have to eat, don't you?"

She shook her head. "No, I can't go out with you if I'm treating you."

His stared into space. "I'm not giving up. I'll find a way around this."

She crossed her arms. "I never said I'd go with you."

"You never said you wouldn't." His grin widened at her scowl.

"You're insufferable."

"You're desperate to go out with me."

"Ha! In your wildest dreams, hockey boy."

He eased his left foot into his running shoe. "What? Is there a dancer boy lurking around somewhere? A significant other?" *The guy in the restaurant?*

"No." She whirled around and headed for the door. "I have to go. My next patient's waiting. Make an appointment on your way out."

A slow smile spread across his lips. No plus one. Why was she playing hard to get then? Had he totally misjudged the situation? "Okay, but don't think I'm letting this go."

She huffed out of the office, her long ponytail swishing back and forth as she practically hit the hallway running. He smiled to himself. Excellent. He enjoyed a good chase.

* * *

Shelby had heard the smile in his voice, but she didn't dare turn around. She inhaled deeply, hoping to calm the blood racing through her veins. It didn't work, because every time she thought of him, her heart threatened a coronary. He'd been serious about a date. A little bit of hope peeked through her heart's walls. *Rein it in, Shelby, because you don't need a broken heart.* Tristan would eventually go back to the NHL, and she'd be left behind. She wasn't letting that happen. She shoved any hope into the depths of her being where it couldn't disappoint her. Again.

CHAPTER TWENTY-FIVE

SHELBY FLUFFED THE PILLOW AND THREW IT ONTO THE QUEEN-SIZED BED IN her guest bedroom. A muted grey paint softened the light in the room, and the pretty pink accents made it feminine. Dropping to the bed, Shelby settled against the pillows she'd fluffed and stared at the white ceiling. She'd tacked a picture of the Eiffel Tower up there so anyone lying on the bed would see it. A little juvenile, but it made her happy. What would her mother think as she slept in the room this weekend? Would she see the charm or criticize?

Shane Tivoli travelled the world and stayed in pretty swank hotels and mansions. Shelby's little guest bedroom felt like home with touches like the log cabin quilt on the bed she'd bought when she'd toured Amish country with Coco in the spring. They'd visited a market, and Shelby had fallen in love with the blanket. The bedside tables were a dark wood, she didn't know what type, but she'd bought them at a thrift store here in Wyattsville. They'd seen a few decades of life, which gave them character. The little crystal lamps sitting on top were the only glitzy things in the room. She'd completed the look by hanging a photograph of the theatre at the Royal Opera House.

Shelby sighed as she got up and ran her hand over the quilt, straightening it where she'd wrinkled it. It had been her mom's request to come and stay with her this weekend. Shelby couldn't compete with posh hotels and mansions. Another way she didn't measure up. She crossed the room and shut the door softly behind her. The quiet apartment filled her with peace and contentment, but would her mother's arrival smother it? And tonight, she had a date. She groaned softly.

Why had she agreed to go on another date with Ryan? *I should cancel. I don't want to lead him on.* A nice guy, but there wasn't any sizzle between them. He'd make a great friend or brother. She chuckled softly. Probably not what he wanted to hear. She bit her lip, staring at her phone. She should call, tell him it wouldn't work and be done with it. But wouldn't that be better done in person? The clock ticked away as she stood, paralyzed by indecision. Too late to call now. She threw her hands up in surrender—she was going on a date with Ryan, but she'd let him know that friends were all they could be.

Ryan was picking her up in ten minutes. Shelby put on her earrings and then stared at her reflection. *Not bad.* Ryan had wanted to surprise her and hadn't told her where they were going, so she hoped she'd dressed appropriately.

The buzz of the door jarred her, and she reached for her pink lipstick. Ten minutes early? Someone needed to school this guy in women etiquette. She buzzed him in and opened the door, then ran back for the clutch she'd left sitting on her bed.

"Hi, darling. You shouldn't leave your door open—anyone could walk in."

Shelby dropped the clutch onto the bed at the sound of her mother's voice. *Mom?* What was she doing here a day early? She rushed out into the living area.

"I thought you weren't coming until tomorrow."

Her mother elegantly slipped out of the white wool coat, like a snake shedding its skin. "Shelby dear, your manners are atrocious." She stopped, coat in hand, and stared wide-eyed at Shelby. "Are you going on a date? The same young man from before?"

Was that hope she heard in her mother's voice? *Oh brother.*

Shelby didn't like the gleam in her mother's eyes. "Um, yeah, It's not a big deal. We're friends. But you didn't answer my question—why are you here today?"

"My meetings finished early, and I didn't want to stay in a hotel room another night. I assumed you wouldn't be busy." Her mother's lips curved up in a big grin. "But I'm delighted to find out you are."

"I'll cancel."

"You most definitely will not. I'll be fine here by myself, and then you can tell me everything when you come home."

Yeah, right. "Mom really, it's not a big deal." She reached for her phone, but the doorbell rang. Her heart sinking, Shelby buzzed Ryan in. She didn't want to deal with her mother *and* Ryan.

Since she still stood in front of it, Shane opened the door, smiling widely as Ryan strolled in. His dark jeans and blue button-up, opened at the collar, highlighted his good looks. The leather jacket didn't hurt either. Her mother's brows rose practically to her hairline. Shelby ignored her. *What is wrong with me that I am immune to your charms?* Handsome, kind, probably every girl's dream. He'd be great boyfriend material. She checked her pulse, finding it normal. *Rats.* Not a blip. Every girl's dream except hers.

Her mother ushered him farther into the apartment. *Oh no. Need to nip this in the bud.*

"Hi, Ryan, ready?" She turned to her mother. "Make yourself at home. I won't be late."

Her mother winked at her. "Don't come home early on my account."

Heat climbed up her neck as Shelby returned to her bedroom to retrieve her clutch. After gathering her wits, she emerged from the room and grabbed Ryan's arm, steering him out the door.

Her mother wiggled her fingers in a wave. "Have fun!" Her voice sing-songed.

Shelby closed the door and rested her forehead against the cool wood. Turning sideways to face Ryan, her head still pressed to the door, she sighed. "Sorry, I wasn't expecting her until tomorrow." She heaved her body away from the door.

"Do you think she'll be—"

"She'll be fine. Let's go." She clutched his arm, directing him away from her apartment and her mother.

* * *

Tristan surveyed the crowded arena. Why was he expecting a small crowd? The place was jammed with excited families, teenagers, and grandparents, ready to cheer on the Wyattsville High School hockey team and, judging by the pointing and gawking going on, catch a glimpse of Tristan Kelly. He waved to a couple of young boys who sported his number on their Renegades jerseys. As he swivelled on the team bench, he tried to ignore several couples sitting nearby, whispering intimately, sharing secret smiles. Obviously date night. *Ugh.*

He mentally ran through the roster as he sipped his ice water, hoping to freeze out the pain in his heart. Hundreds of people surrounded him, but he'd never felt more alone. Jason's girlfriend sat behind them, the seat next to her empty. It mocked him.

Jason approached him, looking pale. Probably nerves. Even Tristan's blood was pounding through his veins, giving him a heady rush. And he wasn't playing.

"I'm running to get some more water. Can I grab you anything?"

Yes, a miracle in the form of a certain physical therapist would be nice. He shook his head. "Thanks, I'm good."

Jason maneuvered around him and headed into the stands. People shouted encouragement as he raced up the stairs. Small towns weren't so bad.

Tristan crossed his arms as he followed the opposing team's warm-up. Wyattsville was playing their rival, Reinholt. The Reinholt guys were huge and had excellent skills. He schooled his features into a blank canvas, but his mouth was parched. Picking up his water bottle, he took a swig, enjoying the coolness on his throat.

Wyattsville had five more minutes of warm-up, so Tristan gave the signal to the team's captain. Jason was making his way to the bench with a tray of water bottles. Normally Tristan would've helped, but he'd only ditched the crutches a day ago, and working his way through a crowded venue was pushing it. Jason's girlfriend ran to help him. Would Shelby come to his games if they dated? Hockey was his life. *I wish I could share this with her.*

He hadn't been able to get around the ethical rule about her not dating patients. He'd have to wait to finish his treatment before he could take her out. If she'd even go out with him then. No. He'd win her over. That wasn't usually a problem. People fell over backwards to give Tristan Kelly what he wanted. *Not her.* Tristan repressed a groan. He really needed the little voice in his head to shut up.

The guys filed onto the bench, crowding the small space. Jason clapped his hands. "Okay, guys, this is it. Everything counts from here. Take every opportunity that you get. Reinholt is rated third overall, so we have to execute our plays and get the puck into their net."

The smell of sweat from the guys and popcorn from the concession stand wafted over Tristan—the smell of home. This was one of the few places he felt like he belonged. He clapped with the team, shouting "Go get 'em!" as the first string skated out to centre ice. Tristan lowered himself onto the bench. His ankle wasn't going to like it if he stood the whole time. A clipboard sat beside him and he picked it up, checking a few stats. A flash of pink to the left caught his attention and he lifted his gaze from the page. Blood rushed through his veins. *What's she doing here?* Then the person with her registered. Same guy as the last time.

He narrowed his eyes as he studied the two of them. Shelby was stunning in a light blue puffy coat and pink toque. Her companion looked as though he'd be more at home at a concert. Way too dressed up for a hockey game. Were they dating? Friends? She'd said no plus one. The desire to know almost pushed him out of his seat and over to their row. *Don't be an idiot and embarrass yourself.*

The clash of sticks roused Tristan from his musings, and he rolled his shoulders in an attempt to loosen the tight muscles. He picked up the clipboard. *Get your head in the game.*

* * *

"Nothing to hang your heads about. You played hard and that's what counts." Tristan encouraged the guys, who sat around the locker room in varying stages of dress. No one was talking. Clearly they thought they were a bunch of losers. *Time for that to change.* A 3-1 loss was nothing to feel ashamed of, especially since Reinholt had a winning record so far this season. A butt whooping was what he'd thought they'd get and they didn't. *I'll take it.*

The guys trudged past him on their way out. Once all the players left, he and Jason tidied up the room.

"Don't feel bad. I think it was a positive first step in moving forward and improving." He held out his hand to Jason.

Jason shook it. "I know you're right, but a loss still stinks."

"It does, but the guys held Reinholt to three goals. From the stats, that's impressive. They're creaming other teams by six or seven."

Jason chucked a wet towel in the laundry bin. "You're right. I need a new perspective."

"You're doing great. Keep it up. I'll see you later." Tristan grabbed his coat and backpack and slowly headed down the hall toward the exit. A few people still gathered around talking to players. A pink toque stood out among the lingering crowd. *She's still here.*

Don't do it. But he couldn't stop himself from walking over. She stood with her friend—Tristan refused to call him a date—and a player, obviously from the other team.

Both guys' jaws slackened as Tristan approached their small group. Shelby must have noticed her companion's reaction, because she turned his way. He inclined his head in her direction. "Shelby." He stuck his hand out to the guy. "I'm Tristan."

Shelby's friend grasped his hand. Tristan was tempted to squeeze it so hard he'd make the guy wince, but he resisted the urge.

"I know who you are. I'm a big fan. Ryan." He pointed to the young man. "This is my nephew, Chris."

Tristan shook the kid's hand. "Nice game." He read the number on the kid's coat. "Number 17—you scored two of the goals against us. Impressive."

The kid's ears turned bright red. "Thanks. I-I'm a big fan. It's good of you to coach the high school team."

"I'm only assisting until my ankle heals."

Ryan eyed Tristan's leg. "Sorry to hear about your injury." A light bulb appeared to go on in the guy's head, and he touched Shelby's arm. "Are you treating him?" Ryan held up a hand. "Actually, I know you can't tell me, but I assume that's how you know him?"

Shelby tugged her coat zipper higher. "No, that's not how we met."

Time to turn on the charm. "Shelby and I go all the way back to our teens. She showed me up at a sports camp."

She tugged her toque off and ran her hand through her hair. "That's your story now, is it?"

"It's the truth. You taught me that dancers are elite athletes too."

"Wow, maturity. Will wonders never cease." She smiled at him sweetly.

A pulse beat at Tristan's temple, and he rolled his tongue over his bottom teeth. Ryan and his nephew were still clearly in a fanboy fog and oblivious to the tension rising between him and Shelby.

"We have pictures of Shelby hanging at the school in her glory days. One of Spencer's best dancers." Ryan wrapped his arm around Shelby's waist.

Tristan clenched his fist. Maybe there *was* a dancer boy in her life or one waiting in the wings. "Did you go to Spencer?"

Ryan laughed. "Oh no. I have two left feet. I teach science there."

Okay, so no dancer boy. "Teaching is tough. Sort of like coaching, I'd imagine."

"Yeah. I coach Chris's soccer team. A few similarities."

"One coach kept me on the straight and narrow at the time I needed it. If it wasn't for him, I'm not sure if I'd be here today." Tristan shifted his backpack on his shoulder. Why had he said that?

"Yeah, me too. I used to play soccer and my coach in high school taught us not only soccer skills but integrity and honour. I've seen it go the other way too. Coaches can make or break you."

Shelby glared at him. *Time to go.* "I should get going. Nice seeing you, Shelby. Nice to meet you, Ryan. Chris, keep up the great work." He slapped the young guy's shoulder before hobbling to the exit.

Maybe Shelby hadn't been glad to see him, but the guy and his nephew were fans and seemed nice. His heart squeezed as he thought of Ryan and Shelby together, maybe entwining their hands, laughing at inside jokes. *Stop it.* He jerked open the door to his truck and climbed in, his ankle throbbing like his heart.

* * *

The lobby's warmth suffocated Shelby. She needed fresh air. Ryan was walking Chris out to the team bus, so she made an excuse about using the restrooms and then detoured out into the cool air. She needed a couple of minutes alone. Cold air filled her lungs and cooled her flushed cheeks. Tristan had a lot of nerve, interrupting her date. *Who does he think he is?* Only the hottest goalie in the NHL right now. Oh yeah, right. She stared at the stars, marvelling that she could see them here in Wyattsville. In the big city, the light pollution blocked such starry skies. Tonight they were tiny diamonds winking at her from a deep velvet background.

"What are you doing out here?"

Shelby whirled around. "Tristan. I thought you left."

"I was about to when I saw you come out." He rubbed his hands together, blowing on them. "I wanted to make sure you were okay."

Her pulse quickened, and she crossed her arms. "Why wouldn't I be okay? You think you have that kind of effect on me? Your arrogance is astounding." He did have that kind of effect on her, but she wasn't about to admit it.

A shadow crossed his face. "Your words, not mine. I wanted to make sure you weren't sick or something. Ryan's treating you okay?"

"I'm perfectly fine. Ryan is a gentleman. I wanted fresh air—the place was stuffy." It sounded lame even to her own ears.

"Okay." He fingered his truck keys. "I'm sorry. I wasn't trying to upset you."

"You interrupted my date—are you sure you want to go with that?"

He sighed. "Whatever. I'll see you at the clinic."

"Don't slip." Shelby huffed. Infuriating didn't even begin to describe Tristan Kelly. *Stop it. You're with Ryan tonight, and you owe him the courtesy of keeping the hockey guy out of your thoughts.* She flexed her fingers a couple of times before plastering a smile on her face and trudging to Ryan's car in the next lot.

Between her mother and Tristan, the evening was already a disaster, and now she had to let Ryan know that they could only be friends.

CHAPTER TWENTY-SIX

TRISTAN SHIFTED IN THE VINYL CHAIR IN THE BUSY WAITING ROOM OF THE clinic. A mother sat with her teenage son who wore a Wyattsville basketball jersey, his foot taped up. Tristan exchanged a sympathetic glance with the guy. *Injuries are the worst.* Beside them sat an older gentleman with bruises around his cheekbones and eyes. Tristan winced. The lighting in the room was dull as rain clouds threatened outside the window.

"Tristan." The voice was male—definitely not Shelby's. He jerked his gaze away from the window. A guy with a shaved head and glasses stood in the entrance to the room, waiting for him. Tristan stood gingerly then followed the therapist to the treatment rooms.

"Hi Tristan, I'm Jake. I'll be taking care of you today."

"Where's Shelby?"

"She had a double booking. Someone messed up at the desk. Sorry."

Sure they did. "No problem."

Jake clapped his hands and grinned. "Let's get to work."

Tristan followed the big guy down the hallway, a grimace on his face. Where was Shelby? Working with Jake was different than working with her. Both were excellent at what they did, but Tristan relaxed more with Jake, for obvious reasons. When his appointment was over, Tristan took his time making his way along the hallway where the offices were located. The door to Shelby's office was cracked open. Not giving himself time to think about it, he stepped closer and knocked, hoping that, if she invited him in, she wouldn't hear his hammering heart.

"C'mon in." Her voice was muffled.

He nudged the door open with two fingers. Her head was buried in a clinical book. "Hi."

She jerked her head up as if someone had poured cold water down her neck. That wasn't the reaction he'd hoped for.

"Tristan, uh hi."

"I saw your door open. I... I'm sorry about Friday night."

She dropped her pen on top of a stack of papers. "You're lucky Ryan is a big fan and not the jealous type."

"I get it." He rested against the door jamb. "So Jake treated me today."

"I heard."

"Wipe that smug look off your face. I'm feeling it. Was that payback?"

"That would be unprofessional. I really couldn't make the appointment, but Jake was more than willing. He's a fan."

"I missed you."

She shelved a textbook on the shelf above the desk, ignoring the comment. "How did you like Jake?"

"He seemed to know what he was doing."

Shelby shuffled the charts around on her desk. "He's excellent at his job."

He chuckled. "I know, but he's not the only one excellent at his job. You are too."

"I wasn't fishing for a compliment. Jake is good and you should trust him."

"I only wanted you to know that you are a good physical therapist. By the way, trading with Jake wasn't so we could go on a date, was it?"

She picked up her pen and opened a file. "No, absolutely not. They double-booked me."

"Since I'm getting close to the end of my treatment, maybe Jake can take over. Then you could go out with me. Problem solved."

"A little over confident that I'll say yes, aren't you? What if I take offence that you'd so easily throw me over for Jake?"

He loved verbal sparring with her. "I'm not, but I want to go out on a date with you more." *And I'll be leaving when I get better. It'll be too late to go out with you then.* "Say yes."

She pointed her pen at him. "Wow, you've resorted to begging? The great Tristan Kelly, NHL star, is pleading for me to go out with him."

I'll get down on my knees if I have to. "Not begging, asking. Politely and fervently hoping you'll say yes."

Her blue eyes locked with his and his breath caught in his throat. She bit her glossed bottom lip. "Yes."

He pushed away from the door. "What?"

"I said yes. I'll go out with you. Jake can take over your care now. My schedule is getting full with new patients, anyway."

Adrenaline coursed his body. He wanted to jump up and down. Instead, he said, "Okay. Awesome." *Play it cool.* He pointed to her phone. "I'll be in touch with plans."

"Great. I'll talk to you later."

He left the clinic as quickly as he could, afraid he'd jinx it. A wide grin slid across his face. *What about distractions?*

Opening the truck door, Tristan climbed in, shoving away those thoughts. A date was not going to side-track him from his mission to return to the NHL. At least, that was what he kept telling himself as he drove home.

* * *

Jessica waved a hand in front of her face. "Earth to Shelby. What is going on with you? You've picked up your water glass three times now and set it down without taking a sip."

Shelby blinked, hoping to free her mind of the whir of thoughts. "Sorry Jess, I'm distracted."

Her co-worker tilted her head. "Hmm. By a hot hockey player who obviously has eyes for you, perhaps?"

Shelby chased a piece of lettuce on her plate with a fork. "No, that's not it."

"You are a horrible liar, Shelby."

Does she read minds?

Jessica bent forward and grabbed her hand across the table. "Why are you totally in denial that he's into you? A lot."

"No, he's not. He—"

"He is. I see how he looks at you when he comes into the clinic, like someone on a desert island who hasn't had water in too long. And in this scenario, you are the water."

"That's ridiculous. And a horrible analogy, by the way."

Jessica wadded up her sandwich wrapper. "It's true. Now tell me why you're hesitating. He's gorgeous, he's a famous NHL goalie, and he's super nice."

"The fact that he's a famous NHL goalie is the problem. I've lived that life with my mother, and I don't want to do it again. The career, fame, and fans always come first. I don't want that in a relationship. Not to mention all the women who hang around him."

"He doesn't seem like a player."

"I don't think he is, but who knows? He doesn't have to be a player to have women drooling all over him. I don't think I can share."

"So you like him?"

"Did I say that?"

Jessica used her fingers to make quote signs. "I don't think I can share."

"Doesn't mean anything. Besides, we knew each other a long time ago, and he chose hockey over me." *You chose dance over him.*

Sunlight flooded the room, warming Shelby's face as she sat staring at her salad. Jessica covered her fingers with her hand. "You were kids. You didn't know any better. What was he supposed to do? He had a promising future in the NHL. You were going to be a famous ballerina."

"I know, but he vanished—dropped out of my life completely. No emails or texts or anything. Just gone." Shelby bit her lip. "What if he does a repeat performance?"

"That's a risk you'll have to take."

Shelby sipped her water. But did she want to risk her heart?

CHAPTER
TWENTY-SEVEN

TRISTAN CHECKED HIS FACE IN THE MIRROR, PICKED UP HIS KEYS AND WALLET from the nightstand, and strode out of his apartment. His heart beat rapidly against his chest, and his stomach flip-flopped like a beached fish. He inhaled deeply, calming himself.

It's a date. You've been on lots of dates. This is no different. That rebellious fish did another flip. *Yeah, right.* Facing Gretzky in a shoot-out wouldn't be as nerve-wracking. He climbed into his truck and started the engine, its smooth purr soothing the fish. He reversed out of his parking space and drove to Shelby's apartment.

Apartment 430. He stuck his finger on the buzzer.

Her voice floated clearly out the speaker. "I'll be right down."

Okay, guess he'd meet her here. He propped a shoulder against the brick wall and checked his phone. Lots of texts from his coaches and agent, but he didn't want to talk to them right now. He shoved the device into his jacket pocket as Shelby emerged from the elevator. His jaw dropped before he remembered himself and snapped it closed. The word *stunning* didn't do her justice. Her long, blonde hair hung in loose waves around her shoulders, and her eyes were brilliant sapphire orbs. Her modest green dress fit in all the right places. He smiled. "Wow. You're beautiful."

"What? You don't enjoy the scrub chic at the clinic?"

"You make anything look good, but I like this the most. Can I help you with your coat?" He held out his hand for the coat draped over one arm.

"Thank you. It was too hot to put it on in the apartment." She handed it to him, and he helped her slip it on, the scent of her orange shampoo teasing his nose. The desire to reach out and touch her hair had him stuffing his hands deep into his coat pockets. They strolled to his truck, and he assisted her into the cab.

Sitting beside her in the small space, he decided he wouldn't need to drink anything other than water tonight. Shelby intoxicated him enough. *It's officially a date.* He didn't let himself dwell on the fact that it was possible one wouldn't be nearly enough.

"Where are we going exactly? Wyattsville isn't all that big."

"I thought I'd take you to Reinholt, if that's okay. There's a really good Italian place there and the food's excellent."

"Sounds good. I love Italian."

He could feel her staring at him, but she didn't say any more. His cheeks heated under her gaze, and he fiddled with the radio dial. "What type of music do you listen to?"

She lifted a shoulder. "Anything."

"Really? Even country?"

She chuckled. "What's wrong with country?"

"Nothing. It's a far cry from what I'm sure you're used to. You know, all that classical stuff."

"Classical stuff?" A memory of him watching her dance at camp came to her. "I'm sure Bach would love you referring to his masterpieces as 'stuff.' What do you listen to?"

"Hey, I listen to classical music too, among other genres."

"You like classical music? I recall you referring to it as a bad taste in music."

He ran a finger over the spotless dash. "I remember. I guess my tastes matured. I'll listen to anything. My mom played a variety of music."

"That's nice. For the record, I enjoy all types of music too. I'm not a dancer snob... anymore."

She said it so quietly he wasn't sure if he'd imagined it.

"Anymore?"

"I was kind of a prima donna in my junior and senior years of high school. And the first part of my career in dance."

Intriguing. "A prima donna, eh? I can't imagine."

She smacked his shoulder. "Not my proudest moments."

"You weren't that bad from what I remember. I've met a few real divas in the sports world, and you didn't come close except for the canoeing."

"Ah yes, the canoeing." She twisted a piece of her long blonde hair in her fingers. "Let's say my drive and focus got more intense after I returned home from camp. As did my mom's. Someday I'll introduce you to my friend, Coco. We were roommates senior year. She'll set you straight."

"I look forward to it." But all Tristan heard was the word *someday*, which indicated they might have more than this date.

* * *

The swanky Italian restaurant in Reinholt was surrounded by fancy cars and even fancier people. The urge to turn around and run overwhelmed Shelby. The stares of people seated in the room bored into her back and followed them to their table. Tristan's hand on her waist warmed her all the way through. Tilting her head slightly forward, she hid behind the waves of her blonde hair.

The low lights cast a golden glow on the room, and the tantalizing smells of garlic, onions, and tomatoes scented the air. Too nervous to have much of an appetite, she'd skipped lunch, and after the long drive, she was famished.

Their server led them to a table in the back covered in a white linen cloth. A single red rose in a vase sat to the side of the table. The server placed two black leather menus down and held out Shelby's chair. She thanked him and sat down. "What can I get you to drink, Mr. Kelly?"

Shelby lifted the rose and sniffed, its delicate scent filling her nose. *Hmmm.* Did everyone in the world know who Tristan was?

"I'll have sparking water please. Shelby?"

"Sounds great. Thank you."

The server smiled before moving off. Shelby stared at Tristan. He ran his fingers over the menu, not meeting her gaze. "Must be a fan."

Let it go. She picked up her menu and perused it. "Everything sounds delicious."

"The risotto or the lasagna is excellent. I've been craving the risotto since the last time I was here."

"Not only excellent but addictive too." She folded her menu. "Sounds sinful."

A tall, bald man approached their table. He held out his hand to Tristan, a big grin on his face.

"Tristan, so great to see you. Where have you been hiding during your rehabilitation?"

Tristan shook the man's hand. "Taking it easy."

Which didn't really answer the man's question. Maybe he did want privacy in his personal life.

The man shoved one hand in his pants pocket and stooped slightly, as tall people tend to do. "How's it going? Will you be returning soon?"

"It's going great, but my return is still up in the air." Tristan gestured to Shelby. "Rick Ames, this is Shelby Wright. Rick supports the Renegades and minor hockey here in Reinholt."

She shook the man's hand. Rick turned to Tristan, eagerly questioning him about the team's chances of making the playoffs. Shelby tuned them out as she gently fingered the rose's petals. A feeling of déjà vu struck her. She was in a restaurant with her mother. People—fans, other artists—dropped by the table, all wanting to see and be seen with the great Shane Tivoli. Her mother barely ate two bites of her meal. Instead, she soaked up the attention while Shelby sat in the corner with her dad, wondering why they had even bothered to go out as a family. She blinked, coming back to the present. *It's one guy. It could happen anywhere with anyone. People run into friends and co-workers all the time.*

Their server stood back, waiting in the wings to take their order. She willed Rick to leave. He must have read her mind, because finally he left for his table. Their server approached. "Are you ready to order?"

Tristan picked up his own menu and glanced at it. "Do you know what you want?"

She held hers out to the man. "I'll have the salmon."

"Very good. Sir?"

Tristan ordered the risotto. Once they were alone, he cleared his throat. "Sorry about Rick."

The contrition was new. Her chest loosened, and her irritation waned. "It's okay."

He picked up his fork and turned it over and over. *Is he nervous?*

"How long did you live here in Reinholt?"

Shelby sipped her sparkling water. Its fizziness tickled her nose. "Reinholt was more a home base. We were rarely here. Mom and Dad travelled a lot with their careers, and I lived at school ten months of the year. Spencer School of the Performing Arts was more a home to me than my house."

"Yeah, I lived with a billet family my senior year. They're families who adopt a player for the season. I played for Edmonton, so I lived there most of the year."

She knew he'd played for Edmonton, but she didn't tell him that. No need for him to know she had stalked him for most of her junior year. He'd never once phoned, emailed, or texted. *Neither did you.* After that year, she had given up and erased him from her life, focusing on her dancing.

"Did you have a nice billet family?"

His grin lit his face as he stared off into space. "The best. The Connollys. Mr. Connolly was really into hockey, and he'd practice drills with me all the time. Mrs. Connolly made chocolate chip cookies that were to die for."

"Sounds very Cleaverish."

"Loved that show. Watched it on reruns."

Shelby ran her hand over the smooth linen tablecloth. "*Leave It to Beaver* did not represent my family."

"Or mine—at least after my dad left."

The server came to the table with their food, which looked amazing. The smell of garlic butter sent Shelby's taste buds into overdrive, and she inhaled. "Mmm, this smells amazing."

The server smiled as he took a step back. "I hope you enjoy it."

Shelby forked a piece of salmon, flaking it away from the rest. Sliding it into her mouth, she tasted the buttery fish and closed her eyes. When she'd swallowed and opened her eyes, Tristan asked, "Good?"

"Mmmm, so good." She wiped her mouth with the burgundy cloth napkin. "Do you see your dad at all?"

A shadow flitted across Tristan's face, and she wished she hadn't asked the question. "I'm sorry. That's none of my business."

"No, it's fine. I always felt my brothers and I weren't good enough, and that's why he left. So I never wanted to hang out with his new, improved family." He picked up a piece of bread and buttered it, avoiding her eyes.

"It's not your fault he left."

He stopped buttering, staring at the piece of sourdough. "I know." The words lacked conviction. "Do you actually—"

"Tristan, my man! It's been ages. Where have you been?"

Tristan smiled at a hulk of a guy standing next to their table. "Roger. How are you?" He stood and shook Roger's hand, pulling him to his chest and slapping his back with the other hand. As Tristan filled Roger in on his injury, Shelby finished her meal and took a sip of water. The two men shook hands again then Roger wandered off to wherever he came from. Tristan stared at his now cold rice.

The server came up to him. "Mr. Kelly, can I heat that up for you?"

"Thank you, I'd appreciate it." Tristan handed the server his plate. When the man had gone, he cupped the back of his neck. "Again, I'm sorry. I haven't seen Roger in a few months. He used to play for the Renegades but moved to Winnipeg last year. He's in town for a conference. He left hockey and now runs his own business."

"That's nice." She didn't know what else to say about a stranger. The server returned with a steaming plate. Tristan thanked him and dug in. Heated-up rice. Shelby shuddered, but Tristan didn't seem to mind. She bent forward to examine the meal closer. Not heated up but a new plate. "He gave you a whole new meal."

Tristan paused, his fork halfway to his mouth, then lowered it. "So he did. Which is fine by me, since reheated risotto is gross."

Shelby narrowed her eyes. "But—"

He waved the fork through the air and a couple of pieces of risotto landed on the tablecloth. "Why choose physical therapy? It requires some serious schooling, doesn't it?"

Clearly he wasn't comfortable talking about the way people treated him with deference. Shelby hesitated before deciding she should probably respect that. "Yes, I spent a number of years in school and then I had to do a placement. I've never regretted making the decision to study physical therapy. Making a difference—giving people back what they thought they had lost—feels like I'm contributing in a positive way. Most patients who come to us have reduced freedom due to restricted movement, pain, or dependence on other people. I get to help them with that, and I find it satisfying."

Tristan set his fork down, his plate clean. "I can see how that would make you feel good about your job."

"It does. I never wonder if it's worth it." She contemplated him. Did he remember their conversation from camp all those years ago?

His eyes met hers briefly, then he pushed his plate away and took a sip of his water. "No, I don't suppose you do."

The server approached the table again. Given his impeccable timing, Shelby guessed he must be watching their table pretty closely. Did he even have any other patrons to take care of? "Can I bring you coffee or dessert?" He picked up their plates.

Shelby patted her stomach. "No thanks. I'm too stuffed to eat another thing. Please tell the chef the meal was excellent."

The guy smiled at her. "Yes, ma'am."

"We're good, thank you." Tristan dismissed him.

Shelby surveyed the room. A young woman in her thirties with raven hair pulled up in a high pony-tail and dressed in a slinky black dress approached their table. Her attention was squarely on Tristan, as though Shelby wasn't even there. "I'm so sorry to bother you, but I had to come over here and meet the great Tristan Kelly."

She doesn't seem sorry. The woman didn't hide the fact that she was checking Tristan out. At least he had the decency to blush as he glanced at Shelby before shifting his focus to the woman. Tristan engaged the fan, smiling and chatting before posing with her for a selfie. The woman plastered herself to Tristan's side. Grinding her teeth, Shelby stood and muttered, "I'm going to the restroom."

Tristan took a step toward her, but the woman grabbed his arm to stop him. The dining room was crowded. Silverware clinking against china mixed with the laughter and chatting of friends to create a din in the room. Classical music piping through speakers in the wall added more noise to the atmosphere.

Pushing the restroom door open, Shelby's eyes widened. This bathroom was nicer than her apartment. A white leather couch and two chairs sat to one side of the door. Why someone would want to sit in a public bathroom and chat, Shelby wasn't sure. A row of highly-polished sinks lined one wall and wooden doors leading to the stalls lined the other. Shelby took care of business then washed her hands. Drying them on a real hand towel, she stared at herself in the mirror. Why had Tristan brought her here? Was he showing off? They could have stayed in Wyattsville and had a quiet dinner with no interruptions. Maybe gotten to know each other. She dropped the towel in the bin and rubbed her temples. *I want to go home.*

Tristan stood talking to the same woman, but now two others had joined her. Shelby reversed her course to the coat check. Standing at the counter, she realized Tristan had their tickets. No coat, no ride. Her eyes met his as she sidled up to the table and slid onto her seat. She ignored the women as much as they pretended she wasn't there.

"Ladies, thank you so much for coming over, but I need to return to my date." Tristan untangled himself from them. They glared at Shelby as they strutted away.

"I'm ready to leave." Her flat tone didn't hide her feelings, but she didn't care. She was so done with this date.

"Sure. Let me pay the bill." He searched the room for the server, then waved his hand. The young man approached. "Can we get the bill, please?" The server whipped out a leather folder from his serving apron. Tristan took it, but instead of handing the man a credit card, he stood and followed him over to the hostess desk.

Shelby watched him, thinking about the replacement meal they had brought him. Why was it that the more fame and money you had, the more people wanted to give you things for free? She'd witnessed it happen to her mom all the time. They kept their famous stars happy so they'd return. Celebrity visits were always good for business, because fans saw pictures on social media of their favourite stars dining and wanted to be able to claim they'd eaten at the same place. Or they came, hoping to catch a glimpse of the rich and famous. *And interrupt their dates. Or family dinners. Or shopping trips.*

Shelby remembered being sixteen, trying on dresses for the formal and waiting in the change room for her mom, who never came back to see her. Teen Shelby stalked out of the room, dress in hand, to find her mother taking photos with a group of teen girls. Shelby had shoved the dress on the rack and left the shop. Her mother had been irritated with her when she found her sulking in the food court. Shelby hadn't cared. She'd felt invisible that day—like tonight.

Tristan returned to their table and held out his hand, but he had a wary look on his face. "Ready?"

She brushed past his hand and stalked to the coat check, her jaw clenched. Tristan procured their coats, and she quickly slid hers on. Stalking out to the truck, Shelby slid into the cab and stared out the window.

* * *

Shelby was ticked, and Tristan didn't blame her. This evening hadn't turned out like he'd hoped at all. He stuck the key in the ignition but didn't start the truck. "I'm sorry. I didn't think—"

"You didn't think what? That walking into a restaurant in Reinholt, where you play hockey, was going to get you attention? Why did you bring me here? To show off?" Her glare seared him, laser-beam hot.

"I... I didn't mean—"

"You know what? I don't care. Just take me home."

The air was heavy between them. His plan to have a nice dinner in a fancy restaurant had backfired in the worst way. Had he been showing off? Maybe. People respected him as an athlete, and a part of him wanted her to see that. He clenched a fist at the sight of her granite face. "I'm sorry."

She whirled to face him. "No, I'm sorry I let you talk me into this date. I knew, *I knew*, it was a mistake. Do you have any idea how many times I've sat with my mother while she ignored me because her adoring fans wanted her attention? How staff fawned over her because of her fame? You wasted your time tonight—I'm not impressed. In fact, you've proven to me that you and I will never work. I can't live this life again. I don't want to. Go back to the NHL and all the adoring fans and perks. You can have them. I don't want them. I'll take boring old Wyattsville any day."

He felt as though she had slapped him. Hard. He'd forgotten about her mother. He swallowed, his mouth dry. "Shelby, I'm sorry."

She held up her hand. "Stop."

Heat flared through his chest. "So you're going to accuse me and then not allow me to explain? All I wanted was to show you a nice evening. Did I know we'd get interrupted so many times? No. Sometimes people approach, sometimes they don't. I never know. I certainly don't ask or expect perks because I play in the NHL."

"But you let people give you free meals because you were too busy talking to eat."

He smacked the steering wheel with his palm. Heat flushed his face. "I paid for the extra meal." *What kind of schmuck does she think I am?*

"It doesn't matter."

"It matters to me. Maybe I did try and show off a bit—sue me. Can't a guy try and impress a girl anymore?"

"The thing you guys never seem to get is that what impresses us is you paying attention to us, not the women who interrupt our dates. We want to feel special instead of ignored."

Tristan opened his mouth then shut it. The women who'd cloyed for his attention coveted photos to post on their social media accounts or online news. People used his status and fame to get what they wanted out of it. Not everyone, but more than he'd like to admit. He rarely took advantage of his celebrity for his own personal gain. Tonight he'd

Face Off

miscalculated—big time. Shelby's hand gripped the door handle, her jaw clenched so tightly he could almost feel the ache himself.

Wrapping his fingers around the keys, he turned the ignition. What was the point? She wasn't going to listen right now. *I guess the evening's over.* The miles clicked by in silence until he braked in front of Shelby's apartment. Words still escaped him. She opened the door. He laid his hand on her arm. "Shelby—"

"Forget it, okay? Forget *me.* Please." She tumbled out of the truck so fast he didn't have time to open his door. After watching her practically run up the walk then disappear inside the building, he slumped back, paralyzed. Somehow this night, this date, had gone totally sideways. How had it gotten so out of his control? Had Shelby and any possible future involving the two of them just slipped through fingers?

The question she had asked him when they'd stood on that beach so many years ago flitted through his mind. Fame, sacrifice, hockey—had it all been worth it? Sitting alone in his truck now, he had absolutely no idea.

CHAPTER
TWENTY-EIGHT

WHIFFS OF STEAM FURLED FROM THE TWO CUPS OF CIDER SITTING ON THE coffee table. The scent of vanilla and cinnamon tantalized Shelby's nose. She snuggled deeper into the comfortable couch as Coco placed a plate of shortbread beside the drinks. Coco and Mike's home was clean but looked lived in. Mike's sports gear was neatly stacked in the corner on the hall by the front door. Their bikes hung from nails in the same hallway. The large windows in the living area made the place bright. Shelby chuckled at their pet rabbit, Whiskers, huddled over the air vent like it was a sauna. The place wasn't posh or decorated by a designer, but it was a home and that's why Shelby loved to visit. She'd searched for a home since she could remember, and this was as close as it got.

But it didn't belong to her.

She picked up her mug and held it in her hands, letting the warmth seep through her cold fingers. Coco grabbed a piece of shortbread and tucked her legs under her. "So?"

"So, what?"

"I'm hearing rumours that you're friends with Tristan Kelly, and the two of you were spotted here in Reinholt on the weekend. Why am I hearing this from other people? I thought we were friends."

Ouch. "Sorry, Coco. It's been a little crazy."

"That's your excuse?"

After placing her mug on the table, Shelby picked up a cookie. "No, I was in denial." She sighed. "I met Tristan before my junior year of high school. We attended an elite sports camp together."

Coco coughed, choking on a piece of her cookie. She took a sip of her hot drink. "Wait. You went to a sports camp?"

"A skills camp—for athletes of all sports. Shane's idea. She thought it would be good to expand my skills and also show up the other athletes with my brilliance at leaping and pointe work."

"I can only imagine."

"I know, right? The footwork drills were no problem, but the hand-eye drills were killer." Shelby pointed to herself. "Are you surprised I'm not a gifted puck-handler or dribbler?"

Coco snickered. "I can't wait to tell Mike this." She blew on her cider then took a sip.

"Don't you dare."

"I've got to tell him how you know Tristan, because he's more observant than you give him credit for. He knew something was up a few weeks back at the restaurant."

"You got yourself a winner, Coco. Make sure you keep him."

Coco winked. "Already put a ring on it. No going back."

A pang went through Shelby's chest. She wanted that too. She wanted someone...

"Soo, you met at the caamp..." Coco motioned for her to keep talking.

"It's a cliché. Girl meets boy, girl and boy spar with each other, then girl and boy realize they're into each other but reality takes over. He was on the fast track to the NHL, and I planned to rule at Spencer as the Belle of the Ballet." Shelby broke a piece off her cookie then set both pieces on the table. "He asked me the last day of camp if I thought it would be worth all the sacrifices. At the time I didn't have an answer, but when I left ballet I discovered a whole new life. I think he's still trying to figure it out."

"But you went on a date with him the other night. He can't be that bad."

"Yeah, against my better judgment. I should always listen to my little voice." Shelby hugged her knees to her chest. "The evening was a parade of people, men and women, wanting a piece of him. I felt invisible. I've had enough of that growing up with Shane."

Coco reached across the couch and covered Shelby's hand with hers. "I'm sorry, Shelby."

"It's okay. Better to know all this now before it amounted to anything."

"Would it have?"

"Well, he pursued me like he would a puck." She made a face then covered her mouth. "Sorry, that was bad."

Coco laughed. "Maybe, but it's probably true. Is he the reason Ryan didn't make an impression?"

"No, Ryan and I didn't have any chemistry. He'd be a good friend." She grasped her mug and raised it to her lips, taking a long drink.

"I won't repeat the friend comment to Ryan. He really likes you." Coco sank against the arm of the couch. "What are you going to do?"

"Me? Go back to my life. Work." She carefully set the mug on the table, avoiding Coco's eyes.

"There's more to life than work, Shelby." Her friend's words were gentle, but Shelby felt the rebuke.

"Maybe."

"No maybe—it's true. I know." Coco nudged Shelby's leg with her foot. She was right. Coco had chased after a dance career, leaving everything behind, only to have it ruined by a career-ending injury. She'd learned a hard lesson. Still, did Shelby want to put her heart out there only to have it ignored? She'd always felt second best with her mother, and she had no intention of repeating the experience.

"Shelby, you deserve to come first with whomever you go out with. I know Shane made you feel you were never good enough, but I hope you know that you are an amazing woman who deserves to come first, to be loved and cherished." Coco finished off her cider and cradled the mug in her hands. "I hope you know God sees you as his prized daughter. He loves you more than you can ever know. You don't need to prove yourself to him. He loves you as you are."

Shelby picked at her thumb nail. Coco grew up going to church—a pastor's daughter— but she didn't typically preach, so the fact she'd said anything indicated it was important. "I find that hard to believe. I've had to prove myself to everyone for so long. Even after leaving dance, I had to show everyone I could still be someone outside of that world."

"I know. But God sees you and loves you whether you dance or are a physical therapist or whatever."

Shelby straightened and stretched her arms over her head. "I need to think about that."

"It's a lot to take in." Coco collected the empty mugs and stood. "You know *I* love you more as a physical therapist, right?"

Shelby threw a pillow at her. "Shut up. You loved me at Spencer too, you just didn't know it because I was such a brat."

"Hmm. A brat? That's what you call that kind of behaviour?" Coco set the mugs down and tossed the pillow back at Shelby. "Speaking of ballet, I've been thinking. Do you want to start working out with me at the barre? For fun. I could use a work-out buddy."

Shelby pursed her lips. "I'm super rusty."

"I highly doubt that."

"Can I get back to you? I have so much to think about at the moment."

"Sure. Let me know."

Going back to the barre intimidated Shelby—it'd been a long time. Contemplating the idea, she realized she'd missed it. The barre, God, Tristan—she hadn't been lying to Coco. She definitely had a lot to mull over.

CHAPTER TWENTY-NINE

TRISTAN WASN'T TAKING NO FOR AN ANSWER. THAT DECISION HAD BROUGHT him to Shelby's apartment parking lot, where he sat in his truck. He wiped his slick palms on his jeans. *Get a grip. You are Tristan Kelly, one of the best NHL goalies, and you speak to all kinds of press and people all the time.* So why did he feel as if he was about to be in a shoot-out? What if she threw him out?

The entrance to the apartment building mocked him as he wiped a hand over his lips. *Coward. Just go ring her doorbell.* When he opened his door, the cool night air hit his warm face. He closed his eyes briefly, then climbed down and strode to the front entrance. *You can do this.*

An older woman leaving the building held the security door for him. He hesitated for a moment then grabbed the door, nodding his thanks.

The woman didn't let go. "When are you returning to the Renegades?"

"Soon."

She lifted her shopping bag a little higher. "Excellent. You better whip that team into shape, because they're awful without you."

He smiled but kept his mouth shut as he hurried inside. The Reinholt Renegades had a losing record without their number one goalie—part of the reason he had to return quickly so they could stay in play-off contention. Taking the stairs two at a time, he thought through what he planned to say. His racing pulse and sweaty palms made him feel like he was seventeen again. Shelby could be unpredictable, so his argument for her giving him a second chance had to be foolproof. She was different than any other woman he'd dated. Even as a teenager, no one had compared to her. Maybe that's why he'd left her—he knew getting involved came with a serious commitment. He opened the door to her floor and breathed deeply. Shelby hadn't changed. If he could only persuade her to take a chance with him.

The royal blue door to her apartment matched the blue in the paisley carpet. Seconds after he rapped, footsteps approached. His heart raced, and he rubbed at the spot. The door opened and her eyes widened as she took him in.

"T-Tristan."

"Hi."

"What are you doing here?"

"Um, I wanted to talk to you."

"Oh, okay. Come in." She motioned him in with one hand. "Have a seat."

"If you don't mind, I think I'll stand." But then he sat on the couch. His brain was a mess. "Changed my mind." He licked his lips then gripped his hands together. Maybe she'd come sit next to him. She remained standing by the door. *Guess not.*

"You're acting weird. What's up?" Her voice was flat and her face was expressionless.

Say something before she kicks you out. "Hear me out." He locked eyes with her in a silent challenge. "Um, can we have a do-over of our date?"

She stepped over to the armchair and straightened a blanket. "I don't think that's a good idea."

"Let me finish. I know I messed up last time, but I'm hoping you'll give me a second chance. I like you, Shelby. You've always been different from other women. When you look at me, I feel seen. You don't care about the hockey or fame." He rested his elbows on his knees. "And we have great chemistry. You feel it too, don't you?" Her cheeks were a rosy colour, which warmed his insides. She didn't respond, so he pressed on. "Please give me another try, Shelby. I'll do better this time."

She bit her lip. "I'm not sure."

He didn't want to lose the inch he'd gained. "What are you doing tonight?"

"Tonight?"

"Yeah, will you go out with me tonight? Please say yes." He couldn't lose this chance. "If it goes nowhere, after tonight, you don't have to see me anymore."

Sighing, she threw up her hands. "Fine. What should I wear?"

He took in her skinny jeans and the pink turtleneck that fit her in all the right places. "You're perfect." She tugged at her turtleneck as though she was hot. He'd meant more than her clothes, and her reaction told him she knew it. The silence expanded and he checked out her feet. "Make sure you're wearing warm socks."

She wiggled her toes. "All toasty and warm." She opened the closet door and tugged her coat off a hanger. "Anything else?"

"A hat and gloves."

She rummaged in a basket on the top shelf and found both. After shutting the closet door, she slid her feet into her boots. She opened the door and they left the apartment. As the lock to the building door clicked, Tristan resisted the urge to pump his fists. Instead, he tugged his keys out of his jeans pockets before opening her door and running around the front of the truck. Settling on the leather seat, Tristan asked, "All set?"

"All set," she echoed.

They drove out onto the street. Tristan kept his foot light on the gas pedal even though he wanted to jam it down and race to their destination.

Shelby tugged her gloves off and laid them in her lap. "Where are you taking me?"

"You'll have to wait and see."

"Sure you don't want to blindfold me?"

He bit his bottom lip. "Tempting."

"I'll figure it out."

"You will. It's no big secret—I just didn't want you to say no."

"I'm not sure I like the sound of that."

He reached over and grabbed her hand, squeezing it gently. "It'll be fun. I promise." Reluctantly, he let go, not wanting to scare her away.

"If you say so." Her low voice reverberated through his body.

"Trust me."

* * *

Shelby traced her finger along the frosted window of Tristan's truck. The scent of his citrusy cologne filled the cab of the truck. She blinked, resisting the urge to lean in and sniff. *Get a grip.*

The truck turned right at the lights. Shelby vaguely recognized the area near the high school. She didn't come this way often since she had no need to. Warning bells rang in her head, and she gripped the door handle.

"We're almost there."

A large oblong building came into view. The arena. The bell in her head peeled again. Loudly. "I'm... No. I don't skate." Her voice trembled slightly.

He parked and turned off the engine. "I know. I'm going to teach you." He said the words matter-of-factly.

"This isn't a good idea. I don't feel like breaking any bones."

"You won't. I won't let you get hurt."

"You can't guarantee that." She stared at him. "Are you supposed to be on the ice yet?" She crossed her fingers.

"Jake gave me the thumbs up." He opened his door. "No, I can't guarantee you won't hurt yourself, but I'll make sure you have the right equipment, and I'll be by your side the whole time."

She slumped against the leather seat. Rounding the front of the truck, he opened the door and helped her down. Then he reached behind her into the back seat and heaved out his hockey bag.

"I don't have skates."

"I brought you a pair. Not figure skates—hockey skates. Way easier to skate in without that pick thingy."

"Really?"

"In my humble opinion, yes." He grabbed her hand with his free one and tugged her to the door. The keys rattled in his hand as he tried to unlock the door. Was the great Tristan Kelly nervous? On his second attempt, he got the door open.

"You have keys to the arena?"

He jangled the keys. "You get the keys when you're a high school advisor to the coach." And an NHL player. He didn't say it, but he might as well have.

"Okaay then."

He flipped the light switch on, illuminating the ice and foyer. Dropping the bag on the bench, he rifled through it, extracting two pairs of skates. Shelby stood by, hesitating. "Seriously not sure this is a good idea, Tristan."

"You told me a long time ago you didn't do sports that could wreck your dancing career, but you don't dance anymore. Don't you want to try something new?" He handed her a helmet.

She sat on the bench and cradled the head gear. "Maybe. But I don't want to fall and take you down too."

He knelt in front of her. "You won't. Let me help you tie up your skates so they are done up properly." He tugged off her boots and loosened up the skates' laces. "Slide your feet in."

She stuck her feet in the skates, and he tied the laces very tight. Then he sat next to her and quickly laced up his own skates. She jammed the helmet on her head. *One can't be too careful.* He adjusted the helmet, tightening the buckles. His warm, minty breath caressed her cheek as he checked the fit. She closed her eyes. His fingers grazed her chin, and tingles spread across her face. He held out his hand. "Ready?"

"As I'll ever be." She fiddled with the buckle on her helmet. "Have you been on the ice yet?"

"I skated with the high school team. Nothing strenuous. And all Jake-approved."

He helped her straighten, waiting while she found her balance on the blades. Once she was steady, they stepped onto the ice. Her heart pounded as the cold hit her face. Tristan glided out onto the hard surface, circling around. He made it look so easy. Her fingers gripped the edge of the boards until her fingers hurt under the gloves. He stopped in front of her and loosened her fingers from the boards. "Hold on to me."

He gripped her hand firmly, but her body refused to move. When he grabbed her other hand, they stood face to face. "I'll pull you along.

Don't do anything. Just follow me. Like you'd let your partner lead you in a dance."

Okay, she understood that. Maybe she could do this.

"Breathe." The corners of his eyes crinkled as he smiled, his face lit up with excitement. Clearly he was in his element here and excited to share that with her.

Shelby exhaled and let him lead her away from the boards. Ever so slowly, he skated backwards, drawing her forward. Dancing on pointe was way easier than this. She shifted and her foot came shooting out from under her. He grabbed her waist, steadying her and stopping her fall. She clutched his arm.

"You okay?"

"Yes," she whispered, afraid to move anything. His strong hands held her as she straightened, then he pushed away from her slightly. When he was an arm length's away, he drew her forward.

"Relax your body," he encouraged. "Better. Find your balance like you would when you dance. The key is to find your centre core. You do it all the time on one foot."

"Not the same thing and that was a long time ago." She was so focused on her feet, she could barely get the words out.

"It's exactly the same, and you're still in great shape. My point is you can do this."

She found her core muscles and lined her body up along her spine until she didn't feel as if she was going to fall anymore. It was a trick they'd used in dance—pretending to pull the cord like a puppet to straighten up. It helped dancers find their centre.

"Excellent. I'm letting go now so find it without me holding you."

He released her hands, and for a moment she wobbled then found her centre. She stood. On her own. Warmth spread through her chest despite the cold of the arena.

He glided around her. "Now slide one foot forward, using your balance to guide you."

Panic surged up her throat. "No."

"I'm right here if you start to fall." He skated in front of her. "Slide your right foot forward, but keep your eyes on mine, not on your skates."

His voice soothed her panic, and she slowly slid her foot forward, keeping her eyes on his beautiful green ones.

"Now the other foot."

She moved the other foot forward, clenching his hands. Slowly they moved across the ice, Tristan encouraging her the whole way. When they arrived back where they started, Tristan transferred her hands to the boards then pumped his fists. "You did it!"

She raised her own fist and bumped his. "I did, but that isn't what you look like when you skate."

"Yeah, I've been skating since I was four. That's a long time." He stared across the ice, his eyes glazing over for a minute, then he shook his head as though trying to clear it. "You're doing great for a beginner. You can't expect perfection your first time out, Miss Over-Achiever. Balance is key, and you've got it in spades from dancing."

"I'm ready to go again."

"Okay, but let's try something different. Trust me?"

"You keep asking me that. I'm on skates, aren't I?"

"And looking fine. Now this time, I'm going to push you from behind. Relax and let yourself glide. Don't fight me or we both go down."

His strong hands gently gripped her waist and she glided forward, Tristan propelling her from behind. They crossed the ice, once then twice. Shelby enjoyed the effortless ride across the ice. At centre ice, Tristan stopped them. "Okay, try it without my help. See if you can skate to the end of the rink where my net would be."

Shelby focused on the end of the rink and moved slowly forward. Wobbling slightly, she found her balance. After several more glides, she grabbed the boards and shouted in triumph.

Tristan laughed. "We'll have you skating by the end of the month."

Some of the warmth seeped out of Shelby. Would he still be around then?

CHAPTER THIRTY

Tristan checked the clock as he took a swig of his hot java. He had a meeting with Jason in a half hour at the school, but if he timed it right maybe he could call Shelby too. A smile ghosted his lips as he thought about their date at the rink. It finally felt as though a few pieces of his life were falling in place. The theme song from *Rocky* interrupted his thoughts. Grabbing his phone, he said, "Hi, Coach."

"Tristan. Glad I caught you. I want to talk timeline for your return."

Tristan set his coffee mug on the kitchen counter. "I haven't been cleared yet."

"Yes, you have. I received confirmation today from the clinic."

Tristan ran a hand over his head. "That's news to me."

Silence filled the air. "Your physical therapist should have called you, but maybe I jumped the gun. I spoke with your physical therapist early this morning."

Tristan stood still. *I should be excited.* Instead, a sour taste filled his mouth. "I guess I'll expect a call from my physical therapist."

"Right. Now that the cat's out of the bag, we need to make plans for you to return. Can you get up here today so we can start to get the wheels in motion?"

Tristan rubbed his forehead. "I'll drive up this morning if that works."

"Do that. I only need you for an hour or two. We'll meet for an hour and then you can see the team doc. Everyone is excited to have you back."

"Me too, Coach." He clicked the End button, then tossed his phone on the counter. His pulse raced as he contemplated returning to the NHL. Did Shelby know? He couldn't wait to celebrate with her.

His pulse skidded to a stop. He and Shelby were finally getting closer. How could he tell her now that he had to leave?

* * *

Shelby twirled a pen between her thumb and middle finger, her mind reliving her date with Tristan the evening before. Giddiness bubbled up from her chest as she thought of their perfect skate date. She relished the challenge of learning a new skill, and Tristan was a good teacher. The fact that there had been no adoring fans or cameras around made it even better. He'd focused on her all evening, and she'd felt special and seen. When was the last time that happened?

A sharp rap sounded on her office door. Jake stood there, a stack of file folders in his hand.

"Hey, what's up, Jake?"

He shuffled file folders, then handed her one. "I cleared Tristan Kelly to play. Just giving you a heads up. His coach called me this morning. Tristan is more than ready, so I gave him the go ahead. Since you worked with him first, I thought I'd let you know."

"Thanks. I appreciate it." *Who am I to question Jake?* He was Tristan's physical therapist now, and he knew best. She wouldn't have trusted Tristian's care to him if he wasn't top-notch.

As if reading her mind, Jake said, "His ankle's one hundred percent. If he keeps doing his exercises, he should be good."

"Sure. Great. He'll be happy." She clicked her pen several times.

"As will all of Reinholt—we need a few wins." He grinned, clearly oblivious to her lack of enthusiasm. "Thanks for giving me the chance to work with him. I've followed his career since he played in the OHL." He slapped the doorframe with his free hand then disappeared down the hall.

The pen she'd been holding dropped to the desk as she stood, glancing out the window. Cars filled the parking lot and people bustled along the sidewalk, but she didn't pay attention to them, only pulled her cardigan tighter. Had Tristan known last night that he was going back and decided not to tell her? Why would he keep it a secret? A deep pit opened up deep inside her, threatening to consume her from the inside out. Was he so excited to get back to his former life that he'd already forgotten her? Second place seemed to be her destiny—she was never going to be enough for him to stick around, was she? *I knew better than to get my hopes up. I'm an idiot.*

The intercom beeped. "Shelby, your next patient is here." Jessica's cheerful voice grated on her nerves.

"Great," she muttered, but she didn't move from the window.

* * *

The phone remained ominously silent. Shelby shoved it away with one finger then covered it with her napkin. Jessica, sitting opposite her, arranged her salad and veggies in an orderly fashion on her plate.

"Expecting a call from your hockey hottie?"

"No," Shelby snapped.

"Ookaay. Touchy, aren't we?" Jessica opened a bag of carrots. After withdrawing one, she waved it towards the phone. "I heard he got the okay to go back to the Renegades. I'm sure he has lots to do."

Shelby shifted on the hard chair, glad no one else was in the room. "I'm not waiting for him to call," she lied. She twirled her napkin around her finger. "But you're probably right. I'm sure he's got an endless To Do list." *Obviously he's so busy, he can't find the time to call me. I guess I didn't even make the To Do list. Nowhere near the top of it, anyway.*

"Why not call him?" Jessica chewed on the carrot stick and swallowed.

Shelby stirred her salad with her fork. She didn't want to discuss Tristan with Jessica. "I told you I'm not expecting to hear from him." She swallowed, hoping she wouldn't choke on the lump forming in her throat. She'd thought Tristan might be different. That maybe he would put her first, especially after last night. But three hours had passed since Jake told her the news, and Tristan hadn't texted or phoned. Of course, he'd had time to do a press conference with the Renegades coach. What did that say about whatever it was between them? Maybe all she'd been was a distraction while he was injured. If that was the case, he deserved an Oscar, because she'd been totally fooled.

She bit her lip, disappointment bursting the happy bubble she'd inhabited since last night with a loud pop.

CHAPTER
THIRTY-ONE

TRISTAN CRANED HIS NECK TO SEE IF HE COULD CATCH A GLIMPSE OF WHAT was causing the stopped traffic on the highway that ran between Reinholt and Wyattsville. An endless line of cars was the only answer. He thudded his head against the seat's headrest. *Please move.* As if it would help him to will the vehicles into action, he chanted the phrase several times. He needed to get to Shelby.

He stared at the lifeless phone on the passenger seat. As he'd left his apartment this morning to report to the team doctor as well as his coach, he'd dropped his phone in a slushy puddle. He'd tried to juggle too many things at once—keys, paperwork for the team, and a duffle that he'd wanted to drop off at his apartment in the city. As a result, he hadn't had a phone all day.

Added to the annoyance of the dead phone, his coach had scheduled a press conference unbeknownst to Tristan. What he'd thought was going to be a short trip to the city had taken the better part of his day. And now traffic. He clasped his hands behind his head and sighed. If there was a God, he could intervene at any time. Why hadn't he called Shelby as soon as he got off the phone with the coach this morning? *You're a coward, that's why.* He hadn't wanted to face her disappointment. And he hadn't wanted to rush their conversation. Now he was trapped in a traffic jam, going nowhere, with no phone. *What is she thinking?* Whatever it was, it couldn't be anything good.

The shouts of kids walking past his building, their coats and hats adding colour to an otherwise grey day, barely made an impression on Tristan as he ran up the walkway to the entrance. He halted at the figure standing outside the door.

Shelby stood clutching her car keys in a white-knuckled grip, her pale face drawn tight. "I've been waiting for your call."

"I'm so sorry. I had to drive to Reinholt and I dropped my phone and..." He stepped closer, reached out his hand, but she moved back.

"You've had a busy day—meetings, press conferences, celebrating."

He dropped his arm. "I know what it looks like, but I would have called you if my phone had been working."

"Let me get this straight. You never saw a phone you could use, *all day*? Not one of your teammates or coaches had a phone you could borrow?"

"Shelby, the coach had me booked every minute. I didn't even know about the press conference until I got there."

"I believe you." Her eyes glassed over, and she swiped a hand over them. "That's the problem. You'll always have things that come up—people wanting you to do this or the coach needing you for that. A press conference at the last minute."

He winced. All of that was likely true.

"That's not even counting all the time away for games and practices. Today you proved I will be the last person on your list. I told you I didn't want to repeat that kind of life. It's hard enough with my mom." She brushed past him.

"Wait." He'd wanted to speak to her so badly, but now, standing in front of her, he couldn't find the words. "Come inside and we'll talk."

"I can't stay." Her voice was flat. Not anywhere close to the excited woman from last night.

He repressed a sigh. She wasn't going to make this easy.

Not that he blamed her. He had caused that flatness. If he admitted the truth to himself, he'd been so excited about the news of returning to the team that he'd shoved her down his priority list. Not only because he was afraid of her reaction, but because, deep down, he was terrified of a serious commitment. He drove his fingers through his hair. Bottom line—he'd blown it.

Her eyes had gone ice-blue and had as much warmth in them.

"I'm so sorry. I never meant to hurt you."

"I know, but here's a little advice. It's been my experience that this is how fame works. You're never in control—it controls you."

His chest tightened. "Shelby." He hesitated, unsure how to counter that. After all, she spoke the truth—he had little control over the media or what people said. Not even over getting news about his own health before his coach did.

"There's nothing you can say." She shoved her keys into the pocket of her jacket. "I can't do this." She pointed between them. "It wasn't ever going to work. We have different goals and lives. I want to live a normal life—spend holidays at home, go grocery shopping without it becoming a spectacle. I want to be the first person you call when you have news. Not the last. I don't want to share you with the world. Been there, done that—don't want a do-over."

He scratched his neck. *What can I say to convince her?* "Most of the guys' wives and girlfriends do live fairly normal lives out of the spotlight. You can too."

She closed her eyes and shook her head. His chest clenched. It hadn't been easy having Shane Tivoli as a mother. Would she really refuse to be with him because of the way she was raised?

He grabbed her elbow. The tightness in his chest clawed up his throat. "Wait! Just like that—it's done? We can't even discuss it? I know I messed up, but don't just leave."

"I'm sorry." She extracted her arm from his tightening grip. "This was a mistake. I thought maybe... but today reminded me that nothing changes, and I don't want that life."

"Don't do this, Shelby. We can work it out." He'd get down on his knees if it meant it'd keep her here.

"I'm sorry, Tristan. I... I wish you all the best." Whirling around, she strode down the walkway. She was leaving him for good. And all he could do was watch her go.

* * *

Don't cry, don't cry, don't cry. Shelby forced her stiff body to move, one foot in front of the other, all the way to her car. After flinging open the door, she slid onto the driver's seat and slammed the door, encasing herself in the small space. Her bottom lip trembled like a traitorous soldier, so she bit down on it. *You knew he'd leave. He's married to the NHL and you don't want that life. Remember?*

She swallowed against the lump in her throat. No crying. She picked up a bagel wrapper from the passenger seat, balled it up, and threw it on the floor. *Always second best, never good enough.* A memory of her mother at her last benefit concert at Spencer came to her. Shane spoke with Coco, then her co-star Eric, and everyone else first. She barely said two words to her own daughter. Shelby had danced her heart out for her mother that night, and it hadn't been enough. *You will always be a loser.* She pressed her fingers to her eyes, trying to block out the images. Tristan wasn't any different from her mother. She'd never come first. She slapped her hand against the steering wheel, accidentally hitting the horn. It beeped and Shelby cringed. *Idiot.*

Shoving all thoughts out of her head, she cranked the ignition. *Who needs him?* She cleared her throat and wiped her eyes. *Who needs any of them?* She didn't and she'd prove it, not only to them but to herself.

CHAPTER THIRTY-TWO

Three Weeks Later

THE PUCK SLID ACROSS THE ICE FROM ONE WINGER TO ANOTHER, COMING closer and closer to the net. Tristan settled in his crouch position, his arms and legs spread like a butterfly. His eyes tracked the puck. His defenseman skated toward an opposing team member, but he passed the puck away from him. *C'mon, guys.* The sound of a body hitting the boards had the crowd yelling. Sticks, bodies, and skate blades whirled, but Tristan's eyes never left the puck.

Here it comes. The player came close and shot. Tristan dove to his left, grabbing the puck out of thin air with his glove. *Gotcha.*

The crowd roared and adrenaline pumped through his veins. Toronto was going to know Tristan Kelly was back by the end of the night. He wanted the win so badly he could almost taste it. Because if he didn't win, if he didn't prove he was the best goalie in the NHL, then he'd have to ask the one question he didn't want to contemplate. Was it worth it?

Focus. Tristan shut his mind down as play resumed, following the little black orb back and forth. *No distractions.*

* * *

Shelby blew her nose, wincing at the pain in her sinuses. She'd gone through several boxes of tissues in the last few days as she battled the flu. She gently rubbed lotion around her red nostrils, hoping to avoid sneezing for a few minutes to let it soak into her raw skin. The down pillow cushioned her aching muscles as she stared at the ceiling of her bedroom, willing her body to feel better. She felt around the lumpy comforter for the remote, finally locating the cold plastic device. After turning on the TV, she flicked through the channels, stopping when a familiar figure filled the screen, guarding his net on Saturday Night Hockey. The remote slipped to the comforter. Her lungs refused to work, and it wasn't due to the flu.

He's playing. Even though it hurt to see him, her eyes hungrily scanned him. His physical presence crowded the net. *It's a mystery how anyone scores against him.* And he looked good—even under the mask and the equipment. *Good grief! Get it together.*

Her finger hovered over the next button then she dropped the remote. Why not watch the game? She could assess his recovery. *Yeah, right.* Tristan lunged for the puck, and she covered her mouth with her hand. Reaching out with his long arms, he snagged the puck out of thin air. No goal. She pumped her fist.

Her phone buzzed. Coco's picture stared up at her. Shelby picked it up, her eyes returning to the game. "Hi, Coco."

"Hey, you sound much better."

"I ate your soup, and it was a magic potion."

"Right? Maybe I should sell it and make a million bucks."

Shelby grabbed a tissue and wiped her dripping nose. "You couldn't leave Spencer and you know it."

Coco sighed. "No, I couldn't. What're you doing?"

"Watching hockey."

Silence filled the line. "Is he playing?"

"Yeah, he's in goal tonight against Toronto." Shelby grimaced as one player smashed another into the boards. *Ouch. He's going to need therapy.*

"What happened to moving on?" Coco's tone was curious, not judgmental.

"I'm watching sports. That's it. Don't make a big deal out of it."

"Yeah right," Coco scoffed. "Talk to me, Shels."

"I don't know. That's my problem. What's wrong with me that I can't get this guy out of my mind and life?"

"Maybe it's because you don't really want him gone."

Shelby pulled her comforter to her chin and snuggled deeper into the pillows. She had no answer for Coco.

"You want my opinion? I think you really like him, but you're letting fear win here. You're so afraid of Tristan being like Shane that you've already decided what the future looks like. You're terrified of not being good enough, that he'll love hockey more. But sweetie, that's something you need to deal with. You are good enough. Period. Even if it doesn't work with Tristan, that doesn't take away from who you are."

Shelby's gaze followed the action on the TV screen. "I never feel good enough." Her voice was low, and she wasn't sure if Coco heard her.

"I know. Remember when I got injured? I thought dancing gave me my identity—without it I was no one. I had sacrificed so much to make those dreams come true."

"Yeah, I remember, but what does that have to do with not feeling good enough?"

"It's about identity. I thought dance defined me. But it didn't. Losing my career made me realize that I needed to find my identity not in my passion or a career but in a God who created me and loved me no matter what. It took time to believe it with my whole heart, but once I did, I felt at peace. The same can be true for you. You are good enough—you don't have to prove yourself to anyone, because God loves you as you are this minute. To Him you're exactly who you're supposed to be."

Shelby rubbed her temples. "It sounds simple yet really difficult."

"It's hard and it can take time. You've believed these lies for how long?"

"Since childhood. Maybe. I don't know. And how does this apply to Tristan?"

"I think you need to figure that out before you get involved in any relationship. You deserve happiness, and you're good enough for any man, but you'll always second guess where you stand with Tristan or whoever because you're basing your worth on him—his actions and opinions. Believe in yourself first. I think you'll only do that if you discover that God loves you as a daughter. Only His opinion counts, and He's already said *yes* to you." A pause. "Am I making sense?"

"Yeah. I need time to process, though."

"Absolutely. And you need to rest and get better. No one ever saved the world while they had the flu."

Shelby laughed. "True. My brain is mush. Thanks, Coco. You're a good friend."

"You're welcome. Feel better."

Shelby hung up and sat staring at the TV. After a few minutes, she turned it off and sat in the darkened room. *God, are you out there? I don't know really how to do this, but Coco says I'm your daughter and you love me. Is that true? Because I've never measured up with my mom. If I could only believe that I measured up with you, maybe I could figure out how to be in a relationship with someone else.*

CHAPTER THIRTY-THREE

"TRISTAN KELLY!"

The low, smooth voice drew him like a magnet. Searching the crowded foyer of the arena, Tristan spotted his old friend Kyle waving to him. Fan Appreciation Day had wrapped up half an hour before, and Tristan was heading home. He stared for a few seconds, incredulous, before striding over to his friend. Two strong arms enveloped him, his friend slapping his back a couple of times.

"Kyle! It's great to see you."

His old camp bunkmate slid his arm around the waist of a tall woman beside him. Her dark hair was pulled back in a low bun, and her smile was warm and welcoming. "This is Kenesha, my wife, and this," he held his hand out to Tristan, "is the great Tristan Kelly."

Tristan balked at his words, but Kenesha reached out an elegant hand, bright pink nails sparkling, and shook his.

"Great to finally meet you, Kenesha."

"Likewise. I've heard so much about you over the years. I think Kyle is your biggest fan."

"Well, I'm *his* biggest fan. He's done amazing things with the kids in Chicago with his football camps." Tristan gestured to a table in a corner, out of the way of the clean-up crew. The three of them sat down. "What are you doing in Reinholt? Were you at Fan Day?"

Kyle shrugged out of his winter coat. "No, but had I realized you'd be here, we would've come. We've got a meeting with city council to discuss bringing camps here. The Reinholt Raiders football organization has great camps already, but we're trying to see if we can help them reach kids who can't necessarily get to camps like that."

"Wow, that's awesome."

"Yeah. If you ever want to help out, we're hoping to get a number of hockey camps started eventually."

"Yeah?" The hockey team from Wyattsville High came to mind. "I might do that. I had a taste of coaching in Wyattsville while rehabbing the ankle. Helped out the local high school team."

"Nice. You'd be great at it. You always were good with the other campers at Ross's."

"There is one thing. I'm not into God—does that matter? I know you talk about faith at camp, but that's never been my thing."

Kyle scratched his temple. "No, it doesn't matter. But can I ask why faith isn't your thing? Just curious."

Tristan's shoulders stiffened. "My dad pretended he was a Christian, but he certainly didn't act like one. He left my mom, me, and my brothers for another woman. If that's being a Christian, then I figure I'm not interested."

Kyle ran a large hand over his jaw. "Man, that's tough. I'm sorry. I never knew that. But not every person who's into God is like that, you know. I'm not. Maybe you need to find new examples of people who follow Jesus. Or better yet, read a bit about Jesus in the Bible. He's the perfect example of how we should be."

A janitor swept up several streamers lying on the floor near their table. Tristan followed his movements as he thought about Kyle's words. "Maybe."

Kyle pointed to Tristan's feet. "You don't seem any worse for wear, considering you've been out with an injury."

His friend's change of subject had Tristan mentally catching up to the conversation.

"I had a great physical therapist."

"Oh?"

"Remember Shelby Wright from Ross's camp your first year?"

Kyle tilted his head to one side. "The dancer?"

"The one and only."

"Wait. She's your physical therapist? Why isn't she dancing?"

Tristan loosened his scarf. "She said it didn't give her much satisfaction, and she wanted to make a difference in people's lives. So she switched careers."

"Didn't she have a famous mother? I remember someone mentioning that after the fact."

"Shane Tivoli."

Kenesha, who had been watching the janitors and stragglers in the foyer, straightened. "Shane Tivoli, the prima ballerina?"

Kyle angled toward his wife. "You know her?"

"Uh yeah. I know who she is, anyway. I was obsessed with the National Dance Company growing up. She was their shining star. You know her daughter?" She slapped Kyle's large bicep. "Why have you been holding out on me?"

Kyle grabbed her hand. "Hey, I didn't know."

She pointed at Tristan. "So you really know her daughter?"

Tristan nodded. "We all went to camp together. It was weird because she was this elite ballet dancer at an athlete's camp."

Kyle nudged Tristan in the ribs. "You were the only one who had a problem with it as I remember, until sparks seemed to fly between you two."

Heaviness washed over Tristan. "Nothing happened at camp. We were too preoccupied with our future careers." *And we still are.*

Kenesha's gaze laser-focused in on Tristan. "Nothing happened at camp, but what about now? You said she's your physical therapist? And you had the hots for her at camp? I smell a romance here."

Tristan ran his fingers under his T-shirt collar. *Hate being a redhead.* "We went out a couple of times. But she didn't want to enter the complicated world of an NHL goalie. She'd had enough of that with her mother growing up."

Kyle winced. "Ouch."

"She's probably right. I'd be travelling a lot, and it'd be hard to maintain a relationship." He rubbed at his chest where a small ache had started. The foyer dimmed as the sun went under a cloud. *Wonder what's she doing now?*

Kenesha stared at him. "That's the stupidest thing I've ever heard. Do you like her? Does she like you?"

Did he like her? That was a no-brainer. "I do. She's smart and beautiful and feisty. I think she has feelings for me, but she's scared. So am I."

Kyle drummed his long fingers on the table. "Relationships are hard, but if they're right, they're worth it. If you like Shelby, then do the work to win her over, to make a relationship work." He lifted Kenesha's hand, still clasped in his. "You think this just happens? We've been together since ninth grade, but that doesn't mean we haven't had our challenges. It takes work. The good stuff always does."

Kyle kissed Kenesha's temple and she beamed at him. Tristan's heart rate quickened. He wanted that. Could he have it? Was it worth the work to go after Shelby?

CHAPTER THIRTY-FOUR

THE RINGING OF THE PHONE INTERRUPTED SHELBY AS SHE VACUUMED. SHE brushed off her hands on her shirt as she grabbed for the device sitting on the table. Her mother's picture stared at her, and Shelby groaned. Pick up or not? If she didn't deal with her mother now then she'd be avoiding her all day. "Hi, Mother."

"Shelby, why do you sound out of breath? Are you working out?"

"No, I'm vacuuming. What can I do for you?"

"I'm flying to London tomorrow, and I want to see you before I go."

A pain shot through her heart. "Mom, I'm working today—the late shift. How long have you known you were leaving for London?"

"Since last week."

"Why didn't you phone me sooner? I can't drop everything when you call."

"Can't you reschedule your appointments? I'm sure your patients understand that life happens." Impatience filled Shane's voice.

Shelby's eyes burned. What had happened to their truce? "No, I can't. When will you be home again?"

Her mother cleared her throat. "In six months."

The burning in her eyes turned to blurring. Shelby sank onto one of the hard dining room chairs. "What? Why are you going? Aren't you starting at Spencer?"

"No, I changed my mind. I'm moving to London and taking the position of ambassador of dance for the Royal Opera House."

Ambassador of dance? What kind of role was that? Shelby slumped against the chair. *Why do I expect her to change?* "Okay, well, I guess I'll see you in six months then." She swallowed over the lump in her throat.

Her mother's loud sigh came through the line. "You know, Shelby, if you hadn't given up dance we could be doing these things together."

I sincerely doubt it. Her mom may have apologized, but she hadn't changed her behaviour. Shelby was still second best. "Good-bye, Mom. See you when you get home."

"See you." The sound of silence roared through the line, and Shelby hit the End button. A tear tracked down her cheek, and she swiped it away with a finger. She would never be enough for her mother to stick around for.

You're enough for me. The words were quiet.

Shelby glanced around her apartment. *Who said that? Is my imagination working overtime?* A memory of the same voice on the beach at Ross's camp came to her.

More tears slid down her cheek. Shelby grabbed a tissue and blew her nose, but the waterworks wouldn't stop. All the tears she'd been holding back for years rushed to the surface, breaking free. Wrapping her arms around her stomach, she cried until her eyes dried up. The only sound in the room was the ticking of the clock on the wall. A calm settled over her. Peace. *You are enough.*

Was she? She reached for her phone and dialed Coco's number, hoping her friend could explain a little bit more about this God who thought she more than measured up.

* * *

The wood of the barre was smooth under Shelby's fingers. The hardwood floors shone and the smell of rosin tickled her nostrils. She sighed. "I feel like I never left."

Coco tied the ribbons on her ballet shoes, then tugged them to make sure they were secure. "You spent years at the barre, so it's a second home for you. Maybe you'll find you enjoy it."

"Maybe. I've missed dancing."

Coco stood and pointed her feet, testing the tightness of her ribbons. "I don't understand why you divorced yourself from it altogether."

"It reminded me of my mom. I wasn't sure who I was dancing for anymore, and I didn't want the reminder I never measured up."

"And now?"

"Now I'm starting to believe I'm good enough." She stretched her leg over the barre and extended her body over it. "But it's hard not to let doubts creep in."

"Keep telling yourself the truth. God loves you whether you're having a good day or messing everything up. I know this from personal experience."

Shelby straightened and lowered her leg, shaking it out. "Easier said than done."

"Yeah, but I'll help you. I'll tell you the truth." She nudged Shelby with her pink shoe. "You are a brilliant dancer, Shels. I competed with you because you were the best."

Shelby raised her other leg over the barre. "Is that a challenge?"

Coco, standing in first position, bent forward then straightened. "You have been off for a while. So if you can catch up to me, bring it on!"

"You've got it." Shelby reached for her toes and groaned. "I'm pretty sure my muscles will regret this tonight."

Coco patted Shelby's shoulder. "I won't work you any harder than I do my students."

Shelby grimaced. "Somehow that's not that comforting."

Coco reached for her phone. She scrolled through it, muttering, "We'll see." Music filled the room and Coco took her place at the barre, a few feet from Shelby. "Pliés."

Shelby faced the barre, shaking her head. *What have I got myself into?* Not only with ballet, but with the far more daunting challenge of puzzling through her relationship with God and Tristan.

CHAPTER THIRTY-FIVE

"Kelly, my man!" Tristan's teammate, Louis Gagner, held up a fist and Tristan hit it with his own. "Nice save. That should get you noticed for the Vezina."

A few of his other teammates echoed Louis's comments. The guys were in a good mood after their win, so the locker room was noisy as the players changed into their street clothes.

Tristan shrugged. No point in worrying about awards. He needed to focus on one game at a time so they could make it to the playoffs. Following Louis out of the locker room, he inhaled the aroma of buttery popcorn and spicy hot dogs, the cologne of an arena. His mouth watered, but he didn't need a hot dog—he needed protein and complex carbs. A few fans and family members lingered in the hallway, waiting for players.

"Looks like all the reporters have left the building. Only a few fawning fans left for you, Kelly." Louis bowed elaborately.

He shoved his teammate lightly. He pushed away thoughts of the one person he wished waited for him.

Louis hurried off to his wife, who waited near the fringe of the remaining people. Tristan blinked. *Don't be a fool. You know she's not coming.* Shelby had made her choice and so had he. Again. Spotting a couple of young fans waving to him, he sauntered over to them, glad for the distraction. "Hi, guys. Thanks for coming out."

"That thave was awethome, Mr. Kelly!" The boy offered him a gap-toothed grin. "Will you sign my jerthey, pleathe?"

Tristan took the jersey, along with the Sharpie the boy held, grinning at the kid. "Sure can. I see you lost your front tooth."

The boy's eyes lit up, his smile widening. "Thure did. The tooth fairy left me five buckth!"

"That's a pretty cool tooth fairy." Tristan handed the jersey to the boy and moved on to the girl standing next to him. She smiled shyly and held out her own jersey with his number on it.

Tristan winked. "I like this jersey."

The boy jabbed the girl with his elbow. "She playth goalie like you."

Tristan's eyes met the girl's brown ones. "Do you now?"

"I like watching you play. I try to copy your moves." The words came out in a rush.

The boy—her brother maybe—said, "She's got the betht win record in our league. She had a thut-out yesterday."

Tristan held out his hand to her and she shook it. "Congratulations. That's amazing. You keep at it."

Her face reddened, but her smile lit up her face. He took a picture with them both before hurrying down the corridor to the exit.

"Tristan!"

He swivelled around, his heart pounding as his eyes sought out the source. A roar rushed through his head as he stared at an older version of himself. Same green eyes and auburn hair, although his father's was more grey than red. "Dad." He choked out the word.

His dad stepped in front of him. "Tristan. It's so good to see you."

"What are you doing here?"

"I wanted to see you. It's been a long time." His dad clutched a Renegades toque in his large hands.

Tristan barked a laugh. "Whose fault is that?" He whirled away, but the weight of his father's hand on his elbow stopped him. He studied the man who'd given him half his DNA.

"I'm sorry, Tristan." His dad closed his eyes. "For so many things, but most of all for abandoning you and your brothers."

The corridor closed in around him. "It's a little late for that," he hissed as he jerked out of his father's grip. "I can't do this right now. If you're looking for free tickets, I can't help you." He stalked off, wincing at his harsh comment. *You're better than that.* He growled as he shoved open the heavy exit doors. His father brought out the worst in him. Why was he here? Tristan didn't buy the apology one bit. He yanked open the driver's side door and hauled himself in. His heavy breathing fogged up the windows. *Forgive him? Is he kidding?* Not in this century or the one after that could he forgive his dad for what he'd done to his family.

* * *

The piece of paper shook in Tristan's trembling hands, and he dropped it to the coffee table as if it burned him. He clutched his head, pulling on his hair. He didn't have to see the paper to know what it said. He'd read it so many times since it arrived in the mail this morning that he'd memorized the thing.

> *Son,*
> *I know you're angry with me and I don't blame you. I've made selfish choices over the years. But I want you to know that I am truly sorry for hurting you. Maybe you won't forgive me, but I want you to know that I love you and I would like to sit down and talk with you when you feel ready.*
> *Dad*

What are you up to, Dad? The man's behaviour was confusing. Tristan fumbled for his phone and thumbed his way through his contacts. Finding the one he wanted, he hit send. It dialed then went to voicemail. Leave a message or not?

"Hey, Matt. You'll never guess who showed up at the arena the other day. *My dad.* He apologized for leaving. Can you believe it? I blew him off, but today I got a letter. He's asking forgiveness and wants to talk. I have no idea if he's sincere or if it's a new game of his. I needed to get this off my chest, so you were it. Call me when you get back from wherever you are."

Hitting the End button, Tristan headed to his bedroom. He needed to run—that always helped him think. He changed quickly into a pair of joggers and a long-sleeved T-shirt and left the apartment—and the piece of paper—behind.

* * *

The phone's keypad mocked Tristan, who couldn't decide whether to dial or not. He flipped it over and tossed it amid the twisted sheets of his bed. It had been a week since Tristan received the letter from his dad, and it pricked like a thorn that had caught a piece of clothing—it wouldn't let him go. Added to the complications of his life, his mind and heart wouldn't let go of Shelby. *I'm slowly losing it. I need to get at least one of these things sorted out.*

Snatching up the phone, Tristan punched in his dad's number, holding his breath while it rang.

"Hello."

"Dad," he croaked.

"Tristan. I'm so glad you called."

The phone felt like a hundred-pound weight. "Yeah, uh, can we meet?"

"Absolutely, son. When and where?"

"Do you know where A Cuppa is?"

"Yes, I do."

Tristan closed his eyes. "In an hour?"

"I'll be there."

"See you then." Tristan sank back onto the mattress. *I hope you know what you're doing.*

CHAPTER THIRTY-SIX

THE BUSY DOWNTOWN CAFÉ, A CUPPA, WAS POPULAR WITH THE BUSINESS crowd on weekdays and teens and couples on the weekends. It proved no different on this Saturday. Tristan surveyed the crowded bistro tables for his father. A slight motion at the back caught his attention, and Tristan lifted his hand to acknowledge his father's wave. Winding through the obstacle course of tables and chairs, Tristan arrived at the tall table and slid onto the bar stool. His father nudged a tall cup of black coffee over to him.

"There's cream and sugar if you want it." His dad's cheeks reddened. "I don't know how you take it."

"Black is good. Thanks."

Tristan turned the cup around and around.

"Busy place." His dad cupped his own mug in his large hands. The deli sat on the far left side of the café, the workers serving up smoked meat sandwiches to hungry customers while the baked goods, sitting under domes of glass, tempted everyone who came in to the small space with their sweet, buttery aroma.

Tristan lifted the cup to his lips and took a swig. The steam misted his nose as the hot liquid burned down his throat. "Yeah, it's pretty popular." His father, dressed casually in a pair of jeans and a long-sleeved sweater, looked good. He'd aged, but the silver in his hair enhanced his strong nose and jaw. His face was softer too, a few more wrinkles around the eyes. Tristan shifted his weight on the stool, crossing his ankles. "What changed?"

His dad nodded, as if he expected the question. "I realized it wasn't all about me. And I miss you and your brothers. I want to make amends if I can. I can't redo the past, but I can apologize. I'm sorry, Tristan. I hope you can forgive me—at least one day."

How long had he been waiting for his father to say that? His eyes burned, and he cleared his throat. Mr. Kelly reached across the small table and rested his fingers on Tristan's wrist.

"Take your time. I don't need an answer today. I just needed to tell you that."

The warmth of his dad's large hand on his wrist reminded Tristan of days on the ice rink in their backyard, his dad holding his wrists and hands while he showed him how to hold a hockey stick properly. His heart ached at the memory.

"I thought I wasn't good enough for you to stay. That I wasn't worth your time." He blurted out the words that had been festering inside him for years.

The man sitting across from him sagged like a limp balloon. "No, it wasn't your fault. Your mom and I were young when we got married—we had issues long before I left, but they had nothing to do with you or your brothers. That's the last thing I wanted to do—make you feel it was your fault. I loved ..." he stopped and cleared his throat, "... love you. I'm so proud of you."

Tristan snorted. "You have a funny way of showing it." He rubbed his eyes. The sounds of laughter, a steamer whirring, and the hum of chatter filled the awkward silence.

"I deserve that." His dad fingered the wooden stir stick. "I also wanted to tell you I'm trying to change. I want to be a better man—the one God created me to be."

Tristan stilled, then shook his head. "And there it is." A pounding sounded in his head. He wasn't going to listen to this crap. "You claimed you were a Jesus follower back then, but you abandoned us. Why say anything now? You think it changes things? It doesn't—it only makes me trust you less."

His dad snapped the wooden stick in two. "Tristan, I was selfish. I was only thinking of myself, and I definitely wasn't following Jesus. I pretended for a long time. I'm sorry."

"So you didn't believe, you only pretended? Well, that explains a lot."

"I was a mess. For a long time I went through the motions with your mom, and I was angry at the world. But I never stopped loving you and your brothers. I'm sorry I was a hypocrite. That's not how a man acts. I made poor choices."

"Yeah, well, those poor choices are your wife and family now." The words tasted bitter on Tristan's tongue.

His dad threw the shards of the stick into a pile. He gazed at Tristan. "I love you—you're my son. I made a mess of things, but that never changed how I felt about you. Yes, it's messy and complicated. I love my wife and our children, but they don't make you less important. I know I haven't acted like it. A part of me stayed away because I was ashamed." He gulped his coffee.

Tristan had shut his father out of his life, not caring or thinking about his dad's feelings. *I've missed him.* The thought surprised him. He'd spent so long being angry, he hadn't let himself feel any other emotion. Could he forgive him? Did he want them to have a relationship? "Dad, I need time."

"I know, and that's okay. I'm thankful you gave me time today and that you listened to me."

Tristan stood. "I'll be in touch, okay?"

"Okay, son." His dad stood too and held out his hand. Tristan stared at it then reached out and shook his father's hand.

* * *

The ticket to the first play-off game burned in Tristan's jeans pockets. He'd slid it into an envelope along with a note and rushed out of the box office, eager to get them in the mailbox a block away. *She won't come.* The image of Shelby throwing away the ticket turned Tristan's stomach. His steps faltered. This wasn't going to work. But he had to try, didn't he? He rolled his shoulders and jogged the rest of the way.

Tugging the envelope from his pocket, he shoved it into the mailbox. *Can't undo it now.* Still, he stared into the dark mouth of the mailbox. It was Shelby's decision, but a warmth spread throughout his chest. *Maybe she'll say yes.* He had to try.

If his father's appearance in his life recently had taught him anything, it was that all things were possible. The conversation he'd had with his father swirled around his head. He understood his dad better now and felt more open to talking to him. If that could happen for him and his father, maybe there was a chance for Shelby and him. Hoping for the best, he'd decided to send her tickets to the game. If she was willing, they could try again.

Tristan closed the drawer, the clang echoing in the air. He stepped away from the box, then strode off, hoping he'd get the answer he desired.

CHAPTER THIRTY-SEVEN

"Hey, Shelby, here are your messages." Jessica handed Shelby a stack of pink slips. Shelby jammed the blue envelope she'd been clutching into her tote. She'd stopped to grab her mail as she left her apartment, and the letter, in a familiar handwriting, had snagged her attention as she'd rifled through the pile while walking into the clinic.

Jessica craned her neck, trying to get a glimpse. "What are you hiding in that enormous bag?"

"Nothing." Shelby plucked the messages out of Jessica's hand as she hurried to her office. She needed privacy to open that letter. She definitely did not need Jessica gawking over her shoulder, hoping for juicy office gossip.

She dropped the pink slips on the desk then tugged the envelope from her bag. The handwriting was more of a chicken scratch. She slid her finger under the flap and lifted out a ticket for the first play-off game in the Reinholt against Calgary series. Her heart crashed against her ribs. Shaky fingers unfolded the single sheet of paper, making it rattle slightly.

Dearest Shelby,
Enclosed is a ticket for our game. I'm hoping you'll come. I know you think this won't work between us but I'm asking you to rethink it. I'm sorry I didn't fight harder for you. Please come to the game.
Yours,
Tristan

She set the paper beside the ticket and stared at them. "Shelby."

She jerked upright. Jake stood in the doorway.

"Sorry, didn't mean to scare you. Have you—" He pointed at the ticket. "Is that a play-off ticket for the Reinholt Renegades?" His voice rose an octave.

She fumbled with the paper, struggling to fold the letter. "Yes."

"Where did you get that? Did Kelly send it to you? Do you know how *impossible* it is to get a ticket? You're going, right?"

She picked the ticket up, checking the date.

"If you don't go, then I'll buy it from you."

She smirked. "I think Tristan would be disappointed to see you in that seat."

"Then you're going?"

She flicked the ticket with her fingernail. "I... don't know. But if I don't go, you can have the ticket."

He pointed the files at her. "I'm holding you to that. But you should go, because if you get together with Kelly it hopefully means more tickets in the long run, right? Because I'm his favourite physical therapist."

She tossed an M&M at him from a bowl sitting on her desk. "Get out of here. And keep this to yourself."

He saluted then laughed as he jogged down the hallway.

Sagging into her chair, Shelby pressed her hands to her eyes. *What am I going to do?*

* * *

"She's going!"

Shelby chuckled as Mike shouted in the background.

Coco's laugh came over the line. "Seriously, you have to go, Shelby. Or Mike is going to freak out."

Shelby stared out the front windshield of her small car. The late afternoon sun provided little warmth on this cool spring day. The clock on the dash told her she needed to get going if she wanted to make the game. "I don't know, Coco. I mean, it's not like anything's changing. He's not quitting the NHL, and I'm not going to suddenly like the spotlight."

"There are lots of girlfriends who stay out of sight and have good relationships. Do you really want to live the rest of your life wondering what if?"

"No," she whispered.

"Well, it sounds like you made your choice. And remember, you're worth it. You deserve to try with Tristan. You deserve happiness too."

"Maybe."

"You do." Coco encouraged her. "Call me after. I want details."

"I want tickets!" Mike said, and Shelby could hear Coco shooing him away. "Don't listen to him. He's being a boy."

Shelby snickered at her friends. "You two are too funny. Talk to you soon."

She dropped her phone into her coat pocket and stared at the ticket sitting on her passenger seat. Exhaling loudly, she grabbed it and stuck it into her purse then turned the key in the ignition. *I'll go and see what you have to say, Tristan Kelly, but I'm not promising anything.* Her heart skipped a beat as she drove out of her parking space.

CHAPTER THIRTY-EIGHT

TRISTAN BANGED HIS GLOVES TOGETHER AS HE SWUNG HIS GAZE TO THE section on his right—to the seat that still remained empty. The large clock on the Jumbotron proclaimed ten minutes to game time. *Calm down. She's got time.*

"Kelly!"

He jerked his head as a puck whizzed right by him. Brett Halman, the team captain, frowned as he skated up to the net. "Kelly, get your head in the game."

Tristan hit his leg pads. *Amateur.* His captain skidded to a stop in front of him, showering his pads with ice. "You okay? We need you here—mind and body. Whatever's going on up here," he tapped his own helmet, "shut it down. Can we count on you?"

"You can count on me." Tristan shoved his mouth guard in and banged his stick on the ice.

"Good." Halman skated away. Tristan settled into the crease, focused on a round black orb rather than the empty seat.

* * *

The cold air wrapped around Shelby's fingers, and she wriggled them in her mitts, hoping to bring feeling back to them. She pulled a tissue from her pocket and wiped her nose. The smell of grease and buttery popcorn wafted through the air, but Shelby had no interest in food. She rose on her boot-clad toes to see the action on the ice better. She sat then stood then sat again. The game was tied 1-1 with five minutes to go. When it was over, she and Tristan were going to talk. *But first he has to win this game.*

The players rushed down the ice toward Reinholt's net, and she leapt to her feet with the other fans as Tristan lunged to the side and blocked the puck with his body. She cheered until her voice cracked. Fans stomped their feet, whistling and cheering so loudly that the place shook. Shelby jiggled her ear. *I'll be deaf before this game ends.*

The puck flew down the ice with a Renegade player. He passed it off and his teammate sent it soaring into Calgary's net. Reinholt was up 2-1. Cheers erupted and fans screamed and hugged everyone around them. The guys in front of her high-fived each other and then offered their palms to her. *Why not?* Shelby high-fived them. Horns went off behind her. Was it possible for it to get louder in this place? How did the players concentrate?

The clock's LED lights slowly counted down the last seconds of the game. Shelby's heart crashed against her ribs as she jumped up and down. The buzzer blared. Reinholt had won their first play-off game of the season. The players shook hands, but only the goalie captured her attention. After he'd made his way through the line, shaking the opposing team's hands, Tristan looked up—the first time he'd glanced her way all game. She lifted her hand in a small wave. His smile lit up his face and he motioned that he'd text her—probably from the locker room. She gave a thumbs up as he skated off the ice, glancing back several times.

* * *

Tristan showered and dressed in record time. Thankfully, the coaches kept it short in the debriefing, and he wasn't needed in the press room. Good. He had somewhere he needed to be. Afraid Shelby would leave, he checked his phone. No text. Whew. After collecting his things, he hurried out of the locker room and into the corridor where friends and family waited for players. He spotted her at the edge of the crowd and strode over to her. She lowered her phone and smiled. *That's a good sign.* Her pink toque and matching mittens made her look like a teenager.

"Hey." He held out his hand to her, eager to get away from the people around them. He normally enjoyed his fans, but tonight all he wanted was alone time with Shelby. She slid her soft mitten into his large hand and he squeezed.

"Hey, yourself. Thanks for the ticket. Great game. You were amazing."

He pushed open the large Exit door and held it open for her.

"Thanks. I've got the best teammates."

"That may be true, but they'd have suffered a loss tonight if it wasn't for you."

"It takes a whole team."

She stopped and peered around the emptying parking lot. "I'm sorry, what have you done with Tristan Kelly, the one who must win at all costs? You know, the one I went to camp with?"

He bumped her gently. "He grew up." His gaze lingered on her face, memorizing every curve. "He finally learned what was worth winning." Settling his hand on her back, he steered them towards the player's parking lot and his truck.

"My car is someplace else."

"I'll have someone pick it up later, okay?" Tristan opened the door to the passenger side and helped her in.

After closing the door, he swiped his slick palms on his jeans. *Is it possible to have a heart attack before the age of thirty?* Sliding into his seat, the faint smell of coconut tickled his nose, reminding him of summer breezes and fresh starts. He could sit here all night long with her next to him. She looked *right*, sitting beside him.

Shelby gazed out the side window. "Are we going someplace, or are we talking here?"

Tristan shifted his weight and turned the key in the ignition. He cleared his throat. "No. Sorry. We're going somewhere." He drove out of the parking lot and into the city to a small bistro, nestled by the river.

Shelby bent forward to peer out the front window, squinting. "I don't think they're open."

"You'll see. Wait and I'll get your door."

He helped Shelby from the truck. Taking her hand, he led her to the exit around the back, praying that he'd be able to persuade her to stay.

* * *

Shelby's eyes narrowed as she stood at the door of a totally blacked-out café. Closed. The sign said so. No other cars sat in the tiny parking lot. She slid a sideways glance at Tristan, who tested the door.

No one's here. "Are you sure—"

The door swung open. A short guy, who looked vaguely familiar, stood with a huge grin on his face.

"Tristan." The man held out his hand and shook Tristan's before pulling the door open wider and motioning for them to come in. Shelby entered the small space, and her host grinned. "Shelby Wright, it's been a long time."

She blinked. "Matt?"

"You remember me!" He slapped Tristan's chest with the back of his hand. "See? She always liked me better. Welcome to my little bistro."

Shelby pulled off her mittens and toque. "You own this place?"

Matt bowed slightly. "I do, but the genius of the place is my wife. I take care of the business end, and she does all the cooking and baking. She has something special for you tonight."

They followed him to a candlelit table in a back corner of the bistro. Twinkle lights were strung along the ceiling. The table was set with funky square plates displaying slices of a delicious-looking raspberry cheesecake drizzled with chocolate. A bottle of sparkling juice and two flutes sat waiting for them.

"Wow, this is amazing!" Shelby sat on the chair Tristan held out for her.

"Thank you. I hope you enjoy. If there's anything else, please let me know."

Tristan slapped his friend's back. "This is fantastic. Thanks."

"Nice win, by the way. Keep it up."

Tristan waved him off, and Matt sauntered into the kitchen at the back of the café.

Shelby pressed her palms to the table. "I don't know what to say. This is... wow."

"I wanted a private place to talk, and I figured there'd be less of a public spectacle here than at a restaurant."

He'd remembered her dislike of the media and fans on dates and had gone out of his way to arrange private time. Her eyes burned, and she blinked. "Thank you." She picked up the cloth napkin sitting beside the plate. "I can't believe Matt owns this."

"Right? It's one of many lucrative businesses he's got going. He travels all over the world. Not too shabby."

"I'll say." Shelby picked up her fork. "Guess he doesn't miss basketball?"

Tristan popped the cork of the sparkling juice and poured her a flute full. "He coaches at one of the youth centres, and that seems to scratch the itch."

"Nice." She set her fork down, taking the flute by its delicate stem. "Thanks."

He poured himself a glass, and she raised her own. "To many more wins."

He clinked his glass and sipped the liquid, his eyes never leaving her. She took a sip and set the glass down.

He folded the napkin in half. "Thank you for coming."

"Thanks for the ticket—I fought off Mike and Jake for it. You're lucky it's not one of them here enjoying a romantic evening with you." She forked a piece of cheesecake. The creamy concoction slid down her throat.

He chuckled as he picked up his fork. "Yeah. I could only get one ticket, but I didn't really want to have any extra people here tonight." The candlelight flickered, making shadows dance across his handsome face. He took a bite and swallowed. "Wow, that is really good."

"One of the best I've ever tasted." The slight awkwardness that had been building between them disappeared.

"Maria, Matt's wife, is one of the best bakers in the city. I think she studied in France."

"That explains it then." Shelby took another bite then set her fork on the plate. "Is that where they met?"

Jennifer Willcock

"Ironically it is. She was there studying and he was on business. They had to fly across the ocean to meet."

"He seems happy."

"He's the most content I've ever seen him." Tristan scraped the last of the dessert from his plate with his fork, then set the plate to the side. "Shelby, I know you had issues with your mom growing up, and a high-profile lifestyle isn't what you want, but I'm in love with you. I'll do anything to figure out how we can make it work. You asked me once if it was worth it, and I finally have an answer. You're worth it. I love hockey, but you mean more. I'll work hard to keep our lives private and you as my priority. Life is empty without you, and I want you in my world." He reached over and covered her hand with his. "This can work if we set boundaries that we both can live by. Guys on the team do it and have successful relationships. I've talked to them over the last few days and asked them how they manage it. They gave me a few good ideas." He wrapped his fingers around her hand. "What do you say? Talk to me."

His wide green eyes searched her own. *Yes, yes, yes.* But talk was cheap—did he mean it? Could she trust him? "Tristan... I don't know. You think you'll be able to keep it separate, but my mom never did. I've been out with you and fans didn't leave us alone." *And you ignored me.*

"I messed up, but I learned from that. What about the skating?" He peered around the empty room and spread his hands. "And tonight? We're alone and it's private. Being an NHLer has its perks if I want to use it to our advantage for privacy. I've never thought to do it before."

Memories of her childhood—traipsing after her mother all over Europe, spending more time with herself than either of her parents, saying no to parties and sleepovers because she was in Europe with her mom—paraded through her mind. Slipping her hand from his, she sighed. *I don't know what to do.* She wanted this. She wanted him, but could they make it work? "I don't know."

"Please, Shelby, give me a chance. Give *us* a chance."

You're enough. Don't be afraid. The voice whispered deep within her.

Was she enough for Tristan? Two months or two years from now, would she still be enough? She still wasn't enough for her mother to stay home or see her.

Don't be afraid? She was so scared to give her heart away. What if he tore it in two? She circled the flute's rim with her finger. Could she risk it?

She raised her eyes to his green ones. Love glowed in their depths, and kindness and hope. *He's a good man.* Her heart beat out a staccato *yes, yes, yes.*

"Yes."

"Yes?" he whispered.

"Yes," she repeated.

The corners of Tristan's eyes crinkled and his white teeth flashed as a smile lit up his face.

He rose and came around the table, scooping her up in an enthusiastic embrace before she could think another thought. She laid her forehead against his hard chest, enjoying his strong arms embracing her. She tilted her head. "We set ground rules."

"Agreed, but I need you to keep communicating with me. Don't shut me out, because that's when things unravel."

"You're right."

"I'm not going to be like your mom."

"I'm holding you to that."

His breath caressed her face. "I'm counting on it."

His hand cupped her chin, and she closed her eyes as his soft lips brushed gently across hers. Shelby slid her arms around his neck as he drew her closer, deepening the kiss. The sound of a throat clearing jolted her back to reality. Matt smirked from the doorway of the kitchen. Beside him, a beautiful woman with long black hair—his wife, presumably—was trying to shove Matt into the kitchen. Matt resisted her efforts. Throwing a tea towel over his shoulder, he said, "I see you worked it out."

Tristan kept his eyes on Shelby, but his words were directed at his friend. "Anyone ever tell you what lousy timing you have?"

The woman groaned and swatted Matt with her own tea towel. "I tried, Tristan. You two enjoy your evening."

Matt followed his wife into the kitchen. "We'll be in the back. Let us know if you need anything."

"You have good friends." Shelby rested her head in the crook of his neck, not wanting to move. They stood that way for several minutes, until he finally let her go and they returned to their seats to finish their drinks. Time slipped by as they talked and laughed.

Finally, Tristan glanced at his watch. "It's late—we should probably go."

"Yeah, it's a long drive to Wyattsville." Shelby rose.

"I'll take you to your car and follow you home. I still have access to the apartment, so I'll stay there tonight and drive back tomorrow afternoon." Tristan stood and lifted her coat from the back of the chair to hold it for her.

"Really? I'd love that. I planned on attending church tomorrow with Coco and Mike. Want to come?"

He ran his hand down her spine. "I don't have practice until later, so maybe I will. I wouldn't mind learning more about God. As long as you don't mind," he whispered in her ear, sending shivers across her arms. "I might get recognized."

"We can sit at the back and sneak out. I've attended a few times, and the people seem pretty cool." She zipped up her coat. "Mike might be the biggest problem. He's a huge fan. And I guess we can't hide all the time."

Tristan wrapped his arm around her as he escorted her to the exit. "I like how you think." He kissed her temple and a warmth spread through Shelby. For the first time in a long time, contentment filled her. She liked herself, and the place she was at in life. She was enough. Added to all that, the person she loved most was by her side.

EPILOGUE

Laughter and the exuberant chatter of an hundred teens filled the large, open room. Shelby stood rubbing the goosebumps on her arms. Strong arms encircled her, and she settled against Tristan's hard chest, his smell cocooning her in a little bit of heaven. He kissed her neck then whispered, "Excited?"

"Yes, but not as much as you."

"I loved camp. Especially the one where I met a feisty dancer."

"Knocked your socks off, did I?"

"Hmm." He kissed her ear lightly.

"Better watch it, or you'll be getting us both in trouble with the director."

He ran his nose gently along the other side of her neck. "I'm personal friends with him, so I think we're good. Besides, we're hidden away in this back corner. The kids are too busy meeting new people to care about us."

"I can't tell which teens are here on scholarship."

"Nope, that's the whole point. We sent out the camp gear early, so everyone comes wearing their camp T-shirts. They're all starting on even footing with everything they need."

"How many scholarships?"

"We raised enough money for ten and then my teammates came together and matched that number, so twenty altogether."

"That's so great. I love your teammates."

"Everyone should have the chance to play sports and attend camp."

"Or dance, paint, play music, and go to camp." Shelby ticked them off on her fingers.

"Exactly. Is the arts camp all set to go next week?"

"Ready for action. Coco's about to burst." She chuckled. "Mike thinks we should have a math camp—Coco told him to stop being a nerd."

"Those two are quite the pair." His arms tightened around her. "There she is."

"Who?"

"The prima donna." He nodded to the left where a group of boys stood, bouncing a soccer ball on their knees. A pretty girl with dark red, French-braided hair stood with her arms crossed and a bored expression on her face.

Shelby tilted her head to the left. "What are you talking about?"

"We had a dancer apply to this sports camp rather than the arts camp next week. Her mother said she needed a challenge."

Shelby glanced at the girl again then tipped up her face to Tristan. "Oh my. I'm not sure whether to feel sorry for her or to warn all the others to watch out. I know that look, and I understand the feelings behind it."

"I know you do. That's why I'm hoping you'll connect with her. She might need a friend."

"I really hope her mom's not like Shane." Shelby settled back against Tristan.

He squeezed her shoulder. "Me too. Either way, I think you'll have a lot to share with her based on your own experience."

"If she'll let me." Shelby stood on tip toe, swivelling her head from side to side.

"What are you doing?"

"I'm searching for the hot hockey dude who's going to get his butt kicked." She scooted away from him but wasn't fast enough.

He caught her arm and drew her close. "I didn't get my butt kicked. I think you have a very selective memory." His low voice caressed her ear.

She opened her mouth, but before she could respond Kyle whistled through two fingers, getting everyone's attention. "Welcome to Ross's Elite Camp for Athletes and Artists! I'm Kyle, the camp director, and I hope you have one of the best weeks of your summer with us.

We're so glad you're here, and we hope you grow strong in both your sports' skills as well as mentally this week."

Shelby clapped along with the kids. "Kyle is so great at this."

"He's a natural." Tristan rested his chin on Shelby's head. "Was it worth it, Mrs. Kelly?"

Shelby didn't even have to think about her answer. "You bet."

The End

Sign Up for Jennifer's Newsletter

Stay up to date with book news, connect with Jennifer, and subscribe to her email list at

jenniferwillcock.com

More from Jennifer Willcock

Exit Stage Right
978-1-4866-1932-0

She wants to dance, and she's willing to sacrifice everything, *everyone*, to get it.

Coco Bradley is a talented ballet dancer, and when an opportunity arises for her to audition for the prestigious Spencer School of the Performing Arts, she's not about to let anyone stop her— including her parents, her friends, and any of the prima donnas of the art school. A pastor's kid, Coco has grown up serving God and people, but gaining entry to Spencer means leaving behind all the expectations that come with growing up in the pastorate, as well as the dead-end town of Wyattsville.

Coco lives by the creed "Ballet First," but she's about to find out in a painful way that there's more to life than dancing.

Opportunities, fame, and love all come calling as Coco chases her dream. But in going after what she wants, will she lose the things that matter most?

Lightning Source UK Ltd.
Milton Keynes UK
UKHW021143240621
386004UK00021B/805

9 781486 621194